THE WOLF OF WHITEHALL

JASPER WYCHWOOD CHRONICLES, BOOK 2

JACK CURRAN

HAWK'S FLIGHT PUBLISHING

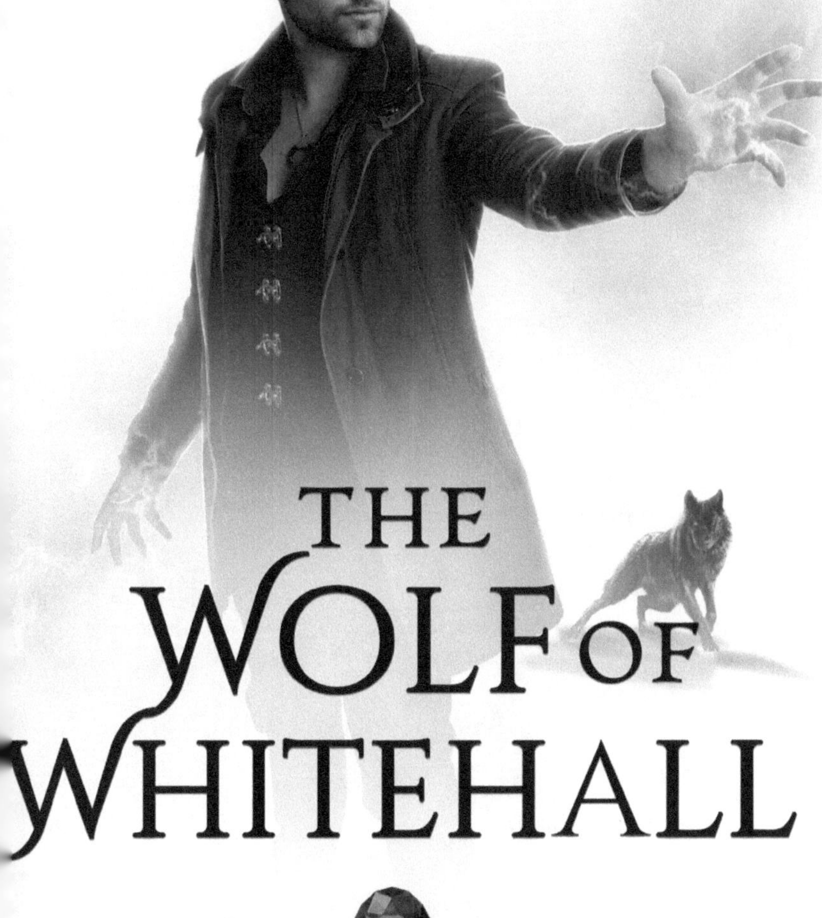

THE
WOLF OF
WHITEHALL
2
A JASPER WYCHWOOD NOVEL

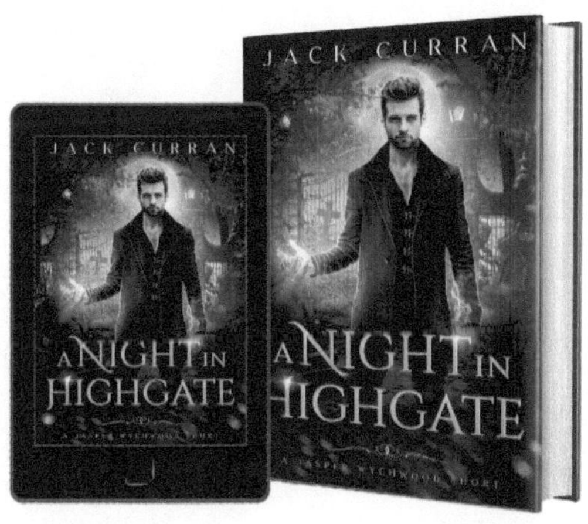

A VICTORIAN GRAVEYARD.
A DEADLY MONSTER.
A NIGHT TO REMEMBER...

Trainee wizard Jasper Wychwood is sent to London's famous Highgate Cemetary to search for a deadly monster. With no backup and no coffee... will he survive the night?

Get your FREE copy of the prequel story here:

www.jackcurranwrites.com

CHAPTER I
THE ISLE OF ISLAY, WESTERN SCOTLAND.

CALLUM NERVOUSLY PRODDED THE fallen cow with his muddy boot to see if it would react. It barely moved—the cow felt rigid and heavy as stone. He wondered how long the carcass had been here. There was a whiff of manure in the air and a fresher, saltier tang alongside it—the smell of the sea—but that was all. No stench of decomposition. So the cow had probably died recently.

Coming around to the front, Callum tensed when he saw the cow's throat. It was a ragged red mess. The grass nearby was dark and sticky with blood.

What could have done this? A wolf? Or something else?

Callum scanned the field for any sign of movement, but it was empty apart from a scattering of cows with their heads low to the ground, chewing grass. They'd moved to the far side of the field as if afraid to be near the bloody mess.

Callum went to the slate wall at the edge of the field and walked along it, trailing his hand across the raw stone. It felt cold and solid against his skin. The familiar stone walls and wooden fences felt like protection against the mysterious predator, whatever it was, even though he knew they weren't really. The wind was howling, making the yellow gorse shiver and the broken kissing gate snap backwards and forwards against its posts as he passed it.

He considered his options. He ought to return home and tell Murray about the dead cow, but he couldn't bring himself to go back yet. That would mean Murray had won. He knew that was a stupid, childish way of thinking, but after their latest argument, every fibre of his being screamed that it was too soon to return.

So, what was his plan?

At the end of the argument, he'd yelled that maybe he wouldn't come home this time. In response, Murray had merely shrugged his shoulders and told him to suit himself. Callum had stormed out with no real idea of where he was going, but his feet seemed to be leading him towards the old, abandoned church at Kildalton.

He couldn't see it yet, but he knew exactly where it was, hidden behind a small copse of trees. Others found the church creepy, but not Callum. For him it was his safe place, a home away from home. Tourists sometimes visited the site in the daytime, but after sunset it belonged to him exclusively.

Kildalton church wasn't just a random place of refuge. After several pints of Guinness, Murray had once told Callum he'd found him in a moses basket outside the church. A helpless baby, abandoned and apparently unwanted. That was how Murray had come to adopt a boy he wasn't related to. It was a story that had seemed believable at the time, but which Callum questioned more and more as he got older. It sounded too much like a fairy tale.

Murray never elaborated on the story, but nor did he disavow it. He did not say who Callum's real parents might be. Did he know? Was the story about the moses basket real, or an attempt to conceal Callum's true origins? These questions went unanswered until eventually Callum gave up asking them.

Despite his warm feelings towards Kildalton church, he reluctantly accepted that going there now was a bad idea and he'd have to return home instead. He wasn't a stupid kid anymore, even if Murray often accused him of acting like one. He was seventeen and nearly an adult. Sulking inside the church was a childish act, so instead he resolved to return to the farm with his head held high and give Murray the silent treatment for a few days.

Callum kicked a loose stone into a tuft of long grass. Murray's only real friends were his dogs, who he cherished far more than his adopted son. When Callum was ten, Murray had announced that it was high time he stopped using childish words like 'dad', 'daddy', or even 'father'. The directive had stung more than Callum would ever admit, but he'd obeyed it resentfully.

He sometimes wondered if Murray had a psychic connection with his dogs and the other animals on the farm. It wasn't such a far-fetched idea. Murray would have laughed—or perhaps sworn an oath on his battered copy of the King James Bible—if anyone had called him a wizard, but Callum had seen him use magic on the farm. He knew the kind of spells that could cure a sheep of disease, or calm a panicking horse, or make vegetables grow in barren soil. He often murmured under his breath and made subtle movements with his hands when he thought Callum wasn't looking.

Magic had been the subject of their latest row. After years of privately studying and practising on his own, Callum had taught himself to levitate small objects and conjure shimmering marbles of werelight. With his new skills, he was desperate to attend one of the great magical colleges in Edinburgh, Oxford, or Paris, but Murray would hear none of it.

'Your place is here, tending the farm and caring for the animals,' he'd said, staring furiously at his steaming mug of tea. He was sitting at the kitchen table, his chair angled away from Callum, who was leaning against the sink, his arms crossed over his chest.

'But I don't want to be a farmer. I'm no good with the animals.'

Murray didn't bother to contradict him—they both knew it was true. 'Your place is here. You'll take over the farm when I'm gone.'

'You're not listening to me,' Callum said, his voice pitching higher, his body coiled tight with frustration. Murray's attitude was infuriating. Didn't he care *at all* what Callum wanted?

'You never listen to me! I don't *want* to be a farmer, I *want* to learn magic and become a wizard, and live in Edinburgh or London. I want to leave Islay and see the world!'

Murray rubbed his temples and stared at his tea without drinking it. A cold draught blew through the kitchen, causing Callum to shiver in his thin T-shirt. He considered storming off and banging the kitchen door on his way out but didn't want to give Murray more of an excuse to see him as a dumb kid.

This was how their arguments often ended—in a frozen standoff.

Eventually Murray said quietly, 'This isn't what I imagined when you came to me as a wee bairn. You're not the boy I thought you'd be.'

With those quietly wounding words, he picked up his tea and left the room. Murray never shouted, never used his fists, never even stamped his feet when he was angry. He just walked away.

Callum had wandered a long way from the farmhouse after that argument. Now he was nearing home again, he slowed his pace and raised his head to look around. He was so deeply buried in his own thoughts and memories, that he'd almost forgotten about the dead cow and the mysterious predator that had killed it.

He mounted a set of wooden steps that brought him over a wall and into a field that was part of his father's farm. He halted suddenly at the top of the steps, his mouth falling open.

Sheep were strewn across the field, motionless, like clots of foam on a green sea. Some looked peaceful, others had been torn into pieces, stripes of blood darkening their woolly coats.

Callum stood in stunned silence for more than a minute, trying to comprehend what he was seeing. Murray must be told about this right away. Their argument was suddenly unimportant. The remaining livestock must be protected from the creature that did this.

A small voice in Callum's head said: *what sort of predator slaughters a field full of sheep without eating any of them?*

Until now, Callum had kept his cool; more or less.

Then came the howls.

Three ear-splitting, soul-crushing howls that seemed to stun Callum's brain and drive away all conscious thought, leaving room only for fear. His heart thumped a frantic beat in his chest. He struggled to breathe. Terror flowed like poison through his veins.

When the noise abated, Callum realised he was whimper-ing like an abused puppy. His face was damp with sweat and he was clinging to one of the posts that framed the wooden steps into the field. He felt sick. His first coherent thought was that the howls had come from the far side of the field he was about to enter. Which meant that the *monster* was somewhere between him and the farmhouse.

He stood for another minute at the top of the steps, agonising over what to do. The sun was orange on the horizon, darkness was falling over the island. He had to make a decision.

He climbed back down the steps the way he'd come, his heart still pounding. Back at the farmhouse, Murray had a shotgun, and a pair of brawny mastiffs, and a telephone, and magic, but something deep inside Callum simply wouldn't allow him to walk towards those horrible howls. Instead, he hurried back the way he had come, until he came to a little stream choked with grey rocks. He turned left, down a steep slope to a place where he could easily cross the stream.

The old Kildalton church loomed in front of him. The walls of the church were grey but peppered with a few dramatic white stones that looked like teeth. There was no roof but all four walls were still standing and looked reassuringly sturdy. The windows and doors were long gone, but the building still offered decent protection against the elements. A small graveyard boundaried by a low stone wall surrounded the church.

Callum jumped over the wall and dashed inside the church. He stood in the doorway and peered out. There was nothing to see except fields and a few trees. There was no sign of the unknown creature.

The wind hissed through the narrow, empty window frames of the church. Callum walked towards the chancel, where the altar would once have been, and sat down with his back against the wall. As some of his fear abated, he felt a stab of hunger, but there was nothing he could do about that.

Better to stay here and be hungry than venture outside where a dangerous predator was prowling about.

A small, spiteful part of Callum hoped that Murray stumbled on the field of dead sheep and realised his son was in danger.

Let him worry. Let him regret treating his adopted son like a lodger.

Let him *care*.

He eventually slid into a kind of half-sleep in which he continued his argument with Murray while being chased across a rugged landscape by a shadow creature that snapped at his heels with teeth like kitchen knives.

The dream ended abruptly. Callum's eyelids were sticky with sleep, but when he peeled them apart all he saw was darkness. He became aware of a deep, regular, rumbling sound and wondered, sleepily, if a storm was starting outside. Levering himself upright he looked down the nave, where moonlight spilled into the church through one of the narrow, slit windows.

There was something standing in the shadows just beyond the moonlight. A dark shape. As he watched, the shape moved slowly forward.

Callum's first thought was of a huge and strangely-proportioned wolf. It was almost five feet tall while standing on all fours. It had shaggy, black fur tinged with green and huge eyes that blazed like lanterns. The creature stared at Callum, tipping its head to one side, parting it's dark lips to reveal teeth that looked perfectly designed to tear flesh and crush bone.

The monster growled softly and padded towards Callum, its green eyes glittering in the moonlight.

CHAPTER 2

THE STRAND, LONDON. TWENTY YEARS LATER.

Jasper Wychwood hurried down Fleet Street and onto the Strand, towards the imposing architecture of the Royal Courts of Justice. He passed a rather alarming statue of a dragon rearing up behind a mediaeval kite shield and hoped it wasn't a bad omen for what he was about to face in court.

This feels like a trap. But who has set it? And why?

A grey-faced official had appeared in his communication orb that same morning to convey a stern message:

Mr J.S. Wychwood, you are required to attend a hearing at the Royal Courts of Justice, today, at 11am sharp. High officials of the Office for Paranormal Affairs will be presiding. You are politely advised not to be late, or judgement will be rendered in your absence.

The official refused to give any more information or answer his questions, but a couple of minutes later, a scribbled note had arrived from Rasmus, Jasper's friend and mentor:

Jasper—I'll be at the hearing today, and will do what I can to help you. Make sure you turn up—and try not to be late. I'll explain what's going on as soon as I can. R.

That was hardly what you'd call an explanation, but it was some comfort that Rasmus would be there and seemed ready to take his side.

If the court looked imposing from the outside, it was even more impressive on the inside. The cavernous entrance hall had a mosaic floor and a high, vaulted ceiling which made it look more like a cathedral than a courthouse. Jasper felt a flutter of nerves as he passed the many statues and portraits of the kings and queens of England which lined the hall.

'Mr Wychwood?'

The speaker was a dark-haired man in a business suit, who looked unremarkable in every way, except one: he was wearing a bootlace tie threaded through a brooch containing a large sapphire. The tie and the jewel marked him out as a seeker working for the Paranormal Office—London's magical government.

'Follow me, please, Mr Wychwood.'

The man spun around and hurried away. Jasper rushed to catch up with him. 'Am I allowed to know what this is all about?' he asked. 'Am I being accused of something?'

Jasper heard the jump in his own voice and hated it, but he couldn't help it if sounded a bit panicky. He *was* panicking.

'You'll find out soon. We mustn't keep the court waiting.'

He said this over his shoulder without even glancing back, his tone making it clear there would be no further discussion. He led Jasper through the grand hall and stopped in front of a marble statue of a man dressed in Tudor costume, with a doublet, tights, and frills around his neck and wrists. There was also a raised oval of marble on the front of his doublet.

The seeker looked around, scanning the area to make sure they weren't being observed. He waited for a pair of barristers in horse hair wigs to pass out of range, then reached out and touched the oval section of marble. For a split second, the oval glowed and transformed into a glittering gold brooch with a glowing emerald jewel at its centre. A moment later the statue slid forward just far enough to allow them to pass through into a hidden tunnel.

'Hurry please,' the seeker said testily, gesturing for Jasper to enter.

The tunnel was only wide enough for them to walk in single file, and the low ceiling forced them to hunch their shoulders and bow their heads. There were no windows and no lights in the tunnel, so both men conjured small globes of werelight to see by.

The air was chilly and smelled of earth and mould. Jasper wondered how long these tunnels had been here. They had none of the grandeur of the great hall above them and seemed more like part of a long lost mediaeval dungeon.

After rounding a couple of corners and descending a narrow flight of stone steps, they emerged into a larger corridor with werelight torches fixed to the walls and doors, and with benches along both sides. A few officials and other wizards were milling around, talking, but they fell silent and stared at Jasper with wide eyes as he passed by. The official led Jasper to a door with a brass plaque on it which read, 'Court of Magical Law: Court 1', and gestured for Jasper to enter.

The courtroom was grander than he'd been expecting after the grim tunnel and dreary corridor: it was wood-panelled, with a high, curving platform for judges to sit at, desks for lawyers and their clients, and wooden benches at the back for the public. The only thing that singled this place out as different from the mundane courtrooms above was the lack of windows and the presence of werelight sconces along the walls, which cast a weird, purplish glow over the room. There was also a large banner hanging down behind the raised platform with a triangular design of three overlapping arcs:

A court official motioned Jasper towards one of the empty tables at the front. As he moved, he scanned the people sitting on the benches. There were one or two he recognised, including a couple of seekers, and a journalist from the *Uncanny Chronicle*, who was frantically writing notes and glancing up at Jasper every couple of seconds.

They've dragged me to a public hearing, Jasper thought, grinding his teeth, *attended by the press, and I don't even know what it's about.*

Just before he sat down, he spotted Rasmus in the crowd. Normally, the old man's fulsome white beard and sparkling blue eyes gave him a jolly appearance, but just now he was frowning hard, as if he didn't approve of what he was seeing. Which hardly boded well.

The hubbub filling the courtroom began to subside as Jasper took his seat. There was a fine-looking crystal glass in front of him, alongside a pitcher of water. He poured himself a glass of water and drank some of it. His mouth had gone suddenly dry.

From behind him, there was a shout: 'All rise!'

Chairs were scraped across the floor as everyone, including Jasper, stood up. From a door at the front of the room, behind the raised platform, three people emerged and took their seats. Jasper recognised two of them, and he could guess who the third one was.

Arthur Sallow took the central seat. He'd recently been elected Minister for Paranormal Affairs, which meant he was in charge of the Paranormal Office and leader of the United Kingdom's magical government. In theory, he answered to the mundane Prime Minister, but in reality the head of the Paranormal Office usually had the final say on all matters that affected wizards and other supernatural citizens. He wasn't much over five feet tall, with a shiny bald head and a neat goatee-beard—the sort of man most people underestimated, sometimes to their detriment.

On Sallow's left was Erin Mayhew, the Paranormal Office's Keeper of Coin. She had a reputation for being a silky-smooth politician, but with a core of steel—someone you wouldn't want to cross. Her hair was pulled back into a severe bun and she wore angular tortoiseshell glasses. She smiled at Jasper as she sat down, but it was a smile that lacked warmth.

The third judge—if that's what they were—was assuredly Patrick Grimshaw, a thickset Glaswegian man with jet black hair, a handlebar moustache, and sideburns. Although Jasper had never met him before, everyone in London's magical community knew who he was. He'd once been a fearsome seeker—a magical investigator—and was now Chief Seeker, in charge of Paranormal Office security. Lately, he'd spearheaded the drive to track and control werewolves through mandatory microchips and tagging. It was rumoured that he'd wanted to go even further by building 'kennels' to imprison large swathes of the werewolf population, but Sallow had stepped in to curb his plans.

All three officials were wearing large jewels mounted in brooches around their throats. In addition, Jasper noticed they were all wearing what looked like matching signet rings with identical symbols. He was too far away to make out the symbols, but he guessed they would be the same as the one displayed on the banner behind them.

After what felt like a long lull in which Sallow cleared his throat and drummed his fingers on the desk in front of him, the Minister for Paranormal Affairs said, 'Thank you all for coming. This hearing is part of an investigation led by the Triumvirate—that is to say, by myself and ministers Mayhew and Grimshaw—into allegations of *espionage* within the Paranormal Office.'

A tense silence followed Sallow's pronouncement. Jasper felt sick. *Espionage? Really?* Was he about to be accused of spying? Or did they think he had information that implicated someone else?

Sallow continued. 'In the interests of transparency, this hearing is being held in public. In front of the *paranormal* public, that is,' he added with a genial smile. 'Witches, wizards, supernatural citizens, we are here to root out a threat to our collective security. I ask you to treat these matters with the seriousness they deserve.'

There were some coughs and murmurs from the crowd, but otherwise they remained in rapt silence. In his understated way, Sallow held their attention expertly.

Jasper could almost feel the crowd staring at the back of his head, wondering—as he was—what part he would be called on to play in this unfolding courtroom drama. They wouldn't have to wait long to find out. With his pronouncement out of the way, Sallow looked directly at Jasper for the first time.

'I call Mr Jasper Wychwood to the witness box.'

The wooden floorboards creaked noisily under his feet, shattering the silence as Jasper walked to the witness box. Once there, he sat down and tried to ignore the massive crowd of onlookers, focusing instead on Sallow.

'Thank you for coming, Mr Wychwood. Your testimony will be most helpful, I'm sure.'

Jasper nodded tightly.

'Are you aware of the violent attack on the Paranormal Office headquarters which took place in November last year, orchestrated by the lich assassin known as Blade?'

Jasper was, of course, well aware of the attack. Blade had committed several murders using blood magic before Jasper had tracked her down and put an end to her killing spree. Unfortunately, he'd only been able to catch her after she'd led a group of werewolves to attack the Paranormal Office headquarters on Whitehall.

'I'm aware of it, yes.'

'Infact, you crossed paths with Blade around that time, did you not?'

'Yes, but not until after—'

'And prior to that, you visited the liches' native realm and spoke with several associates of Blade, including the lich queen Celeste?'

'Yes, but—'

Erin Mayhew interjected, cutting short Jasper's answer. 'We appreciate your eagerness to assist our inquiry, Mr Wychwood, but there is no need to make elaborate statements. A simple yes or no answer shall suffice.' Mayhew's voice was as smooth as polished glass, and when she'd finished, she beamed at Jasper with brazen insincerity.

Jasper bit back a sarcastic reply. He was tempted to tell Mayhew and Sallow what he thought of this sham hearing, but that would do him no good. If they were about to stitch him up—and he felt sure they were—he was better off keeping his mouth shut, at least for now.

'And perhaps I can reassure you that we're merely interested in establishing the facts,' Sallow said. 'We don't intend to bring criminal charges against you as a result of these proceedings.'

'Unfortunately,' Grimshaw said, his voice a deep rumble. His arms were crossed over his broad chest and he was shooting Jasper a filthy look.

'That's very reassuring,' Jasper said. Somebody in the crowd behind him chuckled.

'As I was saying,' Sallow continued, choosing to ignore Jasper's sarcasm, 'you had several conversations with Blade and her associates. Did you discuss the Paranormal Office and its activities?'

Jasper paused before answering, wondering where they were going with this. 'Yes, but only in the most general terms.'

'Did you tell them about our security measures?' Grimshaw bellowed, leaning forwards. 'Did you tell them how to break in?'

'Of course not! I wouldn't *know* how to break into the Paranormal Office—I don't work there.'

'But you used to?' Sallow asked.

'Many years ago, yes.'

'Would it be fair to say that you bear a grudge against the Paranormal Office? After all, we sacked you from your job, banned you from practising magic, and, at the time in question, accused you of the murders Blade was responsible for.'

This is ridiculous. They can't possibly think I leaked infor-mation to Blade, could they?

'Look, I risked my life to defeat Blade. Why would I do that if I was in league with her?'

'No-one is suggesting you meant to betray us,' Mayhew said, her smile fixed in place. 'But we think you may have inadvertently given Blade information which allowed her to circumvent our security measures.'

'We have considered other explanations for these leaks,' Sallow added, before Jasper could protest any further. 'But you, Mr Wychwood, seem to be the most likely source.'

The noise from the crowd grew from a few hushed whispers to a wall of sound as people reacted to Sallow's accusation. Jasper turned around in his chair and located Rasmus among the crowd. His old friend looked him in the eye, a grim expression on his face, and shook his head slowly. His message seemed to be: *there's no point in contesting this—keep your powder dry for now.*

And he was right. This wasn't really a fact-finding hearing. Sallow and the others had already made up their minds, and nothing Jasper could say would alter their conclusions. He was their scapegoat. The purpose of dragging him here was to ensure the whole magical community of London knew he was to blame for this security leak. A useful idiot who unwittingly helped an undead assassin. The fact that it was all nonsense wouldn't matter—people would believe it anyway, especially since Jasper had a dodgy reputation in the supernatural community to begin with.

Sallow was banging a gavel on the desk in front of him, trying to silence the crowd.

'Quiet please! That will do for today, I think. We will have to ask Mr Wychwood some of our more... sensitive questions on another occasion, behind closed doors.'

'Wait a minute,' Jasper said, standing up and glaring at Sallow. 'You're not planning to drag me into court again are you? This circus has gone on long enough already.'

'The young fool has a point,' Grimshaw barked. 'If we want to question him again, we'd better keep him here until we're ready for him.'

Jasper looked from Grimshaw to Sallow, alarmed. 'You don't mean...'

'I'm afraid my colleague makes a good point,' Sallow said, shaking his head with what Jasper thought was probably feigned regret. 'If we let you leave, there's no guarantee you'll return voluntarily. We'll be forced to '*drag you*' back here, as you put it.'

Sallow looked towards a pair of seekers who were guarding the door. 'Please escort Mr Wychwood to the cells.'

CHAPTER 3

Two male seekers frogmarched Jasper out of the courtroom. He didn't resist—he suspected they'd slap handcuffs on him if he did.

The journalist from *Uncanny Chronicle* shouted questions at him as the seekers led him away.

'Are you really the source of the leaks? Did you mean to betray the government? Do you think you've been treated fairly?'

Jasper ignored her. Any answers he gave would be twisted to make him look even worse than he already did. This whole episode was a nightmare—a horrorshow. He'd thought that after the messy business with Blade, the authorities had accepted he wasn't a killer, or traitor, or some kind of lunatic.

Apparently not.

The seekers pushed him—none too gently—into a cell with bare stone walls, a grim-looking toilet in one corner, and a threadbare mattress on the floor. Before they shut the cell door they searched him—not a strip search, thank Merlin, but a distressingly thorough one nonetheless. They found and confiscated his small ruby ring, which contained a limited store of magical energy. Again, he didn't resist. What was the point? It wouldn't do any good.

Five minutes later, Rasmus arrived and stepped inside the cell. His jaw was tight and his eyes shone with anger, which Jasper felt reasonably confident had been provoked by the actions of the Triumvirate rather than himself. Some of the tightness in his chest lessened.

'I hope you're here to get me out, Rasmus. That so-called hearing was a complete farce. I have no idea how Blade and her werewolf mates broke into the Paranormal Office. I didn't even meet her until after—'

Rasmus put his palm up to silence Jasper. 'I know all that. This has all been a bloody circus—a show trial. The Triumvirate knows you aren't the source of the leaks, but, as usual, they're playing political games.'

'Then what's this all about? What are they playing at?'

Rasmus sighed heavily. 'Shall we sit down? This might take a while to explain.'

There were no chairs, so they both sat on the thin mattress on the floor and made themselves as comfortable as possible—which wasn't very comfortable at all. Rasmus had a bushy white beard and was wearing a long purple hued coat with bright, multicoloured buttons (he had unique, some would say garish, fashion taste). He reached inside the coat and brought out a metal flask, which he offered to Jasper.

'Thanks, but I'm trying to cut down.'

'It's coffee, lad. You look like you could use some caffeine.'

Jasper took the flask and sipped greedily. It was dark, bitter and delicious, with a hint of something spicy over the top. Rasmus was something of a coffee connoisseur, and it showed.

'So what's going on? I thought after what happened a few months ago, I was in the Paranormal Office's good books. Or at least no longer on their hit list.'

'Believe it or not, you *are* in their good books. That whole performance was just that—a performance. Sallow and the rest know you're not responsible for leaking government secrets.'

'So why publicly accuse me? I noticed a hack from the Uncanny Chronicle in the crowd, so we know what tomorrow's headline will be.'

Rasmus took a long drink from the coffee flask before answering. His expression remained grim, his mouth pinched into a thin line. Rasmus wasn't the kind of guy to take things too seriously most of the time, so he must be genuinely worried.

'The thing is, they're dealing with a lot more than a few leaks.'

He held Jasper's gaze and dropped his voice. 'There's a supernatural spy at the highest level of government who's been leaking information to the local werewolf packs, inciting them to violence. It's been going on for months now, and last week the press got wind of it. The *Chronicle* has been threatening to go public, pressing the Paranormal Office to comment, which is why they're acting now, trying to make everyone think they've identified the culprit.'

'Me?'

'I'm afraid so. Everyone with an ounce of sense knows it's nonsense, but your record is against you. I tried to talk them out of it, but it seems I don't have the same influence at the Paranormal Office I once had. The best I could do was to persuade Sallow to imply you might have given away information accidentally.'

Jasper laughed dryly. 'Fat lot of good that will do. Don't get me wrong, I'm grateful for your support, but the damage is done. The supernatural community now thinks I'm either a traitorous spy, or an idiot. Or both.'

'I know, I know,' Rasmus said tersely. 'It was the best I could do.'

'Instead of chasing their own tails, Sallow, Grimshaw and Mayhew should rethink their werewolf policy. It isn't leaks that are stirring up the werewolves—it's the fact that the government wants to forcibly tag and microchip them like dogs.'

The new policy of tagging and tracking werewolves had been the talk of London's magical community for months. It was a divisive issue. Many saw it as draconian and discriminatory, but others felt the government needed to take action to prevent werewolf attacks, which had increased in recent months. Jasper was firmly in the former category.

'I agree with you,' Rasmus was saying, 'but there has been little appetite for compromise since Ironclaw pack ransacked the Paranormal Office headquarters a few months ago. Rumours of a spy in their own ranks has only made the government more paranoid. What's more, there have been several wolf attacks on mundane citizens, so the mundane prime minister is apparently pushing for a crackdown as well.'

'So, is this spy a werewolf?'

Rasmus shrugged. 'No-one knows. It could just be someone who sympathises with their cause. Or the spy might have an entirely different agenda, which is somehow furthered by instigating a werewolf uprising.'

'Wheels within wheels' Jasper muttered. 'Great. But how does framing me help sort any of this out?'

Rasmus fiddled with the lid of his coffee flask. 'Because it buys time. They can pretend that the leaks are over and the situation is under control.'

'Except it isn't. Won't this all blow up in their stupid faces when the leaks continue while I'm incarcerated?'

Rasmus dipped his head and grimaced. 'You won't be incarcerated for much longer.'

Jasper frowned, wondering what Rasmus could possibly mean.

Then the penny dropped.

'Wait a second—you're not about to ask me to investigate this spy, are you? After that travesty of a hearing?'

'I'm afraid that's exactly what I'm about to ask. Remember, this wasn't my idea. You can say no if you want to.'

Rasmus offered the flask again, but Jasper refused. He'd had enough coffee—he was already feeling wired and tense, and more than a little angry. He stood up and paced the small cell. This was typical of the Paranormal Office leadership. Rather than simply asking for help, they'd manipulated the situation so that Jasper had little choice but to go along with their plan.

'Believe me, I share your frustration,' Rasmus said. 'But remember, in their own weird way, Sallow and the others are showing that they actually do trust you. They believed your explanation about what happened with Blade—and they credit you for saving London from her.'

'Then why drag me through the mud? People already suspect me of being a traitor—now they'll feel certain of it.'

Ramus stood up and put a hand on Jasper's shoulder, bringing his pacing to a halt. 'I said all this to Sallow and the others this morning. Got quite shirty with them as a matter of fact.'

'Do you really think I should agree to it?'

'Yes. But I think you should extract a handsome premium for your services.'

Jasper looked into Rasmus's face. For the first time, the old man smiled, his blue eyes gleaming bright.

'What do you have in mind?'

'Sallow, Mayhew and Grimshaw have agreed that if you catch the spy for them, they'll officially restore your right to practise magic, and invite you to become a seeker again. They also agreed—after some haranguing from yours truly—that they'll state publicly that you are not, and have never been, a traitor or a spy.'

It was a tempting offer. As a child, Jasper had dreamed of becoming a seeker and using his magic to protect the world from dark wizards, vampires and other unsavoury types. But when he'd finally achieved his dream, it hadn't worked out as he'd hoped. Now, he was being offered a second chance—a fresh opportunity to lead the life he'd always longed for.

And the final part of their offer—to publicly restore his reputation—was just as important to him. Ever since Jasper had been accused of treason and fired as a seeker, people had assumed he was a dark wizard—a dangerous creep who would sell his own grandmother for an ounce of power. If the Paranormal Office publicly proclaimed their renewed faith in him, it would go a long way towards bringing him back into the bosom of the supernatural community. He wouldn't be an outcast anymore.

But could he really trust this offer? Could he trust the likes of Sallow and the other magical leaders not to double cross him?

Even if he agreed, there was the small matter of actually catching this werewolf spy.

'If I'm going to do this, I must be allowed to use magic during the investigation—not just in emergency situations. Sallow can't expect me to search for a potentially dangerous spy with one hand tied behind my back.'

'Quite right,' Rasmus agreed. 'That would be most unrea-
sonable.'

With a flourish, the old man reached into his purple coat
and brought out a brooch containing a large, faceted ruby
surrounded by a circle of diamonds. It was far bigger than the
ruby ring Jasper had been forced to surrender earlier.

'I charged it up this morning,' Rasmus said. 'I'm afraid I don't
have a chain for it, but it's best if you don't wear it prominently,
anyway.'

Jasper took the ruby-and-diamond brooch and felt its considerable weight in his hand. He smiled, in spite of himself.
The thought of investigating again, with a proper store of
magic at his disposal, sent a pleasant prickle of trepidation
through him.

'Alright,' he said, placing the brooch in his pocket. 'I'm in.'

CHAPTER 4

THE PRIME MINISTER LOOKED tired, overworked, and out of his depth. His hair had gone from untidy to positively dishevelled over the course of the day. There were dark circles under his eyes. His purple paisley silk tie lay discarded on a nearby chair. Still, Callum had to give him some credit. It was after ten o'clock at night and he was still in his office at Number Ten Downing Street, working on affairs of state.

Callum hadn't knocked before entering the PM's private office. The Right Hon. Joseph Bingham MP barely looked up from his notes as his principal private secretary placed a steaming cup of black coffee on the desk in front of him.

A few moments later, Bingham finished the note he'd been writing, inhaled deeply, and smiled. 'Coffee! Just the thing. You're a good man, Callum. I don't know what I'd do without you.'

You'd make a mess of Prime Minister's Questions, for one thing.

Callum didn't rate Bingham as a leader—not that his views on the subject mattered much. Callum was a civil servant, not a politician. He served the government and prime minister chosen by the British people, whoever that might be. He'd worked for three successive PMs, and found Bingham to be the least impressive of the bunch. It was a mystery what the public saw in him. He was the sort of politician who tried to be chummy with everyone, a regular bloke-down-the-pub (despite being privately educated at great expense), but he was useless at leading the country. He simply muddled through each day trying to avoid getting deposed or losing his precious popularity.

Another way of putting it would be to say that Bingham was easy to manipulate. Which was rather convenient, as that was exactly what Callum intended to do.

'I don't mean to disturb you, prime minister. I can see you're busy.'

'Burning the midnight oil and all that,' Bingham said with forced joviality.

'I just came to see if I could take some of these policy papers off your hands. For instance, if you're ready to sign off on the...' Callum dropped his voice to a whisper '...werewolf policy.'

'Ah yes, I wanted to talk to you about that. Have a seat, there's a good chap.'

Callum sat down stiffly. *This doesn't bode well. Is the prime minister about to express an opinion on one of his government's policies? God help us...*

Bingham blew out a breath, puffing his cheeks and causing his flabby lips to wobble. 'You know, I still can't get my head around all this hocus-pocus business,' he said.

'No, sir.'

Bingham slurped down some of his coffee, then stood up and started pacing the room, forcing Callum to swivel in his chair to keep him in view.

Why did he ask me to sit down if he was planning to pace around the room like a caged lion?

'Wizards and vampires! Werewolves roaming the royal parks at night! Here, in London, under our very noses! It's incredible—literally *unbelievable*. When you arranged for me to have a secret briefing with that chap—Anthony, or whatever his name was—I thought he was going to tell me something about MI6 or Trident. Instead, he calmly informs me that there's a secret paranormal world operating parallel to our own, kept quiet from the public, run by a department of my government that I never even knew existed. It's barmy!'

'I'm sure it was a shock, sir.'

'It certainly was. I tried to tell Juliet about it, but somehow I couldn't get the words out. Probably for the best I suppose—she'd think I was off my trolley.'

Callum smiled to himself. The real reason Bingham hadn't been able to tell his wife about the Paranormal Office was that *Arthur Sallow*—the Minister for Paranormal Affairs—had put a spell on Bingham preventing him from blurting out anything about the supernatural community. Only a select few within the mundane government knew about the paranormal world, and they were subject to strict protocols preventing them from telling others what they knew. When Bingham left office, he'd soon forget everything he knew about wizards, werewolves and vampires.

'If it's any consolation sir, all prime ministers struggle with this at first. In my experience, the Paranormal Office is extremely self-sufficient. They take care of themselves without much need for intervention from the rest of the government.'

'That's the thing,' Bingham said, resuming his seat. He sat with his legs wide open and arms crossed over his paunch. His jowls continued to wobble as he spoke. 'Last time I met Sallow, I urged him to support this new werewolf policy, as you recommended. The idea that there are werewolves running freely around London, biting innocent citizens, is frankly alarming. Sallow seemed happy to go along with it—microchipping the blighters and so forth—but he did mention that the wolves are getting a bit restless. Organising themselves, staging protests. Although God-only-knows what a werewolf protest looks like.'

'I think they get together and do a lot of howling, sir.'

'Gosh. Well, anyway, Sallow is worried they might go further and start a violent rebellion if we push forward with microchipping. Can you imagine? I can't go down in history as the PM who allowed Londoners to be savaged by wolves. The idea is positively mediaeval!'

Callum felt a nervous twinge in his gut. He'd worked hard on the werewolf policy, canvassing support in both the mundane and magical branches of government. This was no time for the PM to get cold feet.

'Everything you're saying is exactly why we need to get a grip on the werewolves, sir. They're getting out of hand. Microchipping them gives us the best chance of keeping the situation under control.'

'So you've said before, but I think we need to tread lightly here. I'm sorry Callum but I'm going to put my foot down. I think Sallow will agree to bin the policy—or at least water it down—if I withdraw my support. He'd better—I'm still his boss, even if I didn't appoint him personally.'

Despite his bluster, there was a trace of doubt in Bingham's voice. In truth, he wasn't Sallow's boss in any meaningful sense. The supernatural authorities cooperated with the mundane government, but they did so on their own terms.

Callum leaned back in his seat and tried to stop his leg from shaking. A bead of cold sweat dribbled down his forehead. His symptoms were getting worse. Stressful situations aggravated them even more.

Why won't this upper class twit do as he's told?

Callum forced himself to remain calm and consider his options objectively. He reminded himself that Bingham was barely competent and, when it came to supernatural matters, out of his element. His ideas were shaped by fear—fear of werewolves, fear of his political opponents, fear of the supernatural world that he'd only recently found out about and which he didn't understand.

That train of thought gave him an idea.

'I feel I should warn you that concerns have been raised that the werewolves might try to assassinate a member of the government if this policy goes through. The previous PM was afraid of being attacked personally.'

'That old goat! I'm sure he was, but I'm made of sterner stuff. I'm serious about this Callum—I want to ditch the poli cy.'Bingham's jaw was set and he was frowning. There was no point in arguing further. The PM was digging his heels in and it would be hard to budge him now.

Hard, but not impossible. Callum just had to increase the fear factor. And he already knew exactly how he was going to do that.

'I understand perfectly, sir. I'll set things in motion.'

'Good man,' said Bingham, looking relieved. 'At least I won't get accused of U-turning again in parliament, since this paranormal business is so hush-hush. Honestly, if you'd told me about werewolves and wizards when I was still a backbench er...'

Bingham chuntered on contentedly, while Callum pretended to tidy up some papers on the desk, waiting for an opportune moment to leave. It was frustrating, though not surprising, that the PM had changed his mind. Bingham was notorious for flip-flopping, especially when things got tough. It never ceased to amaze Callum that Bingham and many of his political colleagues craved power with an almost messianic fervour, yet didn't know what to do with it once they got it. They often seemed relieved when a civil servant like Callum took decisions out of their hands.

Callum hadn't got where he was today by letting others make decisions for him. If he had, he'd still be mucking out pig pens on Murray's farm. When he'd finally left the Isle of Islay, he realised that his intelligence and bookishness—which for so long had seemed like a sort of handicap, a weird quirk that got in the way of good, honest farmwork—was actually an asset. He realised there were many things a bright young man could do which would bring him success and status. His sharp mind had allowed him to secure a scholarship at Cambridge and afterwards ascend the Whitehall hierarchy quicker than most of his peers.

His sharp mind—and his powerful friend on the *other side* of Whitehall.

Callum politely turned down the offer of a whisky from the PM and left his office. He'd need to be quick if his plan was to work. Now that he'd made a decision (just the one), Bingham wouldn't spend much longer in his office. He'd throw back his whisky and then go upstairs to the private flat he shared with his wife.

Callum made his way downstairs to a meeting room on the ground floor that was rarely used. He threw open the window and looked out. The Downing Street rose garden was gloomy, but since it was the middle of July, not completely dark. *Perfect*. Bingham would have a good view.

Callum locked the door of the meeting room and stripped off his clothes, leaving them in a neat pile on a chair.

Then he thought about home.

The windswept island, the waves crashing noisily against jagged rocks, the fresh, salty air blowing in off the sea. He pictured the lost souls floating around Murray's farm, looking for a guide to lead them to the beyond. He remembered Kildalton church, a place of safety and comfort despite being open to the elements and clogged with weeds.

The desire to return to Islay was almost overwhelming.

To run across the open landscape, bare his teeth, howl at the silvery moon.

And kill.

He took control of the yearning and mastered it. This part was becoming more difficult. Every time he transformed these days, it became harder to control. He was afraid that one day he wouldn't be able to stop the rush of canine instincts that threatened to vanquish his human thoughts. But that was a problem for another day.

Bristling hairs burst out of Callum's skin and his mouth stretched into a snarling snout full of razor sharp teeth. His pasty skin gave way to a coat of deep black of fur that shimmered with a green tinge. He grew vicious claws and put on several kilograms of weight—muscle, sinew, claws, and fangs.

He leapt out of the open window and landed softly in the Downing Street rose garden. The air outside felt fresh on his fur. The pleasant smell of roses filled his sensitive nose. He padded into the shadowy bushes. He wanted to be seen, but not by just anyone. There were already rumours fizzing through Whitehall of wolf attacks in the capital—which those few who knew about the paranormal community realised were werewolf attacks. Callum had fuelled some of those rumours himself, but he didn't want people thinking there were werewolves actually stalking the grounds of Downing Street.

Except, of course, for one specific person.

He found a comfortable spot and lay on his front, resting his snout on his paws. It wasn't easy to keep still and quiet—it went against his canine instincts. He realised he was growling and forced himself to stop.

Once settled, he scanned the windows. There were only a handful of lights on in the building. The empty meeting room was one. The prime minister's private office was another.

In this form, he had excellent eyesight, far better than human Callum's, who wore glasses with thick lenses. He got a bead on the PM. He was strutting around his office, raising his glass of whisky in an imaginary toast, opening and closing his mouth. Perhaps he was talking to someone on speakerphone, but more likely he was reciting a speech and imagining—optimistically—that he was getting a rapturous response from his audience.

Suddenly, Bingham stopped in his tracks. He wheeled around, his eyes darting around his office and then turning toward the window. He knew he was being watched.

Callum inched forward, poking his head out of the bush.

He knew from experience that his wolfish eyes were unusually large and glowed like green spotlights.

Bingham's gaze snapped to him. His eyes bulged with fear.

Slowly, ever so slowly, Callum crept forward, coming fully out of the bushes, unfolding himself, revealing himself to be far larger than any wolf. He peeled back his black lips to show his teeth.

Bingham turned white. The whisky glass dropped out of his hand. For a long moment, he stood frozen in place. Then he turned and lurched out of the room.

Callum retreated into the bush, pleased with his work. He'd wait until tomorrow morning before urging Bingham to change his mind on the werewolf policy. Let him spend a sleepless night stewing in fear.

Everything was going to plan.

CHAPTER 5

WYCHWOOD BOOKS HAD BEEN doing a roaring trade for several weeks, and it was driving Jasper mad.

He knew he should be more grateful for the increase in custom. The money from those book sales would come in handy, filling up his black hole of an overdraft, but he found dealing with the public difficult. In his experience, many customers of independent bookshops liked to spend ages chatting with the owner only to leave without making a purchase. He didn't mind people who browsed quietly or inquired about a specific book—it was the blowhards and talkative tourists that really grated. Also, since his bookshop served both mundane and magical customers, he had to be careful to keep the former away from books intended for the latter.

One sarcastic customer asked if he modelled his customer service methods on Ebenezer Scrooge. Rather than refute the accusation, Jasper told the bloke he'd better buy something or bugger off. Fortunately, today he had the perfect excuse to keep the bookshop closed—he had to start his investigation into the Whitehall spy.

It was early in the morning, at least by Jasper's night-owl standards, and he was still in bed, contemplating the day ahead. Now that he was fully awake he slid his feet into furry slippers, wrapped himself in his favourite towelling dressing gown, and went downstairs to make tea and toast.

Jasper was a naturally untidy person, but lately he'd made more of an effort to keep the flat above the bookshop relatively clean and tidy. He did this partly to keep at bay the waves of depression he was prone to, and partly out of a vague hope that he might someday have company in the flat. He'd been on a couple of dates recently—his first for ages—and although they hadn't led to anything more exciting than a fumbled kiss, Jasper was starting to have hope he might not be completely repulsive to every woman in London.

The kitchen, however, was another story. The washing up was piled high, and it smelled as though something that had once been food was now decomposing.

Come on mate, Jasper chided himself. *Get your act together.*

After making a dent in the washing up, Jasper took his breakfast downstairs into the bookshop. *Wychwood Books* was looking less forlorn than it had for a long while. He'd started vacuuming once a week and had evicted most of the spiders that loved building webs in gloomy corners.

Jasper was feeling positively chipper when he went to check his post. There were a couple of bills, but of much greater interest was a letter from the *Wimbledon Centre for the Incurably Delusional.* Officially, and to any mundanes who inquired, it was a psychiatric hospital catering to those suffering from the delusion that they possessed occult power. In reality, it was a high security prison for supernatural criminals.

Jasper tore open the letter and stared at several sheets of paper covered with his own handwriting. It was a letter he'd sent to his brother Tristram the week before, returned to sender. Jasper scanned the pages. At the bottom of the last page, below his own signature, he found a single sentence in Tristram's handwriting:

Debts must always be paid, little brother.

Jasper muttered darkly under his breath. 'Debts must be paid' was a pet saying of their father's. During their childhoods, he'd often made Jasper and Tristram feel like any mistakes they made would be held over them like a bad debt.

If Tristram had intended to make his younger brother feel guilty and anxious, he'd succeeded.

Tristram and Jasper's childhoods had been tumultuous, and they'd fallen out many times, but they'd also shared a close bond. That changed when Tristram joined forces with the dark wizard Yarrow and Jasper joined the Paranormal Office as a seeker tasked with combating Yarrow and his supporters.

As a child, Jasper lacked the ability to cast magic. Yarrow and Tristram both played a role in turning Jasper into a wizard when he was a teenager, so Tristram regarded it as a rank betrayal when Jasper sided with the authorities against Yarrow. Never mind that the guy was a power-obsessed maniac who killed his rivals as ruthlessly as any mafia boss.

Inevitably, when Yarrow was defeated, Tristram was arrested and imprisoned for his role in the rebellion. That was nearly eight years ago—and Tristram's time in prison was nearly at an end. Despite all that had happened, Jasper had hoped they'd be able to get back on friendly terms when his brother was freed.

Debts must always be paid... Tristram's meaning was clear. He believed Jasper was indebted to him and Yarrow. Until that debt was paid, Jasper's attempts to repair their relationship would be rebuffed.

Satisfied that there was nothing else to be gleaned from the letter, Jasper chucked it in the wastepaper bin. He'd invited his brother to come and visit him at the bookshop—to stay for a while, if he needed somewhere to crash—but that was obviously not going to happen. Far from getting over what had happened, he could only assume Tristram was more bitter than ever.

As he was finishing his toast, Jasper's mobile phone—a battered looking old Nokia that was at least fifteen years old—rang. Jasper fished the Nokia out of the pocket of his dressing gown and answered it.

A woman with an American accent said, 'Jasper, I need your help right away.'

CHAPTER 6

Jasper arrived at Bethnal Green police station about forty minutes later. There was a woman with a far off stare and tear-stained cheeks sitting in the waiting area. Jasper swallowed hard and went to the desk, which was protected by a thick sheet of perspex. The copper behind it was about six feet tall, stocky, with a shiny bald head and a challenging expression on his face. Jasper was grateful he'd had the presence of mind to add a tie to his usual ensemble of a crumpled white shirt, dark jeans, and a black overcoat. The next few minutes were going to demand all his powers of persuasion—plus a generous sprinkling of magic.

'I'm here for Ms Alyssa Morgan,' he said.

The copper stared sullenly at him. 'And you are?'

'Her solicitor. Jasper Wychwood, of... erm... Wychwood and Associates, Bloomsbury Street.'

The copper raised an eyebrow, but thankfully didn't question his credentials. 'Have a seat. Someone will be out in a moment.'

Jasper nodded and took a seat next to the tearful woman. He tried to shake off the feeling that he wouldn't escape this place—that the police would guess he wasn't a real lawyer and lock him up.

Ten minutes later a young detective emerged and ushered him through a door into the main area of the police station.

'We're ready to start right away, if you are,' she said, smiling at him in a bland, professional way. She was clutching a steaming black coffee in a red Arsenal mug and was smartly dressed in a blue shirt and dark grey suit jacket. Unfortunately for Jasper, she didn't look like the kind of person who'd be easily tricked. He'd been hoping for a copper who banged their meaty fists down on desks and was easily bamboozled, but she didn't look the type. He reminded himself that most police officers weren't like that these days, and he should probably stop watching cheesy cop shows from the seventies.

The detective showed him to a tiny, windowless interview room where Alyssa was sat glaring at a male detective with blond, straw-like hair and a nasty case of acne. Alyssa herself was in her mid-twenties and had shoulder-length brown hair. She was wearing a leather jacket and a *screw-you* expression, which Jasper assumed was aimed at the detectives rather than himself.

'Are we ready to get started?' the female detective said briskly, taking a seat next to the spotty officer and motioning for Jasper to sit next to his 'client'.

'Let's get this over with,' Alyssa said, before whispering in Jasper's ear. 'Thanks for coming. You can put a hex on them or something, right?'

Jasper smiled tightly and nodded. Out loud, he said, 'Just answer the nice detectives' questions and I'm sure we can sort this out in no time.'

Detective Spotty frowned and narrowed his eyes at Jasper, who suddenly realised that what he'd just said wasn't the sort of thing a real defence solicitor would say.

Damn. Get it together.

'Well then, let's get started,' said the female detective. She pressed a button on the boxy recorder on the desk between them and the device emitted a long continuous beep. She then introduced the people in the room for the benefit of the recording.

Reaching behind her, the detective picked up something heavy and laid it on the table in front of Alyssa. It was a revolver in a clear plastic evidence bag. Jasper recognised it at once. Alyssa had used it to save his backside from super-natural nasties more than once.

'Perhaps you can start by telling us what this is.'

'It's my gun.' Alyssa had her arms crossed over her chest and sounded surly. Jasper wanted to hiss at her to sit up straight and to be civil. If the police were too suspicious or hostile, the spell he was planning to use might not work.

'Do you have a licence for this firearm?'

'No. But I didn't buy it here.'

'You mean you imported it into this country?'

'I brought it with me when I came here, yes.'

'From the United States?'

'Yes.'

'Did you declare it at customs?'

Alyssa paled. 'I didn't think that was necessary, they didn't ask.'

The two detectives shared a significant look.

'So, to be clear, you smuggled this gun into the United Kingdom, and you don't have a licence for it? Is that right?'

'I didn't think it would be a problem,' Alyssa said weakly. She gave Jasper a sideways look that said, *Get me out of this!*

She's not making this easy for me, Jasper thought irritably.

He looked over at the two detectives. He reckoned the woman was in charge—she was leading the questioning—so he focused his attention on her, looking her straight in the eye. As he did so, he put his hand in his pocket and drew power from the ruby brooch that Rasmus had given him. The ruby acted as a kind of magical battery, boosting his magical power. Fire magic was his specialism, but all mages were taught to perform a range of spells, including ones capable of affecting the thoughts and emotions of others. Such spells were especially effective against mundanes who knew nothing about magic.

The female detective's expression clouded over. She blinked and turned her head to the side, frowning at the wall. Jasper gave her his best winning smile and said, 'You've clearly been very thorough in your police work, And my client has obviously made an unfortunate administrative mistake, for which she is very sorry.'

Jasper elbowed Alyssa in the ribs. 'That's right,' she said. 'I screwed up the forms, sorry. It could happen to anyone.'

Detective Spotty laughed humourlessly. 'This is a lot more serious than an admin cock-up. Your client has just admitted to a very serious crime.'

Jasper nodded seriously. 'Ms Morgan was unfortunately unaware of how different the gun laws are here in the UK. Now that you have brought this to her attention, she'll obtain the correct documents as soon as possible. Won't you?'

'Absolutely,' Alyssa said.

Although Jasper was answering Spotty's question, he continued staring at the female detective, not letting his eyes drift away for a single second. She was staring right back at him and her mouth had fallen open, a slack jawed, vacant expression on her face.

Spotty leaned forward and jabbed his finger at Alyssa.

'I've got three witnesses saying you brandished this weapon in broad daylight, Ms Morgan. That's a serious offence in this country, carrying a possible custodial sentence. Even if you had a licence for the weapon, that would not give you the right to carry it in public and wave it around whenever you felt like it.'

The detective flushed red with anger, the copious spots on his forehead and cheeks looking like crushed cherries. Meanwhile, his colleague was slumped in her chair, going cross-eyed.

'Look,' Alyssa said, 'I didn't mean to break the law, but I was being threatened. I have a right to protect myself, don't I?'

'Protect yourself from what?'

'From a wolf. A big one.'

Spotty threw back his head and let out a laugh which sounded more like a cough.

'A wolf? In London? That's your defence, is it?'

Spotty was losing his temper, but that wasn't a bad thing. Meanwhile, the other detective was refocusing her attention on the interview, although her eyes were wide as dinner plates.

'There are lots of wolves in London,' Alyssa said, 'and some of them are really stirred up at the moment.'

Spotty shook his head in disbelief. 'Just to be clear, you're telling us you were brandishing an illegal firearm in public to protect yourself from a wolf? Despite the fact there haven't been wolves running wild in England for hundreds of years?'

Alyssa rolled her eyes. 'I just told you, there are loads of wolves in London.'

Jasper decided it was time to break up this cosy chat. 'My client was acting to protect herself and other innocent bystanders from this wild animal. No-one was hurt in this incident, I assume?'

He glanced at Alyssa, hoping it was true. She nodded.

'In that case, I think we can all consider the matter resolved. My client will get her paperwork in order straight away, won't you?'

'Definitely,' she said.

'Good.' Jasper met the female detective's gaze. 'So we can consider the case closed?'

Spotty looked as if he was about to explode, but before he could respond his colleague said, 'I agree. The matter is resolved.' There was a faraway look in her eye—she looked like someone who had taken a nap and hadn't fully woken up yet.

'Excellent. So my client is free to go?'

'She is free to go, yes.'

Jasper stood up quickly, and Alyssa followed his lead. Spotty stared aghast at his colleague.

'This interview is far from over,' he spluttered. 'Sit down, both of you.'

'I think it's over,' Jasper said.

'Me too,' said the female detective. 'Interview terminated at 11.17.' She pressed a button on the recorder.

Spotty gaped at his colleague, apparently lost for words. His mouth opened and closed but no sound came out. Jasper grabbed Alyssa's arm and steered her towards the exit. The spell had worked and its effects were rather amusing, but they wouldn't last forever. They needed to get out of this police station now, while they still could.

'Kate, what's going on?' Spotty hissed. 'We've got more than enough evidence to press charges!'

'I don't think so,' Jasper whispered under his breath.

'I don't think so,' Kate said.

At the door, Alyssa prodded Jasper and pointed at the gun in the evidence bag.

'Oh, and thank you for looking after the revolver,' Jasper said. 'We'll be taking that now.'

'Yes, of course,' said the female detective, jumping up from her seat and handing the bag to Alyssa. 'Thanks for everything.' She beamed at Jasper and gave him a handshake that was slightly alarming in its enthusiasm.

When he'd extricated his hand from the hexed detective's grip, Jasper whisked Alyssa out of the police station as quickly as possible without actually breaking into a sprint.

CHAPTER 7

JASPER HALF-EXPECTED TO HEAR sirens and see blue lights chasing after them, but ten minutes later he concluded that they'd successfully evaded the long arm of the law. They walked down Bethnal Green Road, past The Marquis of Cornwallis pub, which Jasper eyed longingly before turning into a greasy spoon cafe where he and Alyssa both ordered egg and chips and mugs of dark brown tea.

'I thought you were about to show me a new pub,' Alyssa said, munching happily on her chips.

'It's a bit early for that,' Jasper said. 'Besides, I'm on a detox at the moment. Trying to cut down on the booze.'

Alyssa smiled teasingly. 'Fried egg and French fries doesn't sound like a detox to me.'

'It's my cheat day.'

'I'm not complaining. The fries taste great.'

'Don't they just,' Jasper said, dipping one into a dollop of ketchup.

'Thanks for helping me out with the cops back there.'

'I'm happy to help, but you need to be more careful. Just because you're part of the supernatural community doesn't mean you can get away with waving a gun around in public. This isn't Chicago.'

Alyssa raised her hands. 'OK, OK. Point received and understood. It's not like I'm some kind of gun nut who pulls out their weapon every chance I get. And Chicago's not as dangerous as people like to make out, for your information.'

Jasper nodded, wiping his greasy fingers on a serviette. 'So what actually happened? How did you end up confronting a werewolf?'

Alyssa leaned forward conspiratorially. The cafe was quite busy, with people bustling around and talking in loud voices, but nobody seemed interested in eavesdropping on their conversation. 'I've embedded myself with a group of werewolves from Silverback pack for the last three months.'

'Embedded?'

'Yeah. You know how journalists embed themselves with troops during a war? And some of the werewolves I've been speaking to think they are involved in a war against the government. They're furious about this plan to forcibly microchip them. They see it as an attack on their freedom, and I agree with them.'

Jasper chewed a chip thoughtfully. 'So do I, as it happens. Werewolf numbers have got a bit out of hand recently, but the authorities' response is too heavy-handed. They should work with the wolf packs, not try to control them.'

'Exactly. The wolves are afraid the government intends to go even further and lock them all up in kennels. Somebody in the government leaked a plan to do that a few months ago.'

Jasper held his cup of tea, allowing it to warm his hands. *Could this be a leak from the Whitehall spy?*

'I certainly hope that's not true, he said. 'But, regardless, you've got to be more careful. Werewolves deserve to be treated fairly, but they're still dangerous.'

Alyssa lifted her chin defiantly. 'The ones I've met have treated me very nicely.'

'Apart from the one you pulled a gun on?'

'Apart from that one, yes. Most of them just want to get the truth out. They want more support from the rest of the supernatural community.'

'Is that what you're doing? Spreading the word about werewolf rights?'

'Sort of. I'm reporting on the werewolf rebellion for my podcast. It's called *The Best of Both Worlds*—it's about the often fraught relationship between the mundane and magical worlds of London. I'm getting listeners from across the divide—mages and non-mages.'

'Blimey. The Paranormal Office will have kittens if they find out about this, and there won't be anything I can do if *they* arrest you.'

Alyssa arched an eyebrow. 'Are you about to tell me you don't have freedom of speech in this country, either?'

'Not when it comes to telling ordinary people about the magical world, no.'

'That's the whole point of the podcast. So-called "mundanes" have a right to know the truth. After all, they're the ones most likely to be victimised by vampires, rogue wizards, or werewolves.'

Jasper knew it was pointless arguing with her. Alyssa was on a one-woman crusade to tell the mundane public about magic. He wasn't sure he agreed with her goals—or her methods for that matter—but he respected her determination.

'The trouble is,' Alyssa continued, 'most of my non-magical listeners seem to think the podcast is fictional. They keep calling me a "creative genius" and storyteller, as if I'm making this stuff up. But it's all real!'

Jasper smiled. 'Some would say there are worse things than being labelled a "creative genius".'

'Right. But people are talking about the podcast like it's a radio drama.'

'It sounds like that time they made H. G. Wells' *War of the Worlds* into a radio drama, and some people thought they were reporting a real alien invasion. Except with your podcast, it's the opposite way around. What you're reporting is real but everyone thinks it's fiction.'

Alyssa huffed out a long breath and pushed the remains of her egg and chips away from her. 'I just wish more people would take it seriously, that's all.'

'Maybe they will, eventually. In the meantime, are you learning a lot about the werewolves' grievances?'

'Loads. It's getting serious, Jasper. The packs are determined to make the Paranormal Office change its mind. Some are even talking about overthrowing the government by force.'

Interesting. Jasper knew that relations between wizards and werewolves were getting fraught, but if what Alyssa said was accurate, the situation was more serious than he'd realised. No wonder the authorities were panicking about the prospect of a werewolf-sympathiser in their ranks.

'Any particular reason you're interested in the werewolves,' Alyssa said, 'or are you just being polite?'

Jasper couldn't think of a reason not to tell her the truth. Not only did he trust her, but her contacts among the werewolves might help kickstart his investigation. The Paranormal Office had virtually forced him into helping them, so he felt under no obligation to keep his investigation secret.

'I do have a specific reason to be interested, yes. I've agreed—reluctantly—to search for a spy in the government who is apparently leaking information to the werewolf packs.'

Alyssa's eyes went wide. 'Wow. OK, you've got my attention. Tell me everything.'

Jasper relayed everything he'd been told about the spy, including the fact they were suspected of helping Blade the assassin break into the Paranormal Office a few months ago.

When he'd finished, Alyssa said, 'I think I know who it is.'

Jasper's mouth fell open. 'Really? Who?'

Is this about to become the shortest investigation of all time?

'I don't know their name, but there are rumours of a werewolf ally inside the government. They're supposed to be a shifter of some kind, but they're not a member of any of the werewolf packs. The wolves I've met call them The Stray.'

'If that's true, at least one person within the werewolf packs must know who it is. Could you introduce me to the wolves you've met through your podcast?'

Alyssa narrowed her eyes. 'I'm not sure I approve of helping the Paranormal Office with one of its investigations, since they're the ones infringing on the wolves' civil rights. But as you're a friend—'

'—a friend who just got you out of jail—'

'—I'll do what I can to help. As it happens, there's going to be a big werewolf gathering tonight on Hampstead Heath. The three London packs are meeting to decide what to do next. And they're expecting The Stray to show up.'

CHAPTER 8

IN A POKY OFFICE at Number 10 Downing Street, Callum Kirk was working late. He was a hard-working person by nature, who loved nothing more than reading policy papers late into the night and mastering their intricate details. That was one reason he'd risen so high in the government. He worked hard and strived to be the best informed person in any room, although he avoided making a show of his cleverness. He shunned the limelight and disliked most social events.

That was one side of his nature. The other side was much darker and more animalistic.

As the evening wore on—it was after 8pm already—he tried to settle into a rhythm and put a serious dent in his to-do list, but that was proving difficult. With every minute that passed he grew more agitated. His hands trembled and his handwriting became messier. His mind wandered from the task at hand to other things. The desire to roam freely through the night. The urge to hunt and kill. The exquisite feeling of ripping bloody flesh from bone. The salty, metallic tang of blood. And running through all of it, a burning desire to return home to Scotland and commune with the wandering souls that linger there.

These urges were diametrically opposed to the desires of Callum the hard-working civil servant. It was as though his brain was home to two warring sets of instincts that could never be reconciled.

Callum noticed sweat dripping off his face—a small puddle of it lay on the document in front of him, blurring the carefully considered words he'd just written with a fountain pen.

'For fuck's sake,' he swore. 'Will this never end?'

It was no good—he couldn't stave off the transformation any longer. He opened his briefcase, which contained six small glass vials. Each one had a wax seal, but five of the seals were broken, the contents of the vials already used up. Callum pulled out the last vial and tipped the inky black liquid it contained down his throat.

The taste was vile. He quickly followed it up with a drink of water to wash away the bitter aftertaste.

He sat breathing hard as the potion took effect. Six vials had once lasted him the best part of a year, but he'd got through this latest batch in only a few weeks. You didn't have to be a top civil servant to know that was not sustainable.

Was his contact adulterating the potion, perhaps? Watering it down to bolster her profits? He hoped that was true, for, if so, he could confront her and get the dosage back to normal.

But deep down he knew that wasn't really the problem. He'd been taking the same potion for years, and its effectiveness had waned slowly over time. Even taking frequent doses, the potion was becoming less effective at containing his symptoms. The wolfish side of him was always near the surface now, threatening to take over completely. His greatest fear was that one day it would lay claim to his mind, driving away his human personality for good.

It's like being held hostage by a maniac who could kill you at any moment.

When he was young he'd entertained the notion that the wolfish form might not be so bad and might even have some advantages. Now he had to admit the truth.

It was a horrible curse.

Callum stood up and opened the window as far as it would go. His regular office was on an upper floor of the building, but he worked in this rarely-used meeting room on the ground floor instead when his transformation was near. In a pinch, he could escape into the Downing Street rose garden and hide there, or even, in extreme circumstances, sneak into London, though doing so was fraught with risk.

The potion allowed him to maintain his human form for longer and prevented the canine thoughts from taking over completely when he did transform. But as well as getting less effective it was now also causing distressing side effects: sweating, shaking hands, a sour stomach, yellow fingernails.

Thoroughly distracted, Callum decided he was done with government business for the night. He reached into his briefcase and fished out a letter he'd already opened and read. In his normal life he was known as Callum Murray, but this letter was addressed to Mr Kirk at a PO box on the Isle of Islay. From there, it had been forwarded to London as part of Callum's careful arrangements to keep correspondence related to magic separate from his mundane life.

Dear Mr Kirk,

It is with regret that we must inform you that your latest application for magical training has been refused on the grounds of age and suitability. As you know, most applicants begin training at the age of eighteen, since learning the arcane arts becomes increasingly difficult after the age of twenty-five. Moreover...

Callum had read the letter so many times he almost knew it by heart.

Why do I torture myself by re-reading it? Am I hoping the answer will change?

As well as citing his advanced age—he was only thirty-seven!—the letter explained, in a roundabout way, that shifters were unsuitable for wizard training. He didn't blame them for taking that attitude—he didn't trust shifters either, even though he was one. He didn't trust himself when he changed.

Callum laid aside the letter and took a deep breath. The potion, he judged, had done its work, though not nearly as effectively as it once had. The urge to transform was still there, only now he was reasonably confident he'd been able to remain in control while in his wolfish form. He decided to transform for a short time to scratch the itch.

He undressed quickly and let the transformation take hold.

It was like sinking into icy water. Shocking, intense, and strangely thrilling.

On all fours, he paced the room several times, getting the feel for his new body, stretching his limbs. He could see how some people might enjoy this. It felt freeing—but that feeling of freedom was really a trap. If he surrendered to it, he'd lose his humanity forever.

Before long he felt tired—the potion sometimes had that effect—so he curled up on the floor for a nap.

A strange noise awoke him a while later. It was a horrible sound, like the hissing of some dreadful monster. Instinctively, he hated it. And it was getting closer... it was just behind the door!

Belatedly, with his human thoughts several steps behind his animal instincts, he realised it was the sound of a vacuum cleaner.

Before he could react, the door to the office banged open.

Without looking back, Callum leapt out of the open window and into the rose garden. His heart was pounding, his hackles were up. He darted towards a shadowy spot in the bushes and lay on the ground, his ears pinned back, resisting the urge to whine with fear. Both sides of him were afraid: the wolf feared the hissing monster, and the man feared the consequences of being seen in this form.

He stared back at the window. A cleaner—a middle-aged woman—was running the vacuum cleaner through the office. He'd forgotten to lock the door. How could he have been so stupid? She moved his chair aside to hoover under it. Callum studied her face. She looked tired and bored, which suggested she hadn't seen Callum in his animal form.

Callum's breathing settled back to normal. He still detested the sound of the vacuum cleaner, but the potion allowed his human thoughts to reassure the dog side of him that there was nothing to fear.

He licked his fur contentedly for a while, then something made his gaze snap back to the cleaning lady. She'd switched off the vacuum cleaner and was picking something up from his desk—a piece of paper. His letter. The one denying him access to wizard training.

Panic flooded him.

Abject fear.

If his secret got out, his career—his life as he knew it—would be over.

That couldn't happen.

He bounded back towards the office, intending to transform when he reached the window to climb back in. But—he realised with horror—if he did that, he'd be naked. How on earth would he explain that?

The cleaning lady's hand was on the door handle. She was about to leave, with the letter still clutched in her hand. She was going to show it to someone.

Throwing caution to the wind, Callum leapt through the window and dived towards the cleaning lady. He intended to grab the letter from her, but, still being in his canine form, he used his teeth to do so. He bit down on the letter and ripped it away from her.

Too late, he realised his jaws had also closed over the hand that held the letter.

Blood spattered the carpet.

The cleaning lady stared at him in horror, her hand mangled and bloody. She opened her mouth to scream.

Callum pounced again, sinking his teeth into her neck, silencing her scream, as a hot spurt of blood filled his mouth.

CHAPTER 9

It was nearly 10pm and Hampstead Heath was blanketed in darkness. The clusters of oak and beech trees created thick clots of inky blackness, and there were only a handful of lampposts lighting the pathways that meandered across the grass. Alyssa activated the torch on her iPhone to help light their way.

Despite the late hour, a large number of people were walking through the Heath in the same direction, holding shining smartphones or battery powered torches. Jasper felt a surge of trepidation as he realised they were all werewolves on their way to the same gathering. Some of them gazed suspiciously at Jasper and Alyssa as they passed but no-one bothered them.

'Don't worry,' Alyssa said, as if reading Jasper's thoughts. 'Silverback pack have promised to keep me safe, and they'll do the same for you.'

'What makes you think I'm worried?'

'You're trembling and you keep looking behind you.'

Well, that's embarrassing. He crossed his arms over his midriff to stop the trembling.

'In my defence, the last time I encountered werewolves, they tried to rip my throat out.'

'I know—I was there. But like I say, the Silverback wolves will protect us. Look—here's Niko now.'

Niko was the Silverback werewolf who had agreed to be interviewed for Alyssa's podcast. He had dirty blonde hair scraped back into a ponytail and was dressed in scuffed jeans and an orange tie dye T-shirt. He looked young and spoke quietly when Alyssa introduced them. 'Um, how many people are gonna hear this?'

'Not many,' Alyssa said brightly. '*The Best of Both Worlds* is quite a niche podcast. Most of my non-magical listeners still think werewolves are creatures from fairy tales.'

Niko seemed to relax a little. 'That figures. Most mundanes will go to any length to explain away shit they don't understand.'

'How long have you been a werewolf, Niko?' Jasper asked, thinking how young he looked.

Niko thrust out his chin. 'Nearly two years. I wasn't attacked or kidnapped if that's what you're thinking. I chose this life.'

He spoke with surprising seriousness for someone who couldn't be older than twenty. 'You *chose* to become a werewolf?'

'Yeah. I know most wizards think all young wolves are victims who were bitten against their will, but that's not true. I always wanted to join a pack. It's a good life—you look out for your pack brothers and sisters and they look out for you. I'm not saying it isn't tough sometimes, but it beats getting kicked around at school by bigger kids.'

Jasper noticed Alyssa was recording everything Niko said on her iPhone. *This will make a good episode for her podcast.*

He wasn't sure how he felt about Niko's argument. Although he was almost certainly old enough to get a job, pay rent, and buy alcohol, becoming a werewolf was something that could never be reversed. Once bitten, there was no coming back. He felt uncomfortable with the idea that the packs were promoting their lifestyle to teenagers, assuming that's what they were doing.

Still, he wasn't about to deliver a lecture on the subject. He'd done something even more reckless when he was Niko's age—taking part in a dangerous ritual to gain the ability to cast magic. He wondered if Niko felt the same about joining his wolf pack as Jasper had about becoming a wizard.

'I must admit, I've never thought about it that way,' Jasper said. 'But I'm certainly willing to keep an open mind about the werewolf community.'

'That's all we want,' Niko said earnestly. 'To be listened to, and have the same rights as everybody else.'

'So, what's tonight all about?' Alyssa asked, stepping closer to Niko and holding her iPhone adjacent to his chin.

Niko swallowed hard and looked nervous again, but he answered the question. 'The three big London packs—Silverback, Greyfang and Ironclaw—are coming together to talk about the *situation*.'

'You mean the plans to forcibly microchip all werewolves and track their movements?'

'Yeah. There hasn't been a meeting like this for ages. The packs are normally kind of hostile to one another, fighting over territory. But that's over now. We're getting together to fight back against the *Paras*.'

Niko spat on the ground in what seemed like a ritualistic gesture of contempt for the authorities. Jasper assumed *'Paras'* was slang for the Paranormal Office.

'Do you know what's going to be discussed?'

'Not sure. We'll decide what to do next I guess.'

Jasper gazed around the heath as Alyssa continued the interview. Niko was right—this meeting was highly unusual. Rivalries between the werewolf packs were famously fierce. The *Uncanny Chronicle* had reported on pitched battles between the wolf packs that had resulted in multiple deaths. The idea that Silverback, Greyfang and Ironclaw wolves were uniting in a common cause was, to the best of Jasper's knowledge, unprecedented. He wondered how stable this new alliance was.

'The meeting's gonna start soon,' Niko said. 'We'd better get moving.'

'Of course,' Alyssa said. 'Thanks for the interview—my listeners will be fascinated to get the inside track on all this.'

Niko blushed, apparently embarrassed at this compliment from an attractive, older (from his point of view) woman.

'No problem,' he mumbled, staring at his feet.

Alyssa smiled brightly and started typing on her phone as they walked towards the location of the big meeting. She was probably editing the interview already.

Jasper walked alongside Niko and asked, 'I wanted to ask you a question myself, if you don't mind. Have you heard of a werewolf called The Stray?'

Niko looked sidelong at Jasper. 'Why do you ask?'

'Don't worry, this isn't for the podcast. I won't quote you. I just heard a rumour, that's all. You're obviously knowledgeable about werewolf politics, so I wondered if you knew about it.'

Jasper felt a twist of guilt in his stomach for not being entirely honest about his reasons for asking, but his attempt at flattery seemed to work. Niko puffed out his chest and said, 'Course I've heard of The Stray. It's all anyone's talking about right now.'

'And what do they say about him? Or... her?'

'Pretty sure it's a guy. The pack leaders say they've spoken to him. They don't know his name, but apparently he has a Scottish accent.'

'And he's been helping your cause?'

Niko nodded vigorously. 'He warned us about the *Para's* plan to microchip us; gave us time to organise ourselves.'

'You said he has a Scottish accent—are there any other rumours about him? Is he a werewolf?'

Niko shook his head. 'No. Whatever he is, he's not one of us.'

'Why do you say that?'

'His smell. The pack leaders who've met him all agree he doesn't smell like a werewolf. It's possible he's some other kind of shifter, but no-one seems to know what kind.'

Jasper nodded thoughtfully. Werewolves, like ordinary wolves, had an excellent sense of smell. If they said The Stray didn't smell like a werewolf, they were almost certainly right.

'Is there any chance you could introduce me to someone who—'

'Look, if you want to find out more about The Stray, all you have to do is stick around. He was the one who called this meeting in the first place—he told the pack leaders he was going to show up in person and tell us what to do next. I think he's planning to reveal his true identity.'

CHAPTER 10

THE MEETING WAS HELD in and around a bandstand. Jasper had never seen anything like it. There were hundreds of werewolves, mostly in human form, but also a few who had transformed and were stalking around the heath, sniffing the air with their long snouts and scanning the darkness with their bright yellow eyes. There was a surprising amount of variation in the werewolves' appearance: some looked like real wolves, others looked like muscular monsters from a Hollywood film. Some bounded around on all fours, while others held themselves upright.

Werewolves were allowed to roam around certain London parks at night while they were closed, protected from prying eyes by long standing magical wards. Even so, Jasper doubted a gathering of this many werewolves in one place was legal, never mind the fact that they were planning to discuss overthrowing the government.

The fashion among werewolves was for grungy attire. Some of those in human form could have been mistaken for goths, others for members of biker gangs (not that there were many of those in London). There were a lot of leather jackets and ripped jeans on display. Almost all the wolves still in human form wore patches sewn onto their clothes that displayed either a silver square, a canine tooth, or a paw with sharp claws. Despite the show of unity this meeting represented, the wolves were still keen to display loyalty to their individual packs through these patches.

The wolves were amassing around the bandstand. Three individuals detached themselves from the throng and climbed onto the bandstand's raised platform. Jasper recognised one of them as Lexi Ironclaw. She had a stern, uncompromising face marred by a couple of scars that looked relatively fresh. Some of Lexi's followers had attacked Jasper a few months ago, when they were allied with Blade, the lich assassin. He hoped Lexi had learned from her mistakes, though somehow he doubted it.

Jasper didn't recognise the other two, but they were bound to be the leaders of Greyfang and Silverback packs.

One of the leaders stepped forward. He had a mop of messy grey hair and an equally tangled grey beard. He appeared to be in his sixties, though he looked impressively fit for his age. There were bulging muscles underneath his buttoned-up denim shirt. Such were the risks of life as a werewolf that many didn't make it to old age, so this one had probably survived many conflicts. Jasper noticed a patch with the image of a canine tooth on the front of his shirt. So this must be the leader of Greyfang pack.

'She wolfs and he-wolfs,' he said, in a strong, clear voice. 'I'm glad to see so many of you here tonight. Despite many provocations, we have remained united in our opposition to the *Para's* plans to strip us of our rights.'

The crowd murmured their agreement, some stamping their feet on the ground.

Alyssa said, 'I'm going to get closer and see if I can record some of the meeting. Want to come?'

'Sure. I think we'd better stick together. It all seems friendly now, but things could turn ugly.'

Jasper and Niko followed as Alyssa led the way forward, weaving through the crowd to get closer to the bandstand. She held her iPhone aloft to try to record what was being said. That would normally have been a reckless thing to do, inviting a thief to snatch it away from her, but there were only werewolves around and they were all listening carefully to the speech.

'We've come a long way together,' the Greyfang leader was saying. 'We are more united than ever in our history. The *Paras* know we act as one and speak with one voice. Now it's time we make that voice heard.'

This statement was greeted with a thunderous response. Wolves all around the bandstand roared their approval and stamped their feet. There were even one or two howls. It was clear they were ready for action and eager to fight back.

The Greyfang elder looked slightly startled by the response his words had provoked. *Where's he going with this?* Jasper wondered. *Is he trying to incite them to violence, or keep them under control?*

'As I say, our unity is beyond question. We are strong. We fear no-one. That is why it is time to negotiate peace with the wizarding authorities. I believe we can achieve our goals by sitting down with the Paranormal Office and—'

'Peace?' shouted one wolf, with obvious contempt.

'Negotiate?' shouted another.

'Sit down with enemies who want to lock us up in kennels? Are you serious?'

The Greyfang leader looked rattled. Clearly, he'd misread his audience. The assembled wolves weren't in a mood to make peace—they wanted to fight.

'Friends,' he said, 'You're angry. I'm angry too! It is in our nature to want to fight, to defend our territory with tooth and claw. But there are other ways to fight. I've spoken to Minister Sallow, and he has assured me—'

Whatever assurances Sallow had given, no-one heard them. The rest of Greyfang's speech was drowned out by jeers and angry chants. Even wolves wearing the Greyfang emblem shook their heads in dismay and barracked their own leader. Faced with this angry response, the Greyfang leader paled and retreated away from the crowd towards the back of the bandstand.

For a moment, Jasper feared the angry wolves might turn into a violent mob and attack the old wolf, but that didn't happen. Instead, Lexi Ironclaw stepped forward and held up her hands for quiet.

'The views of us all are clear,' she said, with evident satisfaction. 'No peace with those who want to make us slaves!'

Lexi shook her fist, and the werewolves roared their approval.

'I say we stop wasting time and do what we should have done weeks ago. Ironclaw pack successfully invaded our enemy's stronghold just a few months ago—and we can do it again. But this time, we should leave no survivors. Let's attack now and overthrow the so-called *leaders* of the supernatural community!'

It was clear Lexi Ironclaw meant this to be a war cry, but, just like Greyfang before her, the crowd's response was not quite what she expected. Some wolves cheered, but most looked worried and started talking amongst themselves.

Jasper turned to Niko. He was frowning and looked uncertain. He saw Jasper looking at him and said, 'I think it's too risky. I want us to stand up for ourselves, but I don't want an all-out war with the Paranormal Office.'

'I think that's wise,' Jasper said. 'A full-blown conflict between wizards and werewolves would be terrible for all of us."

A group of wolves were chanting. At first, Jasper thought they were chanting in favour of attacking the Paranormal Office, then he realised they were shouting the word Silverback. Lexi Ironclaw scowled as a female wolf wearing a brown leather bomber jacket with a silver patch on the front came to the front of the bandstand. She was probably in her mid-thirties and had black hair with streaks of purple in it.

The crowd fell silent.

The Silverback leader left a long pause before beginning her speech, as if weighing her words carefully.

'I don't know the right answer,' she said frankly. 'I don't trust the *Paras* one bit, but I also know that an all-out attack would be too risky. We don't want to start a war we can't win.'

'But there are other options. We could ramp up our protests, stopping short of outright violence. We could seek allies among the mages, among other shifters, among vampires—yes, even vampires. I don't think we can be fussy about where we get support from right now.'

Lexi Ironclaw looked furious. She spat ostentatiously on the floor of the bandstand and shouted, 'Another coward arguing for surrender. We need to attack now, while we have the chance!'

But the Silverback leader was voicing what many in the crowd seemed to think. She ignored Lexi Ironclaw's criticism and said, 'When the first werewolves arrived in London, they made decisions by voting. Why don't we do that? Settle this issue with a vote.'

A flurry of talk and debate flowed through the crowd. Lexi looked scandalised, but it seemed that many of the wolves liked the idea of voting. After all, it would give them all a direct say in what happened next.

'See,' Alyssa said. 'Werewolves aren't all violent thugs—they're actually quite reasonable.'

'I never said they were violent thugs!' Jasper said. 'But I must admit I'm surprised—I didn't think wolves were especially democratic by nature.'

'I think they're changing,' Alyssa said. 'Becoming a serious political force. Surely the Paranormal Office will have to listen now?'

Jasper nodded, but he feared they wouldn't.

Just as it looked like the wolves were coming to a consensus, the mood shifted again. There were shouts of outrage from the back of the crowd.

'What's going on? Has a fight broken out?' Alyssa wondered aloud.

Many of the werewolves turned around to see what was causing the commotion.

Suddenly, yellow lights winked into existence in a large, unbroken circle all around the bandstand, encompassing all of the assembled werewolves.

Jasper peered toward the nearest lights. It was hard to see properly in the gloom, but he could just make a group of people holding up what looked like flashlights. He took a few steps towards them to get a better look.

Then he froze in shock.

This is bad. Really bad.

'Are those *wizards*?' Alyssa said.

'Seekers,' Jasper said darkly. 'From the Paranormal Office enforcement division.'

What Jasper had at first taken to be flashlights were in fact large topaz jewels which the seekers were holding above their heads. The jewels were ablaze with yellow light. The wolves nearest the seekers started whining in pain. Mundane police-men were standing side-by-side with the seekers, dressed in riot gear and brandishing batons.

'You've told me how the three primary magic jewels work,' Alyssa said. 'Rubies power up fire magic, emeralds enhance earth magic, and sapphires work with ice magic. What about these jewels?'

'See for yourself.'

The werewolves nearest the seekers were twisting and moaning in agony as their bodies sprouted fur and they grew canine teeth and claws. As each of them transformed into their wolf forms they curled up on the ground, whimpering in pain and unable to move.

CHAPTER II

'THAT'S HORRIBLE!' ALYSSA SAID. 'It sounds like they're in pain.'

'They are,' Jasper said grimly. 'Topaz is used to force shifters to transform from one form to another against their will. Unlike transforming voluntarily, it's quite painful.'

Alyssa swore under her breath.

Some werewolves were trying to escape, but they collapsed as soon as they came within range of the topaz-wielding seekers. Those that had already succumbed to the transformation spell lay quivering on the ground. Jasper watched as a group of Ironclaw wolves transformed voluntarily and charged at the seekers, but the authorities had prepared for this as well: the mundane police flanking the seekers were armed with tasers, which they used to electrocute any wolves that managed to evade the topaz magic.

'Look,' Alyssa said, tugging Jasper's arm. 'In the bandstand.'

Jasper looked where she was pointing. Dozens of werewolves, mostly from Silverback pack, were taking shelter inside the bandstand, trying to organise themselves. Most had transformed voluntarily or were in the process of doing so.

'Why are the authorities doing this?' Alyssa said, her voice shaking. 'They're not trying to arrest every werewolf in London are they? That's crazy.'

It soon became clear why the seekers were kettling and incapacitating the werewolves. As more and more of them fell to the ground, the police went around injecting them using white plastic syringes.

'It's the microchips!' Alyssa hissed. 'All of London's werewolves are together in one place for the first time *ever*, and the authorities are seizing the opportunity to inject them with microchips.'

Jasper was genuinely shocked. Despite the Paranormal Office's obvious hostility towards werewolves, he hadn't imagined they could be this ruthless.

'We've got to do something to help,' Alyssa said. 'We can't just stand around and watch this happen.'

'I'm not sure what we can—'

But Alyssa was already rushing toward the seekers on the far side of the bandstand. Jasper followed reluctantly, worried for her safety as much as for the wolves. In theory, the seekers should recognise that she and Jasper were not werewolves and let them leave, but in the chaos it was more than likely they'd get tasered regardless.

Alyssa stopped a few metres away from a cop who was busy injecting microchips into fallen wolves. Alyssa crouched down and started filming what the police were doing.

Jasper looked back at the bandstand. More wolves were gathering there. Jasper recognised the Silverback leader among their number. She appeared to be rallying her comrades for some kind of counterattack.

'This should be enough to embarrass the authorities,' Alyssa said, nodding to her phone, 'but we need to do something more to try and stop this.'

'I'm not sure there's anything more we *can* do,' Jasper said. 'Even if I was prepared to use magic against seekers—'

'Which you've done before.'

'Which I've done before, against *one* seeker, but there are dozens here. Picking a fight would achieve nothing, and it could make things even worse.'

The Silverback wolves in the bandstand looked like they were preparing to charge. The seekers had spotted them too. Three of the wizards, flanked by riot police, advanced towards them holding their topaz jewels aloft, casting golden light in a wide arc in front of them.

'I know it's risky, but we need to help them,' Alyssa said, following Jasper's gaze.

'Alyssa, *wait—*'

'I'm not going to start a fight, Jasper. I've got a better idea. Just promise me you'll bail my ass out of jail when this is over?'

Jasper groaned, knowing it was pointless to argue with Alyssa once she had the bit between her teeth. In any case, she didn't wait for him to answer. She squeezed his hand, then strode over to the advancing seekers with her phone held high, filming them and loudly adding commentary over the top.

'...this unprovoked attack on a peaceful meeting of werewolves on Hampstead Heath...'

Dammit Alyssa! She loved to rush in where angels feared to tread. Jasper had been accused of doing that himself a few times, but Alyssa took it to a whole new level.

He considered his options. His instinct was to break cover and help Alyssa remonstrate with the seekers, but, given his less-than-stellar reputation, particularly among his fellow wizards, that might only serve to inflame the situation further.

'You can arrest me if you want,' Alyssa was saying, 'but I've been filming what you're doing, and the video will post automatically on YouTube unless I decide to stop it. It won't matter if you take my phone away—the video is already saved to the cloud and scheduled to go public.'

Jasper chuckled. Alyssa could be foolhardy, but she was also cunning.

One of the riot police snatched away her iPhone and started tapping the screen. A look of frustration clouded his face. Meanwhile, one of his colleagues tried to put cuffs on Alyssa, who struggled and shouted at the top of her voice. More police and seekers drifted over to deal with the commotion.

Which opened a gap in their lines.

A gap that the Silverback leader in the bandstand noticed at once.

'Oh shi—'

The Silverback wolves charged, snarling and snapping as they went. Their counterattack took the police and seekers by surprise—several wizards were bowled over, clutching bleeding wounds, while others retreated or cast combat spells which mostly missed their targets.

Chaos ensued. Several wolves were tasered. Some of the police went down after furious bites. Wolves from the other packs leapt into the fray.

Just as Jasper feared it was about to turn into a bloodbath, the Silverback leader—who was now far away from the bandstand, beyond the now broken circle of seekers and police—howled loudly. The wolves battling the police and seekers stopped attacking and sprang towards the sound. In all, several dozen werewolves managed to escape, loping away into the thick darkness of the heath.

The police and seekers regrouped and closed up their lines. Although many of the wolves had been incapacitated before the counterattack, a good number had escaped thanks to the intervention of Alyssa and the Silverback leader. Jasper had to admit he was impressed.

Which reminded him. What had happened to Alyssa?

He scanned the area and saw her being led towards a police van; one of several parked on the grass nearby. She wasn't making it easy—she was wriggling and shouting all the way and refusing to walk, so that two cops had to physically drag her along the ground.

Jasper broke cover and jogged towards Alyssa and the police. 'Excuse me, I'm a lawyer and that's my friend you're dragging away. Where are you taking—'

Intense pain surged through every muscle in Jasper's body. His legs folded as he fell to the ground.

CHAPTER 12

THE PAIN WAS LIKE nothing he had felt before. It was as though his entire body was on fire, every muscle twitching and contracting involuntarily.

Thankfully, the intense pain lasted only a few seconds. When it was over, Jasper found himself lying face down on the grass in shock, confused, aching all over. He felt a stabbing pain in the small of his back that was separate to the aching in his muscles. He reached behind and felt a pair of sharp pins or barbs sticking into him.

He'd been tasered.

Rough hands rifled his clothes, searching for weapons. A gravelly voice above him said, 'Don't move or you'll get another jolt.'

Jasper didn't think he'd be able to resist even if he wanted to. His muscles felt like jelly. The cop grabbed his wrists, bringing them together behind his back, preparing to put him in cuffs.

'Hey, listen—'

Before he could finish his sentence, Jasper felt a rush of air above him, and the cop let go of his wrist. He took the opportunity to haul himself into a sitting position. He saw a policeman in full riot gear sprawled on the grass, surrounded by snarling werewolves. The policeman aimed his weapon, but before he could shoot, a wolf bowled into him from the side, knocking the taser from his hand.

'Can you stand?' growled one of the wolves who had appeared suddenly at Jasper's side.

'I think so.'

Jasper got up slowly. The wolf beside him barked at the others. They disengaged from the police and escorted Jasper away from the mêlée like a roman phalanx.

Jasper looked around for Alyssa, but there was no sign of her.

'Could you help my friend too? The police were dragging her away when I was tasered.'

'We wanted to,' said the wolf who had spoken before, who seemed to be leading the others. 'But we were too late—she'd already been placed in a police van by the time we reached you.'

The wolves led him into a thick copse of oak trees, where they transformed back into their human forms. Jasper averted his eyes, as the werewolves were naked at first, although they didn't seem embarrassed in the slightest. One of them emerged from the bushes carrying a bin bag full of clothes which they distributed among the group. Since werewolves were allowed by law to roam Hampstead Heath on certain nights, they presumably had spare clothes and perhaps other provisions hidden here.

The wolf chief turned out to be Una Silverback—the pack leader who had stood on the bandstand and called for a vote to decide what the werewolves should do next. It was hard to mistake her purple dyed hair and bomber jacket. Jasper introduced himself and thanked her for rescuing him from the police.

'We were only able to escape in the first place because you and your friend distracted some of the seekers,' Una said. 'I'm sorry we weren't able to free her as well.'

'The distraction was all Alyssa's doing really, but I'm still grateful for your help. Hopefully I'll be able to get her out of the police station later.'

'Alyssa... is she the one with the podcast?'

'That's right.'

'So she was here to interview werewolves?'

'Yes.'

'And you? Why are you here?'

The werewolves were staring at Jasper with narrowed eyes. Although they'd helped him escape, they were obviously still suspicious of him. That was understandable. After all, he was a wizard who, on the face of it, had no legitimate reason for turning up at a werewolf meeting. He wouldn't blame Una or her comrades if they suspected him of being a Paranormal Office agent.

'So, why are you here?' Una repeated.

'I can assure you I'm not a friend of the Paranormal Office, if that's what you're worried about. I certainly don't approve of what they've done tonight.'

Una smiled coolly. 'That's good to hear, but it doesn't answer my question.'

Jasper decided to tell the truth rather than lie and pretend he'd come to help Alyssa with her podcast. Technically, he *was* working for the Paranormal Office, but he was telling the truth when he said he wasn't their friend. Besides, he had a hunch that The Stray wasn't a true friend to the werewolves either.

'I'm trying to gather information about the wolf known as The Stray. I came to the meeting to ask if anyone had met him.'

Una spat on the ground. 'I don't know what that creature is, but I assure you he's no wolf. He smells foul, like some kind of demon. And he's betrayed us.'

Jasper had suspected as much. 'I heard he was supposed to be attending tonight. Do you think he tricked you into coming here so the authorities could microchip you?'

'Of course! This is the first time in years all three packs have gathered together in one place. The Stray led us into a trap. We were stupid not to see it coming.'

'Perhaps he is playing both sides?'

'It's more likely he was never on our side at all.'

'How much do you know about him? Have you met him?'

Una nodded. 'Once, near Whitehall, with the other pack leaders. He went to great lengths to conceal his identity, but he is some kind of mutant shifter. After the meeting, I followed him back to Downing Street. He snuck into the building through the garden.'

'Downing Street? As in, the home of the prime minister?'

Una nodded. 'He works there I believe, although I don't know in what capacity.'

Jasper had assumed that the Whitehall spy was part of the magical government, but if The Stray was based in Downing Street, that strongly suggested he worked for the mundane government. Of course, there was no proof that The Stray was the spy he was looking for, but it seemed like a fair assumption for now.

It was also a fair assumption that The Stray had intentionally led the werewolf packs into a trap. But why? Why feed the werewolves information and encourage them to rebel, only to then betray them to the authorities? What kind of double game was he playing?

'We need to strike back quickly against this betrayal,' Una said. 'I'm going to Downing Street tonight to bring this traitor to justice. You're welcome to come with me if you wish.'

'I'm not sure that's a good idea,' Jasper said. 'I understand your anger, but the prime minister's residence is heavily guarded. You'd be leading your remaining wolves into danger.'

'I won't be taking my wolves with me. If I leave my pack behind, I can sneak into Downing Street through the garden. But I'll stand a better chance of succeeding if I have a wizard with me.'

'Even if you manage to sneak inside the building, what are your chances of finding The Stray? Even if you're right and he works in Downing Street, he's unlikely to be there late at night.'

'I think he will be. Every time he has met the pack leaders, it has been late at night near Downing Street. I'll be able to smell him from the garden if he's in the building.'

Some of the other werewolves chimed in, begging to accompany their leader, but Una was insistent she would only go alone or with Jasper. 'The rest of you should go lick your wounds and prepare for the fight to come. Our struggle against the Paranormal Office has only just begun.' She turned back to Jasper. 'So, wizard, do you want to come? I'm not forcing you—my pack mates will see you safely off the Heath if you prefer.'

Jasper had already decided he was going, even though it was a reckless plan. Una was going whether or not he accompanied her, so he might as well tag along and try to steer her away from doing anything too dangerous.

'Lead the way.'

After a short tube ride, Jasper and Una arrived at Charing Cross station and walked down Whitehall. Although it was late at night—after 11pm—it was a warm, balmy evening.

By London standards, Whitehall was a wide street containing many grand government buildings built of pale stone and statues of famous generals and politicians. By contrast, Downing Street was a tiny side road that was surprisingly easy to miss. The famous black door of Number 10 appeared on the news all the time, but it was difficult to see in real life unless you were a journalist or politician with a pass granting access through the tall, black gates that stood across the entrance to Downing Street.

Tonight, there was even more activity than normal around the heart of the British government.

It looked like something serious was happening, or had recently happened. There were police everywhere, with an especially dense cluster around the gates to Downing Street. Pedestrians were being told to cross the road and stay well clear. Police vans were parked alongside the Cenotaph—the giant memorial dedication to soldiers who died in World War One. TV journalists were sprinkled up and down Whitehall, setting up their equipment or recording pieces on camera.

What's happened? A terrorist attack? A medical emergency?

For probably the first time ever, Jasper wished he had a smartphone. If there had been a dramatic incident at the centre of the government, it would be all over the news websites, but his battered old Nokia wasn't capable of accessing the internet.

'I'm afraid our chances of breaking into Downing Street unnoticed have dropped from low to zero,' Jasper observed. 'There are police crawling all over the place.'

Even as he spoke, officers were shooing away members of the public.

'I wasn't planning to knock on the front door,' Una said archly.

'Seriously. Security looks incredibly tight tonight. Perhaps if we consult the other werewolf leaders and come back in a day or two—'

'We have to act now!' Una snapped. 'We can't wait. The Stray believes he's destroyed the packs, which means his guard will be down.'

Jasper sighed. He'd thought Una Silverback was a pragmatist after she took a balanced position at the werewolf meeting, but now he was having doubts about her rationality.

'It won't do your pack any good if you get yourself arrested or killed.'

'That's not going to happen.'

Una strode toward the police vans that were parked around the Cenotaph. Jasper had to jog to keep up.

'If we cause a distraction in the street, no-one will notice me sneaking into the back garden.'

Una found a dark, secluded area at the base of the Cenotaph, away from the prying eyes of the police. She quickly stripped off her clothes and transformed into her wolf form.

'This is not a good idea,' Jasper hissed, picking up Una's discarded clothes. 'If anyone sees you there'll be hell to pay. What kind of distraction are you—'

Jasper soon found out what kind of distraction Una had in mind. She thrust her snout in the air and howled into the night. In the relatively quiet and open street, the sound was startlingly loud.

'What the hell are you doing?'

Una didn't stick around to explain herself. As soon as she'd finished howling, she sprinted away on all fours, moving much faster than any human could have managed. She was soon out of sight, and clearly didn't expect Jasper to follow her.

Of course not, he thought bitterly. *Because I'm the bloody distraction.*

'Stay where you are and put your hands up,' shouted a copper. 'Now.'

The policeman was pointing something at him—a taser?—and more officers were running toward him from multiple directions. Some of them were holding machine guns.

Jasper put his hands in the air. He had no intention of getting shot today. Wizard or not, he was unlikely to survive a round from an automatic weapon.

'Take it easy, guys,' he said. 'I'm cooperating.'

'On the ground! Keep your hands where we can see them!'

'OK, no problem.'

Jasper made slow, deliberate movements, first kneeling on the ground, then lying flat on his stomach with his hands behind his back.

'Don't move!'

'I wasn't going to,' Jasper muttered irritably. One of the cops knelt on his back, forcing the air out of his lungs, while putting cuffs around his wrists.

This is turning into a really lousy evening.

Jasper expected to be dragged to his feet and hauled into a police van, but there was a delay as the cops talked among themselves.

'I don't think that's necessary,' a male voice said above him. 'Presumably you don't think this man is capable of howling like a wolf?'

That clipped, precise voice sounded familiar. *Where have I heard that before?*

There was a brief argument, which Jasper heard only snatches off, then the police removed his handcuffs and pulled him upright. Jasper found himself looking at someone he knew well: a black man with a bald head and a neat goatee beard, dressed in an immaculate, tailored suit.

CHAPTER 13

'Zach!'

Zachariah was a seeker who had once been tasked with arresting Jasper, but since then they had become friends. Jasper was mightily relieved to see him.

'Please don't call me Zach. My mother calls me that and I hate it.'

'Fine. It's good to see you *Zachariah*.'

'I'd like to say the same, but you've appeared at a rather delicate moment.'

'I can see that. Has something happened?'

Before Zachariah could answer, a tall, broad-chested white man with wobbling jowls elbowed his way through the assembled police. He was wearing a crumpled white shirt and a tie that hung loose around his collar. There were sweat stains around his chest and armpits.

'Right then,' he thundered. 'Who the hell are you and what are you doing here?'

Zachariah rolled his eyes and said, 'Chief Superintendent Richards, meet Jasper Wychwood. Jasper is... a colleague of mine.'

The superintendent scowled. 'Colleague? You mean he's a *spook* too?'

Zachariah winced. 'Jasper works with me at SIE. I believe he's here to assist my investigation.'

The SIE—Special Intelligence Executive—was what Paranormal Office employees called themselves when they worked with the mundane police and security services. Jasper didn't know what investigation Zachariah was referring to, but he decided to play along. Whatever it was, it had clearly caught the attention of both the mundane and magical authorities. Which was interesting.

'That's right,' Jasper said, thrusting out his hand in a way he hoped conveyed confidence. 'Good to meet you, superintendent Richards.'

Richards ignored Jasper's offer of a handshake. 'What in God's name was all that howling about? It came from right here, behind the Cenotaph.' Flecks of spit flew out his mouth as he spoke.

'It scared the crap out of me too,' Jasper said, lowering his hand awkwardly.

'I don't care if it made you fill your pants and dance an Irish jig,' Richards shouted. 'Did you see the beast that did the howling? It must have been some kind of dog or wolf.'

'I didn't see anything.'

Richards swore and stalked back the way he'd come. 'Let him go then,' he shouted over his shoulder at his officers. 'Bloody time-wasters.'

Zachariah went after Richards and motioned for Jasper to follow.

'Mr Wychwood has come to help me investigate the more. .. arcane aspects of the incident in Downing Street. He'll need access to the crime scene.'

'Great. Two *spooks* for the price of one.' Despite his clear dislike of 'spooks', Richards seemed to accept that Jasper was to be included in the investigation.

The two wizards followed the superintendent at a distance as he strode down the street.

'So, what's going on?' Jasper asked.

'A werewolf attack inside Downing Street,' Zachariah said. 'One woman was killed, no other casualties as far as we know. Is that why you're here?'

'No, it's just an unhappy coincidence. I assume you've heard about this Whitehall spy leaking information to the werewolf packs?'

Zachariah chuckled dryly. 'It's all anyone in the Paranormal Office talks about these days. The rumour mill has gone into overdrive with speculation about who it might be.'

'Well, strictly between ourselves, I've been asked to look into it. I think Sallow and the rest wanted an outsider to take the case.'

'That makes a certain amount of sense I suppose. Do you think the spy—whoever they are—might be behind this latest werewolf attack?'

Jasper bit his lip. 'I'm not sure. If not, it's quite a coincidence.'

'Get a move on you two!' Richards barked. 'I don't have all night.'

They passed through the police amassed around the gates of Downing Street in silence. The street itself was clogged with cop cars but was free of the TV journalists who usually camped there late into the night. The door to Number Ten opened seemingly of its own accord as they approached. Inside, the heart of the British government was strangely unimpressive. It looked like a typical Georgian townhouse, albeit one furnished in a rather lavish and old-fashioned style. Portraits of dead prime ministers stared down at them like suspicious ghosts.

Richards led them through a warren of narrow corridors and into a poky office on the ground floor. 'Right—get on with it then,' he said with his customary lack of charm. 'I'll be honest, I'd rather the two of you weren't sticking your noses into my crime scene, but the commissioner wants me to cooperate with SIE. And what the commissioner wants, the commissioner gets.'

'If this is indeed a wolf attack, it falls within SIE's jurisdiction,' Zachariah said sharply.

'Yeah, yeah. Just don't fuck up my crime scene with any of your hocus pocus rubbish.'

Jasper wondered how much the Metropolitan police really knew about 'SIE' and its activities. The general population knew very little about the supernatural world, but in some areas the dividing line between the two worlds was very thin indeed. London was one of the most magical cities on the planet, so it was impossible to keep all of its mundane residents in the dark all the time. Some—like the prime minister—were explicitly told about the existence of supernaturals, while others—like Richards, in all likelihood—were given just enough information to do their job. Richards' memories of SIE and werewolves would probably be wiped once the investigation was complete. It was all a delicate dance, but somehow the Paranormal Office made it work.

Jasper turned his attention to the crime scene. It was a wood-panelled meeting room with a long table in the middle surrounded by chairs. There was a vacuum cleaner standing by the door, still plugged in at the wall, and an open sash window that looked out into the garden. A few cupboards and shelving units lined one wall. Near the open window there was a dark patch on the carpet which Jasper assumed was a bloodstain.

'You've taken the body away?' Zachariah asked.

'Obviously,' Richards said. 'Don't want it stinking up the place on a warm night like this. It's with the pathologist now.'

Zachariah looked like he wanted to reprimand Richards for his coarseness. Instead, he said, 'I understand the victim was a cleaner?'

Richards consulted his notebook. 'Hilary Greggs. Forty-seven years old. Resided at 256b Streatham High Road. Divorced. Two kids. Poor old bint came in here to hoover and got her throat bitten out, most likely by one of these wild wolves that have been springing up everywhere lately. Hence you lot have been drafted in.'

Jasper noticed that both Richards and Zachariah had used the word *wolf* rather than *werewolf.* Was that because Richards sincerely believed they were dealing with a normal wolf, or because he and Zachariah were dancing around the supernatural element of this crime?

'Who uses this room?' Jasper asked.

'No-one, as far as we know,' Richards said. 'We checked with the PM's top civil servant. This is a spare meeting room, not assigned to any specific person or team.'

'Do you know if this window was open at the time of the murder?' Zachariah asked.

Richards nodded. 'We think the cleaner—Mrs Greggs—opened it to get some fresh air while she was hoovering.'

'And you think a wolf leaped in from the garden and killed her? That's your theory?'

The sarcasm in Jasper's tone wasn't lost on the superintendent. 'Listen *friend*, that poor woman was savaged. Her head was almost detached from her neck when she was found. Trust me: there's no doubt that a wolf did this. And a big one at that.'

'Yes, but what's the motive? You're saying a wolf hopped in through the open window, killed a random cleaning lady, then hopped out again and disappeared into the night? It just seems like we're missing something important.'

The superintendent's eyes were bulging. Jasper guessed he wasn't used to people contradicting him.

'Motive? You're asking what the motive was? We're talking about a wild animal for God's sake! Animals don't have motives. The only reason I haven't handed this case over to the dog unit is that the attack happened at Number 10, and the commissioner wants to be absolutely sure there was no foul play involved.'

Zachariah shot Jasper a look that seemed to say, *There's no point in trying to reason with this guy*. And he was probably right. How could they explain to a mundane policeman—and this one seemed especially mundane—that werewolves could have motives that were just as complex as anyone else's?

'OK, point taken,' Jasper said. 'Mind if I have a quick look around anyway?'

'Fine—but get a move on. I want to wrap this up soon, and we've still got to get forensics in here. Put these on and don't move anything.'

Richards handed them both translucent white plastic gloves and shoe covers. Jasper put them on and walked slowly around the room, looking for anything unusual. He wondered about the idea that this office belonged to nobody in particular. *That's a bit convenient, isn't it?*

The table was almost completely bare, with only a handful of Number 10 branded pens, pencils and sheafs of notepaper stashed neatly inside a stationery holder.

'The table smells like it was cleaned recently,' Jasper said. 'So no fingerprints.'

Richards sighed theatrically. 'Mrs Greggs was in here cleaning, wasn't she? She obviously cleaned the desk before she was attacked.'

Maybe. Or maybe the killer did it.

'What about the body?' Zachariah asked. 'Anything unusual about it?'

'Apart from the fact her throat was ripped out, you mean?' Richards snapped back. 'Well, she was holding a torn piece of paper when she died. Nothing out of the ordinary, just ordinary paper of the kind you'd find in printers all over the building.'

'Was there anything written on the paper?' Jasper prompted.

'We only recovered a tiny piece in her hand, plus a few fragments on the floor. The paper seems to have been shredded during the attack.'

Then where's the rest of it? Jasper wondered.

Zachariah was evidently thinking the same thing, because he said, 'Have you searched for the rest of the paper?'

Richards scowled. 'I just told you. We only found a few scraps—not enough to see what, if anything, was written on it. It hardly matters though, does it? Wolves don't kill people over bits of paper. Unless you think Mrs Greggs was holding the deeds to a piece of prime London real estate and the wolf killed her to get its grubby paws on it?'

Richards threw back his head and laughed at his own joke, causing his jowls to quiver alarmingly. There was an undercurrent of hysteria in his laugh and his bad-tempered aggression.

Jasper ignored him; there was no point in arguing. If he could find some of the paper the cleaning lady was holding, he might be able to reconstruct the whole thing. And he had a hunch that whatever was written on the paper would provide a clue to the identity of the killer.

Jasper set about searching the room methodically. He lay flat on his stomach and looked under the table and down the sides of the cupboards, but there was nothing there. As a last resort, he'd ask Richards to hand over the scrap they'd found in Mrs Greggs' hand, but he had a feeling Richards would fight them tooth and nail before surrendering that kind of evidence.

Jasper's gaze lighted on the vacuum cleaner standing near the door. It was the bagless kind, with a transparent plastic cylinder containing the dust. He sat on his haunches and stared closely at the cylinder. Among the grey particles of dust and strands of hair were a few white shapes that looked like paper.

It was worth a try. Jasper opened up the vacuum and dipped his hand inside the cylinder.

'What the hell? Stop that now! You'll contaminate the scene with dust!'

Before Richards could intervene, Jasper had pulled out a tiny scrap of paper. It was torn and stained with a splash of dark red blood. Zachariah caught Jasper's eye.

'You'd better keep hold of that,' he said.

Jasper nodded, and tried to slip it in his pocket unobtrusively, but Richards wasn't having it.

'Oh no you don't. If you've found evidence, I want it. I'm required to let you look around, but this is still my crime scene. Hand it over.'

'Why? It's only a piece of paper, which won't tell you anything. But at SIE we might be able to—'

'Oh, pull the other one,' Richards thundered. 'Don't tell me you're going to use some hocus pocus on that paper to find out who the killer is. I'm not that thick!'

'Could've fooled me,' Jasper muttered.

Richards squared his shoulders and thrust out his chin, which made him look even more like an obstinate bulldog. 'Hand over the paper. Now.'

Zachariah stepped in front of Jasper and met Richards' angry gaze calmly.

'I assure you, superintendent, we'll share our findings with your team. We're not trying to undermine you. But the likelihood of supernatural involvement in this crime gives us full jurisdiction over—'

'We'll see about that.' Richards stomped out of the room, slamming the door behind him.

'You think she was killed because of something she found?' Zachariah asked. 'Something written on that piece of paper?'

Jasper shrugged. 'It's a reasonable theory. If not, why would the killer go to the trouble of ripping it out of her hand and hoovering up the pieces afterwards.'

Zachariah nodded. 'And you think this killer is the spy you're looking for?'

'Most likely. If not, it's one hell of a coincidence.'

The door banged open and Richards came back in, flanked by two policemen dressed in bullet proof armour and clutching sleek black machine guns.

'Bloody hell,' Jasper said.

Richards was looking smug. 'Well, what do you know? Look's like we've caught our killer already.'

Zachariah raised his voice. 'Listen superintendent, you'd better stop mucking around. As I've explained, we have jurisdiction over this crime scene as members of SIE.'

'Except that one of you isn't with SIE,' Richards said with undisguised glee, eyeballing Jasper. 'One of you is actually a known fugitive who tricked his way in here on false pretences. And I think I know why. You're mixed up in this murder somehow, and you've come back to the crime scene to hide evidence. Am I getting warmer?'

'You're barking up the wrong tree, mate,' Jasper said.

'Sure I am. Well, we can work this out at the station. Now, hand over that evidence and put your hands where I can see them.'

'Do it. Now,' said one of the armed police, lifting the muzzle of his machine gun.

'Alright officers, let's all stay calm shall we?' Zachariah said. 'Mr Wychwood has already put the evidence in his jacket, and since I assume you'd prefer he didn't go reaching into his pockets, I will retrieve the evidence, OK? Then we can all go to the station without anyone getting shot.'

Richards looked like he was about to object, but then said, 'Fine. Get on with it.'

Zachariah turned his back on the three policemen and stood close to Jasper. His seeker's sapphire was nestled in his hand, aglow with magic.

'Get ready,' he whispered.

CHAPTER 14

ZACHARIAH PRETENDED TO RIFLE inside Jasper's jacket pocket, but left the scrap of paper where it was. He turned around and stepped towards Richards, holding out the sapphire.

Richards frowned. 'What the hell is—'

The sapphire exploded with light, with the power of a dozen camera flashes going off at once.

Jasper realised what his friend was about to do a second before it happened. He shut his eyes and shielded his face with his arm. He felt, rather than saw, the blinding flash of light and turned his face away from it.

With white spots dancing across his vision, he leapt out of the open window, landing awkwardly but remaining upright. He sprinted across the lawn and dived into the bushes on the other side. That turned out to be a mistake. Belatedly, he remembered that the prime minister's garden was known as the Rose Garden. Thorns scratched his face and hands and tore at his clothes.

Turning back towards Downing Street, he saw that the window he'd just jumped out of was now closed. Superintendent Richards was wrestling with the catch on the other side, looking red-faced and furious. Zachariah must have closed the window and sealed it shut with magic. Jasper made a mental note to buy the seeker several drinks when he next saw him.

Despite Zachariah's efforts, he wouldn't have long before the cops forced the window open or made their way into the garden via another route. He waded through the clawing rose bushes, hoping to find a way out without having to run across the exposed lawn. There was a gate built into the garden wall a short distance. It was difficult to see it properly in the darkness, but it looked like it might be open.

As he crept through the bushes, his foot touched something large and heavy lying on the ground. It was the body of a bulky, hairy animal. Jasper took a step away from it, fear and alarm pulsing through him.

As he recovered himself, he realised it was the body of a werewolf, fully transformed... and fully dead.

Could this be The Stray? If so, what had happened to them? Was it possible they'd been injured in their struggle with the cleaning lady, and had staggered into the garden, only to collapse and die among the roses? That seemed far-fetched. A middle-aged cleaner surely wasn't capable of inflicting a mortal wound on a fully-grown werewolf? Jasper bent down and examined the body carefully and realised it looked familiar. He'd seen that face and snout before. Very recently.

It was Una Silverback. It took him a few seconds to be certain, but he was sure it was the same wolf who had led the counterattack in Hampstead Heath. He'd watched her transform from wolf to human and back again and he was sure this was Una in her wolf form.

What had happened? How had she died?

She'd said her plan was to cause a commotion at the front of the building to draw the attention of the police, then creep into Downing Street through the garden. It seemed her plan had half worked. She'd successfully distracted the police, but then she'd been killed in the garden. There were bloody claw marks on her haunches and teeth marks on her throat. Chunks of her flesh had been ripped off. Her fur was matted with blood.

Jasper heard raised voices from Downing Street—Richards and his colleagues must have succeeded in prising open the window. He hurried through the shadows towards the garden gate he'd spotted earlier, keeping his head down. Armed police had climbed out of the window but were fortunately looking in the wrong direction.

Strangely, the gate was standing ajar, its sliding lock lying twisted and broken on the ground. Someone—Una perhaps?—had busted it open from the outside.

Before leaving, Jasper looked back towards Number Ten, Downing Street. The police were still on the wrong side of the garden, fanning out across the lawn, but he had an eerie feeling that *someone* was staring straight at him. He studied the uniform rows of windows along the back of Downing Street. A few were lit, most were dark.

Was The Stray lurking behind one of those windows?

CHAPTER 15
TWENTY MINUTES EARLIER.

Somewhere on Whitehall, a werewolf howled.

Inside Downing Street, Callum froze. The sound cut through him like a knife. The howl felt like a threat intended specifically for him.

If a werewolf had come to Whitehall, it meant at least one of the mangy beasts had escaped the trap that Callum and his Paranormal Office sponsor had set at Hampstead Heath. *Have they come here seeking revenge?*

What was supposed to have been a night of triumph was fast turning into a nightmare. Callum had spent the last few hours preparing the crime scene for the police. The cleaning lady's death had horrified him. He hadn't meant to kill her, but the bloodlust had taken hold and he hadn't been able to stop himself. Every time he thought about it, he felt a strange mixture of revulsion and ecstasy. The hound within him exulted in death and the spilling of blood, while Callum the civil servant detested such barbaric acts.

Still, there was no time to mourn his loss of control. He'd set about making it look like an attack by a random werewolf who had opportunistically hopped in through the window. It helped that the government and the Met police were already alarmed by the growing number of werewolf attacks in the capital. The PM himself had seen a werewolf in the Rose Garden just a couple of nights ago.

During the attack, Callum had inadvertently torn to shreds the letter the cleaner had been holding—the one declining Callum's application for wizard training. He'd picked up the larger pieces of paper and hoovered up the rest. Then he accessed the internal Downing Street CCTV and wiped the tapes that showed him in and around the crime scene that evening.

When the oafish superintendent Richards arrived and started ranting about the dangers posed by feral dogs brought to London by foreigners, Callum breathed a sigh of relief and dared to think he was in the clear.

Now, he wasn't so sure. If a werewolf had indeed come to Whitehall seeking revenge, all bets were off. The howl had come from the direction of the Cenotaph, near the front of Downing Street, so Callum decided he would slip out the back way, through the rose garden.

That turned out to be a mistake.

As soon as he stepped onto the neatly trimmed grass, a large werewolf stalked out of the shadows, its yellow eyes gleaming in the moonlight.

Callum turned and sprinted towards the garden gate. But the wolf was faster. It bounded across his path and blocked his escape.

'Coward,' the wolf snarled. 'You betrayed us to the *Paras* and now you want to run away from the consequences!'

Judging by her voice, this was a she-wolf. 'I d-don't know what you're talking about,' Callum said, stammering with gen-uine fear. 'I'm just a civil servant.'

'A civil servant who knows a werewolf when he sees one. Don't play games with me, Stray. I can smell the magic on you.

But your scent isn't like that of any shifter I've ever met. So, what are you?'

You wouldn't believe me if I told you.

He felt the transformation rising inside him, like a twist of black smoke creeping up a chimney stack. Callum clenched his fists and crossed his arms over his chest. Then he thought: *why resist the inevitable?* Transforming might give him a chance of surviving this encounter.

'I'll show you what I am,' he murmured.

Fur sprouted from his skin. The buttons on his shirt popped out and his trousers split as his body bulked out. When the transformation was complete, Callum stood seven feet tall on his hind legs, dwarfing the werewolf. His vision improved, allowing him to see into the dark corners of the garden. A green aura surrounded him, produced by his glowing green eyes and shiny pelt. He watched with satisfaction as the werewolf's ears pinned back in fear.

'What kind of monster are you?' she said.

'The last one you'll ever see.'

Despite her obvious fear, the she-wolf didn't flee. She growled, showing her teeth, then padded towards him, moving slowly at first, then quickly. She circled around to one side and lunged for his neck. Callum dropped his shoulder and swiped at her with one of his massive paws. It was like a lion striking a house cat. His claws raked her fur, drawing blood. She whined in pain and tumbled onto the grass.

'I have no quarrel with you' he said. 'I'll let you live if you leave now.'

The words were conciliatory, but they belied the bloodlust that was rising rapidly inside Callum. He was growing hungry for the kill. He could smell the she-wolf's blood on his paw and wondered what it would taste like.

'No quarrel? You insult me with your lies, Stray. You led us into a trap.'

The she-wolf approached again, more cautiously this time. She still moved nimbly despite the fresh sheen of blood on her coat. Callum snarled in response, showing his own, much larger, teeth. The she-wolf halted about ten feet away, her body taut, waiting for an opportunity to strike.

The urge to attack was strong. Callum could no longer resist it. He was a hunter, after all, and nobody's prey. He fell onto all fours and darted forward, looking to savage the she-wolf's neck, but she ducked under his attack and sank her teeth into his hind leg as he passed her. Callum yelped in pain and shook his leg to dislodge her.

Anger swept through him, fuelling his desire to kill. He'd been too hasty, but he was far from beaten. *I'll teach this upstart wolf a lesson!*

He limped away from the she-wolf, whining loudly, as if in great pain. The werewolf took the bait, leaping forward and snapping at his neck, but just as she was about to get a grip on his throat, he dodged aside and bit down hard on her shoulder. Blood fountained through his teeth and dribbled off his lips. Bones snapped.

The she-wolf whimpered in agony and tried to wriggle away, but Callum held firm, putting more pressure on her shoulder, crunching through bone and cartilage. Using the immense strength in his legs, he lifted her off her feet and tossed her bodily into the rose bushes.

The she-wolf landed like a rag doll and didn't get up. She made no sound.

The desire to howl and run off in search of more prey almost overcame Callum, but a voice in the back of his mind warned him not to surrender to the bloodlust, not to lose his mind in the savage pleasure of the kill.

Becoming human again was a painful process. During the fight, Callum's worldview had narrowed into a simple set of dualities.

Life and death.

Win or Lose.

Kill or be killed.

Now, more complicated human emotions forced their way back in.

Fear, anxiety, uncertainty.

Dread.

His body ached. The air felt chilly against his bare skin. His leg stung where the she-wolf had bitten him. A cold rush of fear washed over him as he realised he was standing in the garden of Downing Street, naked, alone, and covered in blood.

What do I do now? How do I get out of this mess?

His first task was to hide the she-wolf's corpse. He grabbed both her legs and dragged her as far into the bush as he could. It was hard work—she felt much larger and heavier than she had during the fight. Callum grunted and sweated and prayed no-one was looking out of the back windows of Downing Street.

Next, he needed new clothes. Fortunately, he was in the habit of keeping fresh suits in Downing Street in case he needed to transform and ripped his clothing in the process. He grabbed the clothes he'd been wearing earlier—which were torn and grass stained—and used them to hide his nakedness. His heart was in his mouth as he crept back into the building and dashed down a corridor to a supply cupboard where he'd hidden a suitcase full of fresh clothes. To his immense relief, he met no-one on the way and slipped into a nearby bathroom unseen. He washed himself with soap and a nail brush that he'd stashed in the suitcase. Blood swirled pinkly down the washbasin. He put on new clothes and stuffed the soiled set into the suitcase. He could destroy them later.

Now, what do I do about the dead wolf in the garden?

Fortunately, the beginnings of a rather elegant plan had begun to unfold in his mind as he'd scrubbed at the blood under his fingernails.

The police were in the building at this very moment, investigating the death of a woman they believed to have been killed by a werewolf. And now there was a dead werewolf in the garden. Could he make them think this she-wolf had killed the cleaner, only to die a few minutes later while trying to escape?

It would be tricky, but not impossible. He could find a way to plant a weapon at the crime scene—a pen knife perhaps—and smear it with the she-wolf's blood. The most difficult part would be getting the mundane police to believe that a middle aged cleaning lady could have killed a fully grown wolf.

But his colleague at the Paranormal Office could intercede to deal with that problem. A glamour spell could make it look like the wolf's throat had been cut by a small blade. With a little persuasion, the police could be made to see that there was no need to investigate further. It would look like an open and shut case.

Callum smiled to himself. Against all the odds, he might just survive this dreadful night with his life and freedom intact.

His next stop was a security room filled with banks of TV monitors. He was on friendly terms with the guard on duty, Harry, who immediately began talking animatedly about the shocking events of the evening. The police had 'consulted' him, he said, but he hadn't been able to tell them much. The CCTV showed the cleaner entering (but not leaving) the meeting room, with her vacuum cleaner. No-one else was seen entering the room. It was a terrible thing, he said with relish. Callum took a seat next to Harry, content to let him prattle on while he monitored the police's activities on the CCTV.

Something on the monitors caught Callum's eye. Two oddly dressed men were being shown into Downing street by superintendent Richards. One was a bald black man wearing a jewel around his throat—a seeker. The other was white, with a short beard and wearing a dark green overcoat. He looked familiar but it took Callum a few moments to identify him. Presumably he also worked for the Paranormal Office, although he was not displaying a seeker's jewel.

Then he realised who it was: *Jasper Wychwood*. One of London's most controversial wizards. He'd been a seeker years ago but had been thrown out of his profession in mysterious circumstances. Some thought he'd been a spy working for the dark wizard Yarrow, others thought Wychwood was really a double agent who had only pretended to support Yarrow. More recently, he'd been mixed up in the messy business with the assassin Blade.

What's Wychwood doing here? Has he been brought in from the cold by the Paranormal Office? Have they made him a seeker again?

Whatever his reasons for being here, Wychwood was an unknown element in an already delicate situation.

'That man is a fugitive,' Callum said abruptly to Harry. 'I recognise him from a Home Office file. He must have tricked his way in here.' Callum prodded the relevant monitor, pointing to Jasper Wychwood just as Richards led him into the crime scene.

'Shit, really?' Harry said, squinting at the monitor. 'Are you sure?'

'I'm absolutely certain. We need to warn the police straight away.'

'Yeah, course. I'll tell them now.'

Harry hurried out of the security room, talking into the radio clipped to his shoulder. Callum settled in front of the monitors and watched with satisfaction as armed police prepared to arrest Wychwood. There wasn't a camera inside the room where the cleaning lady had died, but there was one in the corridor outside, so Callum expected to have a clear view of Wychwood being dragged out in handcuffs.

After an agonising wait, a bright flash lit up the screen. It had come from inside the meeting room. Wychwood was trying to use magic to escape the police!

Callum leapt to his feet and ran to a room with a window overlooking the Rose Garden. From there, he watched Wychwood stumble across the lawn and hide in the bushes. A few moments later, he stumbled into the body of the she-wolf. After crouching down to examine it, he made his way towards a gate that would lead back into London, while avoiding the police who were climbing out of the ground floor window and pointing torches into the garden.

Before he completed his escape, Wychwood straightened up and stared back at Downing Street, as if sensing that someone was watching him.

Callum took a step backwards, away from the window, grinding his teeth.

'It looks like I'm going to have to do something about you, Mr Wychwood.'

CHAPTER 16

Jasper returned to Wychwood Books tired and tense. Events had moved much faster than he'd expected. He felt sure The Stray had killed Hilary Greggs and Una Silverback, but he was no nearer to discovering their identity, or even confirming that The Stray and the Whitehall spy were one and the same person.

The Stray had led the werewolf packs into a trap, so clearly their motives were more complex than he'd first thought. At least he'd come away from Whitehall with a clue: a fragment of the paper the cleaning lady had been holding when she was killed. He decided not to do anything with it yet. It would take a nifty bit of magic to force the paper to reveal its secrets, and he was too tired to attempt that just now. What he wanted most was to relax with a cold beer, or maybe a double shot of whisky poured over a single ice cube...

The temptation was powerful, but Jasper had promised himself he wouldn't drink alone anymore—and certainly not when he was tired and stressed. That was a trap he needed to avoid. In the last few months, he'd come to the realisation that booze had become a crutch he'd leaned on far too often in difficult moments. In an effort to get a grip on his drinking, he'd binned all the alcohol in his flat and was restricting himself to occasional drinks down the pub with friends. No more drinking alone, no getting shit-faced. And no more greasy takeaways.

Since he'd started this detox, he felt better… and worse.

He'd started going for runs in St James's Park to improve his fitness. He felt better physically, but his emotions were all over the place. In the past, when he felt depressed, he drank. When he was bored, he drank. When he had something to celebrate, he drank. He was now discovering that it was harder to hide from your feelings when you couldn't drown them in a sea of alcohol.

As he sat down on his squidgy armchair behind the cash till with a hot cup of tea, he reflected on his decision to investigate the Whitehall spy. It was cheeky of the Paranormal Office to even ask him—and worse, they'd basically forced him into it. Despite that, he'd jumped at the offer.

The truth was, he needed a purpose, and this investigation had given him one. Alyssa had previously floated the idea of him becoming a paranormal private eye, and while he liked the idea in principle, he was scared of taking the plunge. He wasn't sure how to go about getting clients, or whether the Paranormal Office would tolerate him moonlighting as a private investigator.

Still, he'd reached the conclusion that he couldn't just let himself rot in this bookshop forever. He needed a reason to get off his backside and go out into the world. He needed to be useful. The carrot that the PO had dangled in front of him if he succeeded—the prospect of becoming a seeker again—was one seriously tempting option that might fill the hole that alcohol had left in his life. But did he really want to work for the government again, with its murky politics and byzantine bureaucracy?

Just as he was finishing up, Jasper's Nokia buzzed. It was a text from Rasmus:

Alyssa fine. I'm with her at Woolwich Police Station. She should be released soon without charge.

Jasper breathed a sigh of relief. He fired off a quick reply, then took himself off to bed. Now that he knew Alyssa was OK, he'd be able to get some sleep at last.

In the morning, Jasper woke to a text from Alyssa asking if he wanted to meet up. He invited her to come have lunch with him at the bookshop. By the time she arrived, he'd thrown together a serviceable pasta salad with feta cheese and cherry tomatoes.

'I'm impressed,' Alyssa said, eyeing the pasta. 'I thought you lived off pies and pints.'

'I do, but pies are too much effort to make from scratch. I can never get the pastry right.'

They ate at the small table in Jasper's kitchen and compared notes on the night before. Alyssa was pleased to hear that her intervention had enabled some werewolves to escape. But she was shocked to learn that Una Silverback had been killed just an hour or so later, most likely by the very werewolf spy Jasper was searching for.

'At least now you know for sure the spy is a werewolf,' Alyssa said. 'You said there were bite marks on Una Silverback's body?'

Jasper shrugged. 'We can't be certain of that. We only know that something with big teeth killed her.'

Alyssa squinted at him over a forkful of pasta. 'If it wasn't a werewolf then what was it? Has a jaguar escaped from London Zoo or something?'

'There are other kinds of shifters besides werewolves, so I'm keeping an open mind. Your friend Niko was very insistent that The Stray didn't smell like a genuine werewolf. Una Silverback said the same thing.'

'And what about this piece of paper you found at the crime scene? What can you learn from that?'

'I was planning to show you after lunch.'

They quickly finished what was left of the pasta, then Jasper got up and found a metal wastepaper bin. He got rid of the contents, then placed the torn scrap of paper and the ruby and diamond brooch Rasmus had given him inside. He put his hands on the rim of the bin and bowed his head in concentration.

There were various ways that wizards could get information from inanimate objects, but none of them were easy. Jasper had been trained as a fire mage, so his preference was to use fire magic. The downside in this situation was that he only had one chance to get the spell right. Whether it worked or not, the paper would be incinerated. He wouldn't get a second chance.

Jasper felt the electric tingle of magic rise up from his core and reach his fingers. His hands grew warm, first from the spell, then from a more conventional source of heat. He looked up and was pleased to see purple fire leaping over the lip of the bin. Staring into the flames, he visualised the shred of paper as a single jigsaw piece fitting into a whole sheet. The fire flared higher, responding to his thoughts.

'Look carefully,' Jasper said. 'There's less chance of missing something if we both stare at the flames.'

'What am I looking for?' Alyssa asked.

'For whatever was written on that piece of paper.'

Dark lines and squiggles appeared briefly in the fire, but they dissolved before resolving into anything resembling words. Jasper controlled his breathing and tried to banish all distractions, focusing only on the shapes in the fire. More dark lines and curves floated up, like bubbles rising to the surface of a lake. Jasper willed them to remain in the centre of the fire. More dark shapes floated up and joined the ones already there, forming letters. Recognisable words started to appear.

Alyssa knelt beside him in front of the bin and started typing on her iPhone as the words became clearer.

...with regret...application...

...at the age of...

...once again...hope you will...

...Mr Kirk...

...writing to you...

A bead of sweat dribbled down Jasper's nose. Although this was an unspectacular piece of magic, it was both difficult and draining. The purple fire started to fizzle out and the words got harder to read. Jasper gripped the lip of the bin tightly and forced a final surge of magic into the spell, hoping to reveal at least one complete sentence before the scrap of paper was lost forever. The fire momentarily flared high above the bin and six words stood out darkly against the bright flames.

Port Ellen, Isle of Islay, Scotland.

Jasper let go of the bin and rocked back on his heels, breathing hard. The fire died instantly. 'Did you get that?' he asked breathlessly.

Alyssa nodded, still typing on her phone.

Jasper breathed a sigh of relief. At least now they had something to go on, and his ill-fated trip to Downing Street hadn't been a complete waste of time. He hauled himself over to his armchair and relaxed for a few minutes while Alyssa continued scrutinising her phone.

'What does professor google say?' he asked.

'The Isle of Islay is in the Scottish inner Hebrides,' Alyssa said, 'and is known as the Queen of the Hebrides. Port Ellen is one of the larger towns on the island.'

'What about this Mr Kirk? Anyone by that name on social media?'

'Loads of people. Far too many to be helpful. I can try looking for someone called Kirk with a connection with the Isle of Islay, but I wouldn't get your hopes up. It seems to be a fairly common surname.'

'We can run it by Rasmus, see if there's anyone by that name working in Whitehall or Downing Street.'

'Yeah, good idea. Meanwhile, I'll research Port Ellen and the Isle of Islay.'

Tired though he was, Jasper smiled to himself. Alyssa was getting invested in his investigation, which was good news for him. Her help could prove invaluable.

'I'll make us something to drink while you do that. What do you fancy? Tea or coffee?'

'A coffee would be great.'

Jasper pottered around the kitchen, digging out a percolator he hadn't used for years and setting it up on the gas stove. He found some small porcelain coffee cups that went with the percolator and poured two strong black coffees. When he came back into the bookshop with the coffee, Alyssa was still hunched over her iPhone, a look of intense concentration on her face.

'Smells great,' she said. 'Thanks.'

'You're welcome. Any luck with the research?'

'Depends how you define luck. I haven't been able to find any Mr Kirks with a connection to the Isle of Islay. But I have found a blogger who claims that in the late '90s there were multiple sightings of a huge black dog in the countryside south of Port Ellen. Seems a bit too much of a coincidence, don't you think?'

'Possibly. Then again, it might just have been a normal stray dog.'

'Maybe, but the blog quotes several witnesses who say the dog in question was huge and had glowing green eyes.'

Alyssa passed her iPhone to Jasper. The screen showed a blog page illustrated with a painting of a furious-looking black dog with shining green eyes and huge claws like a lion.

'According to the blog, locals feared the appearance of the spectral hound. They considered it a bad omen—a herald of death.'

CHAPTER 17
ISLAY, SCOTLAND. TWENTY YEARS AGO.

CALLUM REGISTERED THE BEAST'S glowing green eyes and enormous size without really processing this information. The creature looked like a dog but it was far larger than any breed he'd seen before—it was at least double the size of the two mastiffs Murray kept on the farm.

The beast regarded Callum with interest, nosing forward through the moonlit church. Callum backpedalled, but there was nothing to hide behind and no escape route. Even with his skinny teenage frame, he wouldn't fit through the mediaeval slit windows. Fear squeezed his insides. His hands shook. He felt a scream gathering in his throat, but knew that crying out for help would do no good. There would be no-one nearby to hear him at this time of night.

'Your thoughts are loud, little one,' the beast said.

Callum wondered if he was going mad. Was this all a horrible delusion his mind was conjuring? He squeezed his eyes shut, hoping that when he then opened them the monster would vanish like a card in a magic trick.

It didn't work. The beast remained as solid as ever as it padded towards him.

A warm wetness spread over the crotch of Callum's jeans. 'Please don't hurt me.'

'Is that really what you want, Callum? To go on living? Don't you long for the sweet release of death? I can give it to you, if you wish.'

Callum backed into the wall, feeling the ancient stonework with his fingers, trying to anchor himself in reality. The wall felt rough, bumpy, laced with velvety moss. 'Please don't kill me.' His voice sounded high and strained. 'I don't want to die. Please.'

'Are you sure? That's not what you've whispered to yourself, in the dead of night, when you think no-one can hear.'

This had to be a nightmare. If not, how did this creature have access to his innermost thoughts—his darkest, bleakest feelings?

'I've wanted to die sometimes, that's true. But that doesn't mean I want you to kill me.'

The monster was only a few feet away. It towered over Callum, but made no aggressive moves. Its huge, green eyes seemed like bottomless pits.

'Are you... death? The grim reaper?'

The beast's lips curled back into something approximating a smile. 'Do I look like the grim reaper?'

'You look like a dog. Sort of. A vicious dog.'

Callum instantly regretted his undiplomatic words, but the monster didn't seem angered by them.

'I am vicious,' it agreed. 'But I can also be merciful.'

Callum's terror decreased a notch. The monster seemed willing to speak to him, so perhaps he'd be able to talk his way out of this?

'Are you... a fae creature of some kind? My dad's a wizard, so I know a bit about the supernatural world.'

He didn't add that his dad only used spells on crops and farm animals and had never bothered to teach his son anything really interesting about magic.

'And your mother was a witch.'

Callum reeled. He felt weightless. Stunned. He had never met his mother. All Murray would say about her was that she left him in a Moses basket outside Kildalton church, presumably hoping someone would take him in, as Murray had indeed done. As he got older, Callum started questioning this story. Why would his mother abandon her baby beside an old, disused church? Had she meant for him to die, or be found? And what was Murray doing near the church, anyway?

Eventually, he came to suspect that the Moses basket story was made up and that Murray knew a lot more about Callum's mother than he let on. But that was pure speculation. Murray always refused to answer his questions.

'What do you know about my mother?'

'I knew her in death,' the beast said. 'It is my job, and my burden, to ensure that wandering souls depart the mortal world.'

Callum thought about this. 'Do you mean you took her to... heaven?'

The words sounded childish, and Callum's face grew hot with embarrassment.

The beast was ever so close now. It's breath stank of rotten meat and sulphurous smoke. Callum felt bile rising in his throat. He thought he might vomit pure adrenaline.

'I consumed her soul, as I have consumed the souls of hundreds more on this island who cling to the mortal world when their allotted time is at an end. Through me, they leave this place and enter the Silent Land.'

Callum wanted badly to ask about his mother, and about the Silent Land and the meaning of life and death, but he was too overwhelmed to form the words.

'You needn't cower, little one,' the beast said. 'I sometimes kill for sport, but I'll forgo that pleasure tonight for your mother's sake. Her desire to live was very strong. I consumed her soul and conveyed her to the Silent Land on the very day you were born.'

This was all too much. Callum's last coherent thought was that he must have gone mad—no other rational explanation could account for this experience. He curled up on the cold, wet ground and retreated to a safe place in his mind.

He couldn't have said how much time passed before he came back to himself and looked up to find that the beast was gone. The church was dark and empty. Rain spattered in through the open roof, slicking his hair and dribbling down his neck.

Against all the odds, he'd survived his encounter with the beast of Islay.

CHAPTER 18
LONDON. PRESENT DAY.

ZACHARIAH GOT IN CONTACT later that day via orb. Jasper placed the glass sphere, which was about the size and weight of a bowling ball, on the desk in front of the cash till and wedged it in place with a couple of hardback books. Zachariah's face appeared in the centre of the orb, his features blurring a little at the edges. He was wearing a hangdog expression and there were dark circles under his eyes. Alyssa came in from the kitchen and observed the conversation over Jasper's shoulder.

'The mundane police have just released me,' Zachariah said. 'They were furious with me for helping you escape, but eventually the Paranormal Office intervened and got me out. Still, I thought I was at least going to receive a reprimand from my superiors, but as soon as I mentioned your involvement everything was smoothed over. It seems you have friends in high places these days.'

Jasper laughed dryly. 'Hardly. Still, I'm grateful for your help. And I'm sorry you had to spend a night in the cells.'

Zachariah waved the apology away. 'Don't mention it. I just got in touch to find out if you gleaned anything from that slip of paper?'

'I did.' Jasper told him about the references to Mr Kirk and the Isle of Islay. 'If the cleaner was killed because she'd seen the content of that letter, this Mr Kirk might be responsible. At the very least, he might be able to shed light on the situation.'

'Indeed. I've got access to British government employment files. Give me a minute—I'll run that name through the computer and see if anything comes back.'

Unfortunately, the search didn't yield any results. 'No-one of that name works in Whitehall, for either the mundane or magical branches of government. Of course, it might be an alias...'

'Do you know if the police found any other clues at the crime scene?'

'Not at the crime scene. But they found the body of a werewolf in the garden.'

'I know about that,' Jasper said. 'I almost tripped over her on my way out. It was Una Silverback. She came to Downing Street with me—she was the wolf who howled near the Cenotaph. Her plan was to draw the police to the front of the building so she could sneak in the back.'

Zachariah frowned. 'Why? What did she want at Downing Street?'

'The same thing as me. To find "The Stray"—which is what the werewolves are calling this spy.'

'And she wanted to find this person because...?'

'Because last night The Stray led the werewolf packs into a trap. Most of the wolves were stunned and microchipped. Una escaped with a few of her pack mates.'

'Ah yes, I heard about that. So this spy is playing both sides?'

'It looks that way.'

Zachariah rubbed his chin. 'I wouldn't mind finding out why. There's clearly more to this than meets the eye. Unfortunately, there's very little chance the police will uncover anything else about the murder now.'

'Why not?'

Zachariah scowled, his displeasure obvious even through the distorted image produced by the orb. 'Because they think this dead werewolf—Una Silverback—killed the cleaner. They think she died as she tried to flee the crime scene. They're ready to wrap up their investigation.'

Jasper blew out a sigh. 'That's ridiculous. How do they explain her injuries? Even in the dark I could see that she had bite marks on her neck.'

'They believe the cleaner fought back and managed to deliver a fatal wound before she died. They've found a penknife in the rose garden near Una's body which is covered in her blood and the cleaner's.'

'But Una was bitten, not stabbed. Anyone can see that.'

'I believe you, but I suspect your spy has been doctoring the evidence. If they're able to cast magic, or have an ally who can, it would be relatively simple to fool the police into thinking Una was killed with a penknife. A glamour spell would do the trick.'

Zachariah was right. Fooling the police wouldn't have been that hard, but it would have taken magic to disguise Una's real wounds. Which meant that the spy was either a wizard with a shifter ally, or a shifter with a wizard ally. Both possibilities were alarming.

'Can you convince the police they're wrong?'

'I'll try,' Zachariah said, 'but it won't be easy. As far as they are concerned, they have a neat solution to the crime and they're eager to announce they've solved it. I'll do what I can, but it looks like it's going to be down to you to find this werewolf spy. Who, in all likelihood, is also responsible for the death of this cleaner.'

Jasper thanked Zachariah for his help, and they agreed to share any further information they came across. With that, Zachariah's face vanished from the orb, which filled with grey smoke. Jasper leaned back in his chair, mulling over the situation.

'What now?' Alyssa asked.

'Niko said The Stray had a Scottish accent, didn't he? And now we have a name and a potential link to the Isle of Islay. I'd say that's enough to justify a trip north. It might be a wild goose chase, but it's the only lead I've got at the moment.'

Alyssa bit her lip. 'I wish I could go with you, but I can't afford to leave London right now. I'm still working at the British Library, and in the evenings I've agreed to accompany some of the Silverback wolves on their howling protests. It's great content for the podcast.'

'Do you think they'll press ahead with the protests, even though most of them are now being tracked with microchips?'

Alyss cocked an eyebrow. 'I'm sure they will. What happened at Hampstead Heath has only made them more determined. And more angry.'

'Well, make sure you look after yourself. It sounds like things could turn nasty.'

'Right back at you, Jasper. Stay in touch and let me know how your investigation goes. If you don't text me on that crummy phone of yours every few hours at least, I'll be riding the next overpriced train to Scotland to come and get you.'

CHAPTER 19

THE BUNKER WAS HARD to find—impossible, really, unless you knew exactly where to look. Fortunately, Callum had visited it many times before, so he knew the route through Hampstead Heath like the back of his hand. He turned off the main path into an area of dense bramble. There was a place where the undergrowth had been hacked back just enough to allow passage through to a clearing. Finding the clearing was tricky enough, especially at this late hour (it was nearly 10pm), but now came the really difficult part.

There was no grass in the clearing—it was carpeted in dirt with a few scattered weeds. Callum set about patting the soil with the palm of his hand. It took him a few minutes to find the right spot. Eventually, his fingers closed around a metal ring, which he lifted to reveal a concealed hatch. He lifted the hatch and carefully lowered himself down the hole.

Most Londoners would be astonished to find this bunker—which its owner, Valerie, called The Hide—down here, only metres away from where thousands of people walked their dogs and played with their children. But here it was. In its own strange way, it was cosy. Not the kind of place Callum would choose to live, but it had a certain charm.

The air was thick with various smells, not all of them un-pleasant. Sage and cinnamon. Jasmine. The rich, savoury aroma of a casserole. Roughly cut logs of wood lined the walls. Herbs hung from the ceiling and metal pots and pans dangled on hooks on the walls. There was a camp bed pushed into a corner on which Valerie sat, a candle lantern propped beside her.

'Stop gawping and get over here,' she snapped. 'I've been waiting over an hour for you, wasting good candles.' Valerie was usually bad tempered, but Callum knew she meant no harm. It was just her way.

'I'm sorry to have kept you. I can pay to replace your candles, if you like.'

Valerie harrumphed. 'Don't need no charity from the likes of you, thank you very much.' She was draped in a dark green shawl and there were gold coloured bangles around her wrists. Her silver hair was pulled back in a bun. She was thin, bird-like, lean. She'd survived for years—perhaps even decades—homeless in London, so Callum knew she was tough.

Except she wasn't really homeless. The Hide was her home. Callum had never been able to fathom how she'd managed to build it in the first place, and Valerie would never tell. She guarded her secrets more closely than any of her possessions.

Callum moved closer, but didn't sit down on the camp bed. That would have been presumptuous, and not in keeping with the nature of their relationship, which was fundamentally one of business, of mutual need and grudging respect. At least, Callum respected Valerie. He wasn't sure if the feeling was mutual.

He was about to speak when he noticed a second source of light in the dim bunker. It was coming from the top of a metal filing cabinet pressed against one of the walls. Intrigued, Callum approached it for a closer look. The light was coming from a beaker full of purple glowing liquid standing on top of the filing cabinet. There was a plastic tube connected to the beaker that snaked down into the drawers below.

Callum carefully slid open the topmost drawer. It was full of wires and tubes and flasks that Callum couldn't begin to make sense of. There was a hole in the bottom of the drawer through which more tubes and wires were threaded.

'What is all this?' he asked.

Valerie grinned crookedly. 'That's my present for the government.'

That sounds ominous. 'What does that mean, exactly?'

'See the beaker at the top? That's full of Greek Fire. It's hooked up to a timer, which I can set to countdown any time I choose. And that's just the bit you can see. I've got barrels of gunpowder and more cylinders of Greek Fire buried underneath The Hide.' She stamped her foot on the floor, which was composed of compacted earth covered with a few threadbare rugs.

Callum stared at the device in alarm. 'You're planning to blow up your own home? Why?'

'To teach those born-to-rule chumps a lesson, that's why! They think they can trample all over people like me, but if I can't have this place, they can't either!'

'I don't understand. Has someone from the government tried to evict you?'

'The government, the borough council. Whatever. They're gonna privatise a big chunk of Hampstead Heath and turn it into some kind of *pleasure garden*. Charge people ten pound just to walk around. Bloody cheek! Anyway, once they start developing the land, they're bound to find this place and evict me. But they won't get rid of me without a fight.'

Callum backed away from the Greek Fire device. Was Valerie telling the truth? Was this really Greek Fire? He'd heard of the stuff, but he didn't really know if it was real or just a myth.

He wondered if he should report Valerie and her device to the police. He did work for the very government she was ranting about, after all. Valerie didn't know that, or she might've been more circumspect about her intentions. But if he did report her, the police would ask how he knew her and why he visited her in the dead of night. Awkward questions that he didn't care to answer.

'Please don't use that device, Valerie. You'll probably end up killing yourself, and maybe others.'

'Not a chance, love,' she said. 'I know what I'm doing. But it's sweet of you to worry about me.'

Rather than continue arguing, Callum decided to conclude their business as quickly as possible and leave. He wasn't sure if he believed her boast about cylinders of Greek Fire and barrels of gunpowder buried underneath the bunker. It seemed far-fetched, more like the fever dream of a madman than something Valerie would actually do. But he couldn't be certain. Despite having known her for years, Callum didn't feel he knew Valerie well at all. For example, was she a real witch, or just a mad old lady who had collected the stereotypical trappings of witchery—herbs, potions, cauldrons, spellbooks—like a magpie collecting shiny objects? Again, he just didn't know.

'Don't worry, it's not about to go boom,' Valerie continued. 'Only when I decide the time is right.' She tapped her crooked nose conspiratorially, then stood up from the bunk bed and thrust a vial into Callum's hand.

The vial was sealed with a blob of wax with an imprint of three interlaced arcs, forming a shape that resembled a Celtic knot. Valerie didn't make Callum's potions herself, although she often bragged that she was a skilled potion maker. The Celtic symbol was there to show that the potion had come directly from their mutual acquaintance at the Paranormal Office—a person Callum had never met, but whom he had relied on for years. He didn't even know their name. Valerie sometimes referred to them as The Boss.

'One vial? Is that it? I need more than that. The potions are getting less and less effective.'

'I know dear,' Valerie said, smiling sadly. 'You told me that last time. But I don't make them, do I? I can only give you what I'm given.'

Callum ran a hand through his hair. This was bad. One potion would only last a few days. After that, the hound would reassert itself. Even though the beast had been an unwelcome visitor in his mind and body for years, the transformation still genuinely frightened him. And it was getting harder to resist. When this potion ran out, the urge to return to Islay and prowl the island in search of prey would quickly become overwhelming.

Valerie touched his arm. Despite her perennial grumpiness, she was always kind to Callum.

'I've told you before,' she said gently, 'you shouldn't take that stuff. There's a reason I don't brew it myself—it's nasty. There's bad magic in it, take it from me.'

Callum suspected the reason Valerie didn't brew the potions herself was that she didn't have the skill, but he didn't say that. Deep down, he knew she was probably right. He was no expert on magic, having been repeatedly blocked from attending magical training, but even he could tell that there was more than a whiff of dark power about those potions.

'I'd love to stop taking them,' he said. 'They give me headaches and make me itch all over. But I don't have a choice, do I? I can't let the hound take control.'

'The werewolves manage alright,' Valerie shrugged. 'They have the instincts of wolves and men, and they learn to embrace both. They don't suppress either side of their nature.'

'I'm not a werewolf. The beast inside me will overwhelm me if I let it.'

Callum realised his eyes were filling with tears. He'd been bottling this up, focusing on problems he could surmount, but now his fear and anxiety were starting to spill out.

'Have a seat dear,' Valerie said, steering Callum to sit on her camp bed. As he collected himself, she rifled through some things on the floor under the bed.

'Here we are! This potion will do you nothing but good. Guaranteed.'

She handed him a bottle of Johnnie Walker Black Label, with several fingers of whisky left in the bottom. Normally Callum would have refused the offer—he wasn't much of a drinker—but just now he lacked the energy to argue. He brought the bottle to his lips and took a slug. The whisky burned his throat, and he coughed.

Valerie chuckled and took a swig from the bottle herself.

'I've got a proposal for you, young Callum. But it must stay between ourselves—no-one else can know about it. You must give me your word as a gentleman.'

It was the first time Callum had been asked to give 'his word as a gentleman', which was hardly surprising since he wasn't a character in a Victorian novel. But Valerie appeared to be serious, so he nodded and said, 'Whatever it is, it'll stay between us.'

'Good boy. Now, here's the thing. These potions hardly work anymore and they're making you ill. I suspect The Boss doesn't care too much for your wellbeing. They're only interested in the information you supply them in return.'

Valerie was warming to her theme. Her fondness for making speeches was such that Callum sometimes thought she should stand for parliament.

'What you need is something that melds the two halves of your personality, not this rubbish that temporarily suppresses your wolfish instincts. You get my drift?'

Callum sighed. He reached for the Johnnie Walker bottle and had another swig. This time the whisky tasted less harsh and warmed him pleasantly on the way down. 'I don't see the hound as being part of my personality. It's more like Jekyll and Hyde. I just want Mr Hyde to sod off.'

'That's the problem,' Valerie said with a touch of smugness. 'Mr Hyde is going nowhere—you have to embrace it, Cal! Merge with it. Bring together your human brain and your canine instincts.'

'How?'

Valerie's eyes twinkled. 'I might be able to help you there. Been doing some reading,' She picked up a spellbook that was inside a metal shopping basket beside the bed. She flipped through the pages and prodded at a potion recipe.

'I could make this for you, if you like.'

'This would bring the two sides of me together?'

Valerie nodded. 'It would allow you to change into your hound form without losing your human mind. You'd be more like a werewolf—wolf and man coexisting in relative harmony.'

Callum stared at the potion recipe, but it meant little to him. For about the millionth time in his life, he felt frustrated with his lack of magical education. He was sure he could have become a decent wizard, but both Murray and the magical authorities had refused to teach him. Without a magical education, he had no way of knowing if Valerie's recipe was real or a load of hogwash.

'Having trouble deciphering the recipe?' Valerie asked. 'No problem—let me help.'

The book was suddenly illuminated by purplish light. Callum jerked backwards in shock. A cunning smile appeared on Valerie's lined face. A small globe of shimmering silvery-purple light was hovering above her left hand. *Werelight.*

'You thought I was a phoney, eh? Many people have made that mistake over the years, but, as you can see, I know a thing or two about magic.'

Callum couldn't argue with that. The werelight was proof that Valerie was magically gifted, to some extent at least. 'What do you want in return for making this potion?'

'Well, I want to help you, Cal, but I have my own problems to worry about. Like getting a new place to live when the council find this place and boot me out. I can't help but notice that you're always wearing lovely clothes when you visit me—shiny shoes and suits from Savile row. So I know you've got funds in the bank.'

'So you want money? How much?'

She looked him straight in the eye and said, without a trace of embarrassment, 'Ten grand. I want to get on a flight to Spain and not come back. I need money for the plane ticket and money to set myself up when I get there.'

Callum considered this. He was an important government official, with a salary benefiting his seniority. His expenses were low, since he didn't have a partner or children to worry about. He could spare ten thousand pounds.

'OK, that seems fair. How long will it take to make the potion?'

Valerie looked slightly startled. Perhaps she'd expected Callum to haggle.

'It won't be easy,' she said. 'I need the blood of a wizard to energise the potion, and a token from the place where you first transformed.'

'What kind of token?'

'Anything—a rock, a twig, a lump of mud. But it must come from the place where you first transformed into your hound form. That's crucial.'

'And you definitely need wizard blood? Can't you use my blood instead?'

'Are your ears stuffed with cotton wool? Yes, it has to be the blood of a wizard. If you're not interested...'

'No, I am. I just don't know how I'll be able to get that.'

Valerie shrugged. 'That's for you to worry about. Only, don't take too long about it. I expect those dogs from the council to find me soon—and you know what will happen then.'

She nodded towards the flask of Greek Fire.

Callum had a lot to think about. He didn't mind about the money, but getting the blood of a wizard would be difficult and dangerous. He stood up and went to leave.

'Hang on,' Valerie said. 'Don't you have any information for The Boss? They'll expect it, you know.'

Callum thought about it, then came to a decision.

'Tell them our agreement is over. Their potions aren't working anymore and I'm fed up with this arrangement. I'll be back soon with the blood and the token.'

'And the cash.'

'That too.'

Callum climbed out of the hatch and strolled through a pitch black Hampstead Heath. Was he really going to go through with this? The money wasn't a problem. Travelling up to Scotland to obtain a token from his first transformation would be awkward, but it could be done. He had plenty of holiday saved up at work, and he was senior enough that he could get away with taking some of it at short notice.

The wizard blood was another matter. Harming a wizard was a very serious thing to do. He was sure the Paranormal Office would hunt down anyone who hurt a wizard, especially if they also stole some of their blood.

Unless...

There were a few mages around Britain who lived off-grid, unknown to the magical authorities. Callum knew of just such a hedgerow wizard who lived quietly on a farm in the Isle of Islay and had few friends.

But could he bring himself to hurt the man he'd once thought of as a father?

CHAPTER 20

IT TOOK ALL DAY to reach the Isle of Islay from London. Jasper hadn't driven his car—a 2004 Honda Civic with dodgy suspension—for ages, but he was relieved to find it still ran well enough after a visit to the petrol station and a top up of the oil. He set off early in the morning and reached the ferry terminal at Kennacraig as the afternoon faded into a pleasantly fresh evening. The ferry took two hours to reach Port Ellen on the Isle of Islay. Thankfully, the sea wasn't choppy enough to trigger Jasper's seasickness, and he spent most of the trip leaning against the handrail gazing at the grey blue sea, taking in the beautiful rugged hills and beaches of Scotland's west coast.

Once he arrived at Port Ellen, he headed straight for the Ardview Inn, where he'd booked a room. The place was whitewashed, rustic, with a relaxed atmosphere—Jasper's kind of place. He dumped his bags upstairs and came straight down again to eat a hearty dinner of fish pie with chunky chips and wilted vegetables. It wasn't fancy, but it sated Jasper's appetite. Mindful of his vow to keep off the booze, he washed down his dinner with a lime soda.

Now that he was here, he realised this trip could easily prove to be a waste of time. When he'd seen the reference to the Isle of Islay in the fire, he'd pictured a small Scottish island, a place where everyone knew everyone else. But Islay was one of the largest Hebridean islands, with several sizable settlements and vast tracts of countryside in between.

His initial strategy—if you could call it that—was to hang around at the bar and pump the locals for information. There were a few barflies there nursing drinks, but Jasper decided to start with the landlord, a man with messy black hair and dark stubble, who appeared to be around Jasper's age.

'I'll have another lime and soda, mate,' Jasper said, doing his best to sound genial.

The landlord raised an eyebrow. 'You haven't finished the last one I poured you.'

It was true—his glass was still more than a third full of soda and Jasper didn't really want anymore. His request was just a pretext to strike up a conversation with the barman.

'I will, by the time you've poured me another one,' he said. 'Oh, and I'll have a packet of salt and vinegar crisps.'

The landlord got the drink and the crisps without comment, while Jasper downed the remains of his lime soda. He felt queasy and had to suppress an explosive burp. *Who knew that soft drinks could be more difficult to stomach than the hard stuff?*

After paying, Jasper tried to engage the barman in conversation.

'I came up from London this morning. I'm looking for an old friend, maybe you know him? His surname is Kirk.'

The landlord stared at him. 'Aye, and what's his first name?'

'Erm, I'm not sure.'

The landlord narrowed his eyes. 'You don't know your friend's first name? Cannae 'a' been that good of a friend then.'

One of the barflies laughed gruffly.

Jasper felt stupid but forced himself to smile, eager to keep these guys on side in case they knew something that might prove useful to his investigation. 'I'm terrible with names. He's more of a friend of a friend, but I thought I'd look him up while I'm in the area.'

The landlord shrugged. 'Don't know anyone by the name of Kirk.' He moved away to serve the man further down the bar, who had just finished his pint.

This wasn't going well. If he was going to get any information, he needed to get chatting with the locals, but his posh English accent and apparent addiction to lime soda wasn't exactly helping him to blend in.

'Who is it you're looking for?' It was the man from further down the bar, who had left his stool to come and stand next to Jasper. He was wearing a beanie hat and had a grizzled but friendly face.

'A man with the surname Kirk. Ring any bells?'

The man looked thoughtful. 'It does a bit.'

The landlord returned with a pint of dark brown stout for the man in the beanie hat.

'I'll get that,' Jasper said, handing over a ten pound note. 'And I'll have the same. Been trying to cut down on the booze, but I'm getting sick of this lime soda.'

'That's kind of you,' said the man in the beanie. 'I'm Malcolm.'

'Nice to meet you. I'm Jasper. To be honest, I could do with a friend around here.'

'Well, you've just made one. Cheers!'

They spent the next fifteen minutes drinking together, chatting about the local area and Jasper's line of work (Jasper told him about the bookshop, rather than his sideline investigating for the Paranormal Office). Malcolm was an amiable guy who had lived on Islay his whole life. Jasper was glad of the excuse to have a proper drink after several weeks of abstinence. He told himself it was a necessary evil—there was no way he'd make friends in a Scottish pub if he stuck exclusively to soft drinks.

'Graham, James, come over here,' Malcolm said. 'Do you remember a lad with the surname Kirk? It's ringing a bell but I can't place him.'

Malcolm's two friends came over and propped themselves at the bar. Graham had an expansive beard and looked quite old, while James was middle-aged and wearing a sheep wool fleece.

'Can you be more specific?' Graham said.

'I wish I could,' Jasper said. 'He works for the government in London, but I think he may still have a house up here.'

'Might you be thinking of Callum Kirk?' James asked. 'Stuart Murray's boy?'

'Oh aye, Callum,' said Malcolm. 'I heard he did well for himself down in London. Anyway, he hasn't lived on the island for years, not since he was a boy.'

James nodded sagely. 'No, but Murray died a few months back, remember? So young Callum might have come back to deal with his father's estate.' James turned to Jasper. 'Is that why you're here? Are you one of the beneficiaries?'

Jasper shook his head. 'I didn't even know his dad had died.'

'You don't know much do you, lad?' Malcolm said genially, patting Jasper on the back and glugging his pint.

'Are you a solicitor?' James asked, a trace of suspicion in his voice.

'No. I run a bookshop in London. Why do you ask?'

'Well, I heard there's some legal trouble with Murray's estate. I don't know the details, but there have been solicitors crawling all over the island trying to sort it out.'

Interesting. Jasper wasn't sure if this information had any bearing on his investigation, but he stowed it away for future consideration.

'Any idea where I might find Callum?'

'Well, if he works for the government in London, as you say, you'd probably have a better chance of finding him there than up here. But I suppose you could try visiting the Murray Farm. If he has come home to deal with his father's estate, that's most likely where he'll be.'

'Do any of you know Callum? What's he like?'

James looked sidelong at Jasper, suspicion written across his features. 'I thought he was your friend?'

'Only a friend of a friend. Actually, some of his mates are worried about him, that's why I'm trying to track him down.' Jasper hoped his improvisation sounded convincing.

His story seemed to satisfy James, who shrugged and said, 'He was in the year above me at school. Tall, scrawny lad. Liked reading. Not much like his dad.'

'That's because Murray adopted him,' Graham chimed in. 'I remember now. This was back in the eighties or nineties.'

'I heard he went to California and made a fortune working in social media,' mused Malcolm, his eyes a little unfocused. He'd already finished the fresh pint Jasper had bought him moments earlier.

'No, that's not right,' Graham said. 'He went to work for the government. Either the Scottish government in Holyrood, or Westminster, I forget which. He was a sensitive boy, as far as I can remember. Can't imagine he had much of a childhood with old Murray being so joyless.'

The three men regaled Jasper with half-remembered anec-
dotes and tidbits about Callum Kirk, some of them contra-
dictory. But they agreed on certain things. They were all sure
Murray had adopted Callum and raised him on his farm. They
believed Callum had left the island in his late teens in search
of a big city career. Murray supposedly hadn't left the island
in years and rarely ventured off his farm.

'One more thing, Jack,' Malcolm slurred, a couple of hours
and at least half a dozen beers later.

'Jasper.'

'Sorry, Jasper. Listen.' He put his hand on Jasper's shoulder
and leaned in close. His breath smelled strongly of stout and
salted peanuts. Fortunately, Jasper was five pints deep himself,
so he didn't mind too much.

'If you go to Murray's farm, be careful. There's something
not right about that place. The kids say it's haunted by evil
spirits, and I'm not altogether sure they're wrong.'

CHAPTER 21

DESPITE HIS HANGOVER (MALCOLM had insisted on buying them both shots of local whisky before calling it a night), Jasper forced himself to get up early. He was eager to move his investigation forward. The information he'd gleaned from the local drinkers was intriguing, but he needed something more concrete to have a chance of tracking down Callum Kirk.

He located the Murray farm on an Ordnance Survey map of Islay he'd brought with him from London. It was less than two miles from Port Ellen, so he decided to walk there and try to clear his head in the morning air. Although it was summer, there was a chill in the air at this time of day. The island looked lush in the morning sunshine. The long tufts of grass looked lustrous and green in some places and mustard yellow in others where they were touched by rays from the rising sun. Brown hills and stony cliffs stood out against a pale blue sky that was mostly free of clouds.

The farmhouse was at the end of a long mud track. The hairs on the back of Jasper's neck stood up as he walked down the winding path. He looked over his shoulder several times, unable to shake the feeling that he was being watched.

When he reached the farmhouse, he got the impression that no-one was living there. The building was dark. Spider webs covered the wing mirrors of the old Land Rover parked in the drive. No-one answered the door when Jasper knocked. He walked all around the house, peering through the windows. It looked lived in, but there was no sign anyone was there now. All the doors were locked. What the barflies had said—that Murray had died a few months earlier, leaving his estate in limbo—seemed to be true.

The feeling he was being watched got stronger as he stared through the kitchen window. He turned around in a slow circle. There was no-one nearby that he could see, but there was something strange about the murmuring wind that blew across the farm.

Jasper had given little credence to Malcolm's drunken warning that evil spirits infested Murray's farm, but now he wondered if he might be right after all. Although they couldn't see ghosts with the naked eye, wizards were more attuned to the spirit world than mundanes and could usually sense paranormal activity if it was intense enough and close enough.

Jasper conjured a ball of werelight. At first it cast a purplish light, but it turned silver as Jasper twisted his hand. He drew some extra power from his ruby brooch and fed it into the silver werelight. The ball floated a few feet above his head and flared brighter.

The silver werelight revealed several figures standing within a few hundred yards. They were translucent, blurring away at the edges, like smoke trapped in glass bottles. They were all staring in Jasper's direction. A ripple of fear passed through him, but he stood his ground and told himself not to panic. Ghosts couldn't attack the living directly, and these spirits had no reason to harm him... as far as he knew.

But why were they here? Ghosts only hung around if they had unfinished business. If that was true, they were most likely to linger in places with a strong connection to their life. Did these spirits have a connection with Murray's farm? Is that why they were here?

Now that he could see the ghosts, he felt their presence even more strongly. When he looked towards the muddy track and the countryside, he sensed curiosity and confusion, but when he turned his attention to the farmhouse, he detected much stronger emotions.

Anger. Frustration. Regret.

Rage.

Jasper extinguished the werelight and walked back to the farmhouse. As luck would have it, a window on the ground floor had been smashed, perhaps by an opportunistic burglar. The window led into a downstairs toilet. Jasper climbed inside, carefully avoiding the spikes of glass sticking out of the window frame. Inside, he noticed muddy footprints on the floor. Jasper let himself out of the toilet and walked down a corridor into the kitchen, moving as quietly as possible.

The kitchen was full of clutter. Tea cups, plates, pots and pans, and cutlery, were gathering dust and growing mould on the countertops. Jasper felt a growing sense of foreboding as he scanned the room. The rage and anguish he'd sensed outside the farmhouse felt stronger inside. The air was thick with it.

A cast-iron skillet started wobbling on the countertop. The movement became progressively more violent until the skillet clattered onto the laminate floor. The sound reverberated harshly through the room. It felt like a warning. Jasper took a deep breath and backtracked into the corridor, suppressing the urge to run out of the house.

'Sorry to intrude,' he muttered. 'But I need to find out if Callum has been here recently.'

He found a stack of old letters in the living room, but they were mostly bills and bank statements addressed to Stuart Murray. There was nothing addressed to Callum Kirk, or to anyone by the name of Kirk. Jasper wondered why Callum apparently hadn't taken his adopted father's name. As he was mulling this inconsistency, the living room window flew open and a gust of frigid air blew in.

Undeterred, Jasper went upstairs and entered the master bedroom. Something on the dresser caught his eye: a framed photograph of a teenage boy standing in front of a tractor. The boy was tall and gangly, with sandy blonde hair and freckles. His arms were crossed over his stomach and he was looking at his feet. He was dressed in wellington boots and a dark blue macintosh, but somehow the outfit didn't suit him. He remembered one of the drinkers at the Ardview Inn saying that Callum Kirk had been a bookish boy at school. Had Callum perhaps longed for a different life to the one Murray had in mind for him? Was this a source of tension between father and son?

Jasper picked up the photo and turned it over to see if there was anything written on the back.

The bedroom erupted.

Shoes, clothes, books and coins flew at Jasper from all angles. A brass carriage clock spun towards his face, forcing him to duck out of the way. The windows burst open and unseasonably icy air blew in.

Jasper shielded his head with his arms and shouted, 'I'm not a burglar! I'm just looking for information about Callum Kirk. I don't mean any harm.'

If the ghost understood him, it wasn't satisfied with his explanation. The bed rattled against the wall, and the duvet cover split down the middle, as if someone had slashed it open with a knife. The door banged an angry drumbeat. *This is getting out of hand.*

Jasper conjured a new ball of werelight, turning it silver with a twist of his hand. A tall, muscular man with a dark brown beard and deep-set eyes stood less than two metres away. He looked about seventy, but appeared to be in good shape for his age, not counting the fact that he was dead. Jasper could see the bed quivering through his translucent form. Even though he was lacking in substance, his rage was clear enough. His teeth were clenched and his hands were balled into fists. He looked ready for a fight.

The ghost of Stuart Murray lifted one of his fists, which Jasper now saw held a small gardening fork. He extinguished the werelight and fled down the stairs. It wasn't worth risking his life in the vague hope he might find a clue to Callum Kirk's whereabouts. The whole house seemed to be clamouring for him to leave: doors and windows were banging and small objects all over the house were rattling or smashing against the walls.

Jasper felt a stinging sensation as he climbed out of the toilet window. He looked down and saw blood welling on his hand where he'd caught it on the broken window. Fortunately, the cut wasn't too deep. He decided to be thankful he hadn't come away with worse injuries.

He could understand Murray's ghost being angry with him for breaking in, but the intensity of his rage suggested there was more to it, as did the fact that Jasper had sensed anger and regret radiating from the farmhouse long before he'd entered it. If the barflies were to be believed, Murray had been a quiet, hermit-like man who loved nothing more than tending his farm and caring for animals. Callum, however, had loved books and had gone to work for the British government. Had a rift developed between father and son? Did that account for the rage and resentment displayed by Murray's ghost? Is that why he still haunted the farmhouse?

Even if that were true, it didn't explain why the area around the farmhouse was littered with wandering spirits. Jasper decided to try something else. He found an empty barn a short walk away from the house where he sat cross-legged on the straw and conjured more silver werelight. Nothing happened right away, but he stayed patient, stretching out his legs when they started to cramp, reaching out with his magical senses, trying to tempt one of the wandering spirits to come to him.

After more than an hour of waiting, an elderly man with a cane and watery blue eyes approached him cautiously. His body was translucent and silvery, but the closer he got to the werelight the clearer he became. When he got to within a few feet, he stretched out his hands as if warming himself in front of a fire. His outline clarified further to the point where a casual observer might have mistaken him for a living man.

'Good morning,' Jasper said, remaining seated on the ground so as not to startle the ghost. 'I wondered if I could ask you a few questions?'

The old man smiled. 'Don't see why not. I heard your voice on the wind, young man. That's a clever trick. You'll have to show me how it's done. I won't sit down if you don't mind—if I do I won't be able to get up again, with my creaky old joints.'

'No problem.'

'So few people speak to me nowadays. I see them milling about, but they rarely see me.' The old man shook his head glumly.

The ghost seemed not to understand that he was dead. Jasper decided to frame his questions carefully, so as not to alarm him. 'I just encountered the man who lives at the farmhouse. His name is Stuart Murray, I think.'

'Is it? I didn't know.'

'He seemed angry.'

The old man nodded. 'I'm sure he is. Many of us around here are getting frustrated.'

'Is that because you have unfinished business? Perhaps something connected with Murray's farm?'

'Unfinished business?' The old man tapped his cane on the ground thoughtfully. 'I had that feeling once, but I can't remember why. Have you ever walked into a room and forgotten your reason for being there? It's like that.'

'I think I know what you mean. Is that why you and the others are reluctant to leave this place?'

The old man frowned. 'No, that's not it. You've got it backwards. We all want to leave—me and the other forgotten people—but we're stuck here.'

'You mean you want to leave, but you can't?'

'Exactly.'

It was Jasper's turn to feel confused. Ghosts were usually obsessed with past mistakes, reluctant to let go of their mortal lives. But this man was saying the opposite—that the ghosts in this area were trapped here against their will. Far from resisting the finality of death, they were eager to move on but unable to do so. So what was stopping them?

'Have you heard of a man named Callum Kirk?,' Jasper asked. 'I believe he's the son of Stuart Murray, the man who owns this farm. Are you perhaps waiting for him?'

The old man shuffled his feet and shook his head. 'I don't know who that is. As I said, I don't want to wait here, but I can't seem to leave. I've been hoping someone would come to guide us away, but no-one has seen or spoken to us for years.'

CHAPTER 22

Jasper went back to the Ardview Inn for lunch, where he found a woman waiting for him at the bar. She appeared to be in her late fifties, with grey hair swept back into a bun and held in place by a blue scrunchie. She was wearing a baby blue polo shirt and grey checked trousers, and there was a bag of golf clubs propped beside her. As soon as she saw Jasper she jumped up and grasped his hand, speaking with a Dublin accent.

'I'm Grace Campbell. You'll be the Englishman who's looking for Callum Kirk, is that right?'

'Yes—I'm Jasper Wychwood. How did you...?'

'It's a pleasure to meet you, Mr Wychwood. What is your interest in Callum Kirk, if you don't mind me asking? Malcolm said you weren't a solicitor.'

Jasper felt a little disconcerted with how much this lady already knew about him, but he recovered his composure quickly.

'I'm not a solicitor, no. I'm a friend of a friend. Just hoping to bump into Callum, that's all.'

Grace's smile faltered briefly, probably because his cover story sounded weak and unconvincing.

'Can I get you a drink?' Jasper asked quickly, covering the awkward silence that followed his unconvincing explanation. 'We can compare notes on Callum?'

'That's a grand idea. I'll have a white wine.'

Jasper bought the wine and a pale ale for himself and they sat in a secluded booth at the back of the Inn. They clinked glasses and Grace sipped her wine, watching Jasper over the rim of her glass.

'So you're just an acquaintance of Callum, are you? ' she asked.

In the time it had taken Jasper to get served at the bar, he'd decided on a new cover story, one closer to the truth.

'Actually, the truth is I work with Callum in London. He has quite an important job in government, but he's gone missing. I've come to look for him.' He leaned forward as he spoke, adopting a conspiratorial tone in the hope that Grace would feel he was letting her into a secret.

It seemed to work. Grace's expression softened, and she said, 'I thought it might be something like that. Do you think he might have come home after Stuart's death?'

'Stuart Murray, you mean?'

'That's right—Callum's father. Well, his adopted father.'

Jasper nodded. 'Yes. We thought he might have come up for the funeral.'

'It's a bit late for that. The funeral was months ago. I hope he isn't in some sort of trouble at work?'

Jasper took a pull of his pint to give himself time to think. 'There are some... irregularities we'd like to discuss with him. Information being leaked from the department. I can't be more specific than that.'

Grace's eyes widened. 'Oh dear. Poor Callum.'

It occurred to Jasper that Grace was pumping him for information. He decided to turn the tables.

'So, what's your connection with Callum? Are you trying to find him too?'

'I'm connected with his dad, really. Stuart hired me to help him round the farm, oh, must be eight years ago now. He'd become an invalid and needed help with everyday tasks. I became his live-in carer.'

There was a twinkle in her eye as she spoke, which made Jasper wonder whether Grace had become more than Stuart Murray's carer. But he decided it would be indelicate to ask.

'Did you ever meet Callum?'

'Sadly, no. The two were estranged for the whole time I knew Stuart. It took me years to get the truth out of him, but eventually he admitted they fell out decades ago.'

Jasper thought about the enraged ghost back at the farmhouse. 'Do you know what caused the rift between them?'

'No. Like I said, Stuart was reluctant to talk about it. But I think they had an odd relationship, even before they became estranged. Stuart claimed he found baby Callum in a Moses basket outside Kildalton Church—which is a mediaeval ruin near here. It's quite popular with tourists nowadays, but it was more secluded back then. Anyway, I was never sure if he was being serious. It sounded like something out of a fairytale.'

Grace seemed to relax the more she talked. She soon finished her first glass of white wine, so Jasper bought her another in the hope she might reveal something important.

She took the second drink gratefully. 'What makes it even stranger is that Stuart never seemed to like kids, as far as I could tell. He wasn't very good at expressing his feelings. I always wondered why he adopted Callum in the first place.'

'What about Callum's biological parents? Does anyone know who they are?'

Grace shrugged. 'Stuart claimed not to know who they were. The whole thing was baffling to me.'

'I agree, it seems odd. Finding him in a basket... it sounds almost biblical.'

'Like Moses, you mean? Except Kildalton church isn't very holy, if you ask me.' Grace crossed herself, and Jasper registered that there was a silver crucifix hanging over the top of her polo shirt. 'Horrible, creepy place. I've only been there once and that was enough. There are stories of a monster prowling the church graveyard at night. I'm not saying that's true, but most locals give the place a wide berth. Except for Callum—apparently he liked it there. '

'Really?'

Grace took a big gulp of wine and smacked her lips. Her cheeks had turned rosy. 'Stuart said that as a boy Callum spent more time hanging around that old church than he did tending the farm. As a matter of fact, that's where he got his name.'

Jasper frowned. 'What, Callum?'

'No—*Kirk.* It's the Gaelic word for church. That's why Stuart called him Callum Kirk rather than Callum Murray—because he found the boy outside an old church. Or so he said.'

'Right.' Jasper stared into his pint of pale ale, digesting this new information. 'I suppose that explains why father and adopted son didn't have the same surnames.'

'Yes, but it's a bit weird, isn't it? Part of the reason they didn't get on, I think.'

'And you haven't seen or heard from Callum since his dad's death? I gather there are some issues with the Murray estate?'

'So you *have* been keeping your ear to the ground,' Grace said approvingly. 'Unfortunately, no-one has seen hide nor hair of Callum, but I'm hoping he'll make an appearance soon. You see, despite their estrangement, Stuart made Callum executor of his estate, and left him everything he owned, including the farm and all the adjoining land. Stuart's solicitors have been searching for Callum for months.'

'What will happen to the farm if they don't find him?'

Grace shrugged. 'I don't know, but they're pulling out all the stops to contact him. The farm is worth millions.'

Really? Jasper was used to London's sky-high property values, but weren't prices cheaper in Scotland?

Grace must have read the scepticism in his face, because she said, 'I'm not exaggerating. Land is at a premium on Islay, and several property developers are eager to build new homes here. It's quite controversial locally, as you can imagine. They offered Stuart millions for his farmland, but the stubborn old goat refused to sell. Now that he's dead, the developers want to make the same offer to Callum. The boy is a millionaire and he might not even know it!'

CHAPTER 23
TWENTY YEARS AGO.

Callum didn't tell Murray or anyone else about his terrifying encounter in Kildalton church. But the beast with black fur and glowing eyes occupied his every waking thought and haunted his dreams. Sometimes he wondered if it had all been a dream, or some kind of delusion. Was he going mad? If he told anyone about the beast, they would surely think so.

Then again, if he told people in Port Ellen that his father used magic to grow his crops, they'd laugh and call him loopy, even though it was true. Over the years, Murray had hinted that there were thousands of wizards in the British Isles, concentrated in cities like Edinburgh, London, Dublin, Oxford, and Bath. Callum had begged him to reveal more, or introduce him to people from the magical world, but Murray always refused. His world was the farm and the surrounding countryside. In Murray's mind, everything beyond Islay was foreign and suspect.

Yet a piece of the magical world had found Callum and nearly killed him. Surely it was only sensible to learn more about it, if only so he could protect himself?

He knew if he told Murray about the beast outright his father would explain it away as a nightmare or a stray dog, so he decided to do his own research before broaching the subject. Without asking permission, he took a passenger ferry to Campbeltown in Northern Ireland and spent an afternoon in the public library. Getting there was a mission, but the resources were better than anything on Islay, and the journey was easier than the one to Glasgow. He found the occult section and roamed the stacks for hours. He'd read some of the books here before in the hope of learning more about the supernatural world, with little success. But although most were full of fairy tales or vague gibberish, he had a feeling he'd once read a passage about a creature resembling the beast that had cornered him in the church.

After much searching, he pulled down a book of Scottish mythology bound in black cloth. The library had labelled the book suitable for children, but some of the stories it re-layed were quite sinister, and the ink drawings that illustrated them were downright creepy. Callum remembered finding this book years before—and quickly returning it to the shelf when he saw the disturbing illustrations.

He flipped eagerly through the pages until he found what he was looking for: an ink drawing of a muscular black dog with glowing eyes towering over a small, frightened man. The dog had a scraggly tail and fangs that looked too big for its mouth. The beast's eyes bored into Callum's, as if daring him to read on. With a shaking hand, he turned the page and read the accompanying text.

The Cù-Sìth (pronounced coo-she) is a spectral hound said to haunt the Scottish Highlands and Hebrides. Those who claim to have seen the creature say it has black fur with a green tinge, a coiled tail, and large glowing eyes.

Many fear the Cù-Sìth as a harbinger of death, much like the Grim Reaper. Its role is to convey the souls of the dead to the afterlife, which it does by feasting on their spectral energy. In some tales, this is a benign or even benevolent act, but in others the ravenous hound seeks out unfortunate travellers, savaging their bodies and consuming their souls. There have been many reported sightings of the Cù-Sìth, with witnesses describing its glowing eyes and terrifying howls, which are said to strike fear into the hearts of all but the bravest...

This was it—it had to be! The beast that had cornered him in the church. The hound that could have killed Callum, but who spared his life for his mother's sake.

Excitement mixed with fear in Callum's gut. For his whole life, Murray had kept him away from the supernatural world, but now a creature from that world had sought him out. He'd faced it and survived. And this beast—the *Cù-Sìth*—claimed to have known Callum's mother, and played a role in her death.

Callum checked the book out of the library and took it home on the ferry. He read the chapter about the Cù-Sìth over and over until he knew it almost by heart.

Over breakfast a week later, he plucked up the courage to talk to Murray about it. He decided to take a circumspect approach, knowing that his father was liable to clam up if he thought Callum was trying to learn about supernatural matters.

'Do you remember the night I left the house?'

Murray stared down at his tattie scones and fried eggs. He would know that Callum was referring to the night of their worst ever row. 'Aye.'

'I slept outside,' Callum said. 'Away from the house, I mean.'

'I thought you must have.'

'I slept in Kildalton church.'

Murray looked up, his expression unreadable. 'Why did you go there? It's a bad place. Dangerous.'

Callum gripped his fork under the table, letting the cold metal bite into the skin of his hand. *Why does he think it's a bad place, when it's where he found me?* 'I like it there,' he said. 'It's where you found me, isn't it?'

'Aye.'

'I saw the field of dead sheep on my way to the church. The ones you found the next day.'

Losing the sheep had been a serious blow to Murray. Despite their row, he'd told Callum about the incident a couple of days later and asked him to keep an eye out for foxes and other predators.

Murray stopped eating and stared at his son. 'You never said.'

'No,' Callum agreed. 'But I think I saw the thing that killed the sheep, up by Kildalton church. It looked like a black dog, but it was much bigger than any normal dog, and had glowing eyes.' Callum held back from saying the beast had spoken to him, not wanting to sound totally mad.

There was a long silence. Murray turned his head and looked out of the window. Callum felt a flutter of anticipation. Murray wasn't dismissing him outright. Maybe he would believe him after all. They could go searching for the beast together.

Feeling encouraged, he said, 'It's called a Cù-Sìth—a hound that eats the souls of the dead. I looked it up in a library book. I heard it bark three times and—'

'That's enough of your tall tales, son. You've been filling your head with nonsense again. It was just a stray dog, that's all.'

Callum felt his face flush red. 'It's not nonsense! The Cù-Sìth spoke to me in the church and said it knew my mother. I think it may have killed her.'

Murray stood up abruptly and tossed his dinner plate and cutlery into the sink.

'Why don't you ever talk about her? You knew her! Admit it.'

'Your mother wasn't killed by a fairy, I promise you that. I'll say no more about it.'

Rage bubbled hotly in Callum's chest. Murray had known his mother, he was sure of it. Why wouldn't he talk about her? If Callum never learned anything about his origins, what was he? Just a foundling, an unwanted child. A farmhand who wasn't very good at farming. A pale shadow.

'She must've been a witch,' he spat. 'A disgusting old hag. That's why you never talk about her. You're ashamed.'

Murray was a tall and powerful man, muscled from years working on the farm, but he was not normally prone to violence. Even in their most vicious arguments, he had never lashed out. But this time Callum had pushed him too far. He spun around and swept his arm across the table, sending Callum's breakfast flying. His plate smashed on the floor. Orange juice sprayed into his lap. He sat there, stunned, silent, unable to move.

'Don't ever speak about your mother that way,' Murray said, his eyes blazing with anger, his chest heaving. 'It's bad enough she died bringing you into this world. You won't speak ill of her now she's in heaven.'

CHAPTER 24
PRESENT DAY.

IT WAS THE FIRST time in over a decade that Callum had returned to Islay. He wore a baseball cap and sunglasses and avoided meeting anyone's eye in Port Ellen. It was unlikely anyone would recognise him after all these years, but he wasn't taking any chances.

He'd taken three days of leave from work—a rare indulgence by his standards. It was a short enough absence that no-one would think it odd, even though he'd booked it at short notice. He intended to finish his business on the island quickly and return to London as soon as possible.

However, he still faced a dilemma. If he asked Murray for some of his blood, he was certain the old farmer would refuse. Murray would certainly guess that he needed the blood to fuel a spell. So Callum would have to use force to get it. How far was he willing to go? Was he prepared to kill Murray to get some of his blood? He'd killed the cleaner, but that had been a mistake fueled by the aggression of his hound form. Deliberately killing Murray—the man who had raised him—was something else entirely. It would be coldblooded murder, pure and simple.

If he bottled it, he'd be doomed to live as the hound. But if he murdered the man who raised him, wouldn't that make him a different kind of monster?

On the other hand, maybe he could obtain the blood without resorting to murder. But even that was fraught with difficulties, as Murray would certainly resist him. Although he would be well into his sixties by now, Murray had always been strong, toughened by a lifetime of farming and outdoor work. He was unlikely to be a pushover, even at his age. And Callum wasn't exactly used to physical confrontations, at least not in his human form.

He didn't hang around long in Port Ellen, fearful of losing his nerve or being recognised. He'd brought a sleek, black revolver with him from London, obtained from a friend at the Ministry of Defence. It felt reassuringly heavy and solid in his jacket pocket. Although he had a licence for the firearm, carrying it around for no legitimate reason was against Britain's strict gun laws. Still, it was unlikely he'd be stopped and searched by the police, especially here on Islay.

It didn't take him long to notice that the island was teeming with ghosts. They were everywhere. One of the side effects of his condition was that he could see ghosts clearly. Their bright, silvery glow made them easy to spot against the drab landscape of Islay. If they got close, he could even sense their emotions.

There were a few ghosts at the outskirts of Port Ellen, but many more near Murray's farm. He tried to avoid them, but to his dismay several drifted towards him, calling out to him in dry, rasping voices that no-one else could hear, begging him to lead them away from this place.

Callum quickened his pace, trying to shake off the gaggle of ghosts that now followed him. Would they follow him into the farmhouse itself? Probably—they could float through physical barriers like walls and doors. He'd just have to do what he came here to do as quickly as possible, then leave. Maybe it was better this way. He wouldn't have time for doubts.

There was a leaden weight in the pit of his stomach as he approached the farmhouse. The front door was locked. So was the back door and all the windows. There were no lights on inside. The place appeared to have been empty for a while. This made no sense. Murray loved his farm. It was all he cared about. He rarely left it; he didn't go on holiday. To him, taking the ferry to the mainland was a rare and extravagant excursion.

The weight in Callum's stomach grew heavier. There was one obvious reason the house might be empty.

He soon felt desperate to have his fears confirmed or refuted. With all the doors locked, he smashed the window of the downstairs toilet and climbed inside.

The house was completely silent, yet his adopted father's presence permeated every room, and not just because he'd lived here for decades. He was still here, but not necessarily in a tangible form. Callum stood in the hallway and listened. He realised this was the first time he'd entered this house and not been greeted, or confronted, by dogs. Murray had always adored his dogs. He'd cried bitter tears when his two mastiffs had died. He couldn't live without canine companionship, but there were clearly no dogs living here now.

Callum's emotions were too powerful, and came too fast, to process.

Grief. Loss. Despair.

Resentment.

Rage.

Callum held onto the bannister at the foot of the stairs for support. The rush of emotions felt like a punch to the gut. Some felt new, others felt decades old. It was as though he'd suddenly absorbed a strange set of emotions that were similar to, but separate from, his own.

After a minute clutching the bannister, with bitter tears dripping down his face, he realised what was happening. His emotions were getting mixed up with those of his adopted father. This happened sometimes, when ghosts were nearby: their feelings bled into his own. It was a horrible experience made worse by his own genuine feelings of loss and regret.

Murray's ghost was upstairs. Waiting. An apparition created by bitterness and anger, shaped by pain and sorrow and obsessed by past mistakes and wasted opportunities.

Callum turned away from the stairs and climbed back out of the toilet window. There was no point in staying. His mission was doomed to failure. Murray was dead and had no blood to offer. There were things Callum would have liked to say to his adopted father... but not to his ghost.

The blunt truth was that Murray had not been a good father. Not because he made mistakes, but because he clearly resented having to raise Callum. Throughout his childhood, Callum had wondered why Murray had adopted him in the first place. When he eventually discovered the truth, it had only hurt even more. Even now, two decades later, Murray was still letting him down, failing to provide blood that would have saved his son from a terrible fate.

Callum was so wrapped up in his own thoughts that he almost walked right into Jasper Wychwood. As luck would have it, the wizard was occupied conjuring werelight and staring at the ghosts around the farmhouse. As soon as Callum saw him, he darted behind the thick trunk of a nearby tree. From there, he watched Wychwood approach the farmhouse and try all the doors on the ground floor.

Has Wychwood followed me here from London? Does he know this was my childhood home? What else does he know?

After walking around the house twice, Wychwood found the broken toilet window and climbed through it, just as Callum had. Following him inside would be too risky, so Callum remained behind the tree and considered the implications of Wychwood tracking him to Scotland.

Wychwood had been poking around Downing Street.

Now he'd found Callum's childhood home.

He'd picked up his scent somehow. He was hunting him down.

Why?

Then the answer dawned on him. He was working for The Boss—the powerful mage in the upper echelons of the Paranormal Office who had supplied Callum with potions for years. The Boss knew the potions were becoming ineffective. They'd anticipated that Callum would want to renege on their agreement, so they'd sent Wychwood—a notorious wizard who operated outside the authorities' direct control—to intimidate him. Or worse... silence him permanently.

After their encounter at Downing Street, Callum had wondered why the authorities would send Wychwood to investigate when they had plenty of capable, trustworthy seekers to call upon. Why hire an outsider with questionable loyalty to do their dirty work?

Now it all made sense. Wychwood had been chosen *because* he was an outsider, because in all likelihood he was more ruthless than any seeker.

Callum had spent years supplying information and subtly steering the policies of the mundane government in a direction beneficial to the Paranormal Office, and to The Boss. Lately, he'd bullied the prime minister into taking a tough stance on werewolves in the name of protecting mundane citizens, which in turn had put pressure on the more dovish officials of the Paranormal Office to adopt a repressive approach. In exchange for this, he'd received regular supplies of a potion that prevented his hound form from taking over.

But those potions barely worked anymore. However you looked at it, it was a bad deal for Callum.

And now The Boss had sent a renegade wizard to hunt him down.

A few minutes later, Wychwood emerged from the farmhouse. His hair was a mess, his skin ashen, and he'd ripped his black coat in his hurry to escape. Had he encountered Murray's ghost? Had he dared to climb those stairs?

Callum followed Wychwood at a distance. He entered a barn that had been left open and untended. Callum found a spot just outside the barn where he could see Wychwood while remaining out of sight. Wychwood conjured a ball of silver werelight and waited. Eventually, the ghost of an old man entered the barn. Callum was ready to run, but fortunately the ghost seemed more interested in the silver werelight than in Callum. Wychwood spoke to the ghost for a few minutes, but unfortunately Callum was too far away to hear what they were saying.

Jasper Wychwood was tenacious, Callum had to admit that. If he continued speaking with the ghosts that infested Islay, he would eventually figure out what was really happening on the island.

After speaking with the spirit, Wychwood made his way back to town. Callum followed cautiously, at a distance, but the wizard seemed wrapped up in his own thoughts. When they reached Port Ellen, he went into the Ardview Inn.

Callum paused on the street outside the Inn, undecided as to his next move. After a minute, he decided to risk following Wychwood inside. He pulled his baseball cap low over his forehead and prayed that the wizard didn't know what he looked like.

As he entered the bar area, he saw Wychwood sitting in a booth with a woman in her sixties dressed in golfing attire. They seemed to be deep in conversation. Callum bought himself a pint of lager and sat in the adjoining booth, where he could hear snatches of their conversation without being seen.

CHAPTER 25

Jasper was planning his return to London when Grace hammered on the door of his room at the Ardview Inn.

'I'm packing to go home,' he said wearily. 'I think I'm better off looking for Callum in London.'

'Oh, but you mustn't leave without seeing the ruins of Kildalton church! It's quite a sight, I can tell you. And I've been thinking—it might contain clues to Callum's whereabouts.'

Jasper frowned. Grace looked keyed-up and brimming with enthusiasm, which, frankly, he didn't share. 'You mean because Murray supposedly found him there in a Moses basket?'

'Partly that. Also, according to Murray, Callum spent a lot of time there as a teenager. I was thinking he might have gone there to hide from his problems in London.'

Jasper rubbed his temples. He was keen to get back to London, and Grace's theory didn't sound very compelling. On the other hand, he didn't have much to show for his time in Scotland, so perhaps it was worth one last throw of the dice, while he was here.

'To be honest Grace, this entire trip is starting to feel like a wild goose chase. Is it really likely that Callum is hiding in an old, abandoned church of all places?'

Grace wagged her finger, which was painted with bright pink nail polish. 'You're forgetting that he was a strange boy.

It's a safe, familiar place to him. Besides, it's just a short walk from town. It's got to be worth a look, hasn't it?'

Jasper was far from convinced that a middle-aged civil servant would hide in a ruined church in the middle of nowhere. Then again, Callum was probably a shifter of some kind, so perhaps it wasn't so far-fetched after all.

'All right,' he sighed. 'I suppose it's worth a try. I'll see you in the bar in a few minutes, when I've finished packing my bags.'

Ten minutes later, he found Grace at the bar nursing a glass of white wine.

'I got you a scotch and soda,' she said, offering him what looked like a double whisky mixed with too much fizzy water. Jasper accepted it politely, although he would rather have got moving than remain at the bar drinking.

Perhaps sensing his reluctance to stay for a drink, Grace said, 'You'll need that. I certainly do. Kildalton church gives me the creeps.'

'How so?'

Grace gave him a long, appraising look. 'Has anyone told you about the Beast of Islay?'

That got Jasper's attention. He remembered the accounts Alyssa had found online of a frightening dog stalking the island many years ago. Was Grace about to describe the same beast? He shook his head and hopped onto the bar stool beside Grace.

'The Beast is supposedly a monster that devours lost souls and travellers. I know it sounds like a story to scare children, but years ago we heard it howling in the night. It's the most terrifying thing I've ever heard—I can't even begin to describe it. I remember it made my insides feel twisted up for days afterwards. People said that Kildalton church was its lair.'

'What kind of monster was it?'

'I never actually saw it, but the rumour at the time was that it was a Cù-Sìth—a huge black dog that takes wandering spirits to the afterlife by devouring them. There were stories of it massacring cattle and sheep. People, too.'

'And it lived in the church?'

Grace glanced around to check they weren't being overheard, then leaned closer to Jasper. 'Murray once got drunk and told me he cornered the Cù-Sìth twenty years ago and locked it up in Kildalton church. The building hasn't had a roof for centuries, but apart from that it's mostly intact. The walls are sturdy. Murray claims he kept the beast trapped there for months until eventually it got free and fled the island.'

Jasper blinked, trying to take in all this new information and wondering how much credence to give it. 'That's quite a story. Are you sure you want to go back to this place?'

Grace met his gaze squarely. 'Yes. I want to find Callum, and I'm convinced we'll find clues to his whereabouts there.'

It was early evening by the time Jasper and Grace trundled out of the inn and began the walk to Kildalton church. Since it would be too late to travel back to London by the time they returned, Jasper paid for one more night at the inn before leaving.

He was puzzled by Grace's certainty that they'd find clues to Callum's whereabouts in the church, yet her tales about the Beast of Islay were too tantalising to ignore. If Callum was a shifter, as Jasper suspected, these old sightings of a big black dog might have been real, although they raised more questions than they answered. Jasper had studied fairy creatures as part of his wizard training at Oxford University, but he had never actually encountered a Cù-Sìth. As far as he could remember, they were rare, found only in remote corners of Scotland.

As he walked behind Grace through fields that glowed orange in the sunset, it occurred to him that he might have stumbled upon an explanation for the large number of ghosts on Islay, which were especially concentrated around the Murray farm. If a Cù-Sìth had once stalked the island, it would have spent its time consuming lost souls. Without the Cù-Sìth to convey them to the afterlife, the ghosts were stuck. The Beast's disappearance seemed to line up with Callum leaving Islay as a young man. Did that mean Callum was the Cù-Sìth? If so, how had he managed to retain enough of his humanity to hold down an important government job in London?

Jasper wished he remembered more from his university course on fairy creatures. To compensate, he'd have to look up Cù-Sìths in a bestiary when he got back to London. He was pretty sure he had a relevant book somewhere in his bookshop.

As the church came into view, fat drops of rain started pelting down. The sky was full of dark grey clouds that looked ready to burst.

'Look's like we're in for a soaking,' Jasper muttered grimly.

'Don't worry, we're nearly there,' Grace said, keeping up an impressively fast pace, presumably because she was keen to arrive before the rain completely soaked them both.

The church was mostly intact, as Grace had said. It had four stone walls, a huge heavy door, and narrow, slit windows. It was quite a distance from Port Ellen, in an isolated area with few other buildings nearby. There was a graveyard and a low stone wall around the church. An impressive Celtic stone cross stood in the graveyard alongside several lopsided gravestones.

'There used to be a small village here which the church served, but folk abandoned it centuries ago. Nobody knows why exactly.'

They were coming down a gentle slope towards the church. Jasper stumbled on the path, clutching his stomach. He felt sick. He wondered if he'd eaten something dodgy the night before, but that seemed unlikely. The inn's food had been excellent—one of the highlights of the trip. Maybe he was coming down with a stomach bug or flu.

Grace helped him up. 'Nearly there,' she said brightly.

When they reached the church, Grace withdrew a large iron key from her pocket and opened the large wooden door at the front of the building.

'How did you get a key to this place?' Jasper asked.

Grace seemed not to hear him. She hurried inside and motioned for him to follow. Jasper traipsed after her, but by now he was feeling very queasy. He crossed the threshold and shuffled over the flagstones, which were uneven and split by weeds that sprouted up through the gaps. There were still some pews in the church, though they were covered in mould and partially rotted away. He found a pew that was mostly intact, sat down, and put his head in his hands, riding the waves of nausea.

'I'm feeling a bit ill, Grace,' he said. 'Give me a minute.'

'Take as long as you need, dear,' Grace said. 'We're not in any rush.'

Jasper noticed that the pew in front of him had teeth marks in it. He looked around and realised that lots of the other pews looked like they'd had chunks bitten off them, too.

'Have you noticed these bite marks?' Jasper said. 'If the Cù-Sìth was locked up here once, it must have tried to feast on the furniture.'

Grace didn't answer. Jasper looked up and saw that she was gone. The heavy church door was shut.

'Um, Grace?'

There was no sound except for the whistling of wind through the slit windows.

Dimly, through the fog of nausea, Jasper realised something was seriously wrong. *Why has Grace left me alone in this place?*

He tried to get up, but his head swam and he felt close to vomiting. He steadied himself and sat back down. When the retching stopped, he reached into his pocket to get out his phone and call Alyssa. He hated to bother her, but he was starting to fear he'd wandered unwittingly into a dangerous situation.

But his pockets were empty. His phone was missing. Either he's mislaid it, or someone had stolen it. *Who'd bother to steal a worthless old Nokia?*

A disturbing thought bubbled to the surface of his mind. *Someone might steal his rubbish phone if they wanted to make sure he couldn't call for help.*

He mentally shook himself. He was a wizard, for goodness sake. Magic would get him out of this situation. Slowly, he tried to perform a healing spell on himself to drive away whatever was making him ill.

Nothing happened.

The familiar, warm feeling that normally uncoiled in his core when he performed a spell was entirely absent. He tried again, but the result was the same. His magic was gone. Snuffed out.

Behind him, the church door clicked open, and someone stepped inside.

CHAPTER 26

A STRANGER WEARING A black hoodie and a baseball cap entered the church. Grace trailed behind him, looking sheepish. Jasper tried to assess the situation, but he was on the verge of spewing his lunch on the floor. It dawned on him that Grace had bought him a drink at the pub that he hadn't asked for. He hadn't even seen it being poured—it had been waiting for him at the bar when he arrived.

What in Merlin's name did she put in my drink? He cursed himself for being so trusting. She'd had plenty of opportunities to swipe his mobile, too.

Experimentally, Jasper tried summoning a simple shield. Nothing happened. He could still feel the magic inside him, but he was unable to channel it into any spells. He gripped the ruby brooch Rasmus had given him and tried to draw power out of it, but that failed too. The ruby still contained latent magical energy but something was blocking his ability to make use of it. Whatever Grace had put in his drink must be suppressing his ability to perform magic. The nausea was probably just a side effect. He hoped the effect was only temporary.

Grace and the stranger were whispering together in the church doorway. Jasper—still too ill to stand up and confront them—called out: 'Grace, what are you playing at? What did you put in my drink?'

'Callum just wants to talk to you, that's all,' she said, a tremor in her voice. 'Don't worry, he won't hurt you.'

Callum. The man Jasper had been searching for. In all likelihood, the Whitehall spy.

The tables had turned. The person he'd been seeking had found him first. Despite Grace's assurance, if the murder at Downing Street was anything to go by, Jasper had plenty to worry about.

'Thanks a bunch, Grace. You could have introduced the two of us without poisoning me first.'

Grace lifted her chin and met Jasper's eye. Before, she'd sounded a little sheepish, but now she answered him defiantly. 'I'm sorry for tricking you, but I had no choice. Otherwise I'd have been cheated out of Murray's farm. I spent years looking after that ungrateful old man! He promised to leave the farm to me, but when he died I found out he'd left everything to Callum instead. He was just using me, stringing me along to get what he wanted. Despite everything I did for him he left me nothing in his will—not a penny! Fortunately, Callum's a better man than his father. He's agreed to sign the farm over to me.'

'How nice of him,' Jasper snarled. 'I expect you'll sell it on to property developers and make millions?'

Grace blushed and her voice became high and shrill. 'What I do with my property is no business of yours!'

Callum evidently felt this conversation had run its course. He said, 'I think our deal is concluded now, Grace. Thank you for your help.'

He handed her a lever arch file he'd been carrying under his arm, which presumably contained the deeds to Murray's farm, and whatever else he might have promised her in exchange for trapping Jasper. Grace grabbed the file and hurried out of the church without a backward glance.

Callum lingered in the doorway, seemingly wary of Jasper.

'I think this is the bit where you outline your evil plan and gloat about getting the better of me,' Jasper hissed, gripping the back of the pew with one hand and cradling his stomach with the other. He tried to summon the strength to stand up. If he was going to die he wanted to face his killer properly, on his feet, but the stabbing pains in his belly kept him sitting down.

'I imagined it would be the other way around,' Callum said. 'I'm surprised to see someone like you working for the Paranormal Office. I thought you hated the government. They certainly seemed to hate you, until very recently.'

Jasper grimaced with the pain in his stomach. 'I'm just trying to put a stop to the violence between werewolves and wizards. A rebellion isn't the answer to our differences, nor is microchipping the werewolf population.'

Callum rolled his eyes. 'Not the most constructive opinion. Arguing against both sides without offering an alternative.'

'Do you think what you're doing is constructive? Feeding just enough information to the wolves to rile them up, only to betray them to the authorities?'

Callum walked slowly towards Jasper, his eyes narrowed.

'I'd have thought that you of all people would understand that I haven't been acting on my own impulses. I carry the curse of the Cù-Sìth, but since I'm neither a wizard nor a werewolf, I can't be too picky about who my allies are. The Boss has had me over a barrel. Without the potions they supply, I'd have succumbed to the beast inside me years ago.'

Jasper blinked. '"The boss"? Who are you talking about?'

'Your boss and mine. The one who sent you after me. A high-ranking official at the Paranormal Office.'

'I don't know who you mean,' Jasper said honestly, but as soon as the words were out of his mouth he realised he *had* been sent on this mission by just such a person. Rasmus had briefed him, but the mission itself came from the Paranormal Office and was probably signed off at the highest level.

A small smile curved Callum's lips. 'It looks like you understand who I'm talking about. I won't ask you to name them—I doubt you know their identity anymore than I do. They're too smart to give away that kind of information to foot soldiers like us. I've been working for them for years and I hardly know a thing about them. Unlike you, I don't have many contacts in the magical community.'

The puzzle pieces were coming together in Jasper's mind. Callum worked at Downing Street, which meant he was employed by the regular, mundane government. But the spy—the real one—was based in the Paranormal Office. Callum was merely a pawn moving around the board at the behest of someone much more powerful.

'Anyway, I'd like you to convey a message to our mutual boss,' Callum said. 'Tell them I'm through with them. I want no more of their potions, and I won't be supplying any information in return. I'm going my own way from now on.'

Callum approached the pew and knelt beside Jasper. He removed Jasper's shirt and rolled up his shirt sleeve, exposing his arm. Jasper tried to resist, but he was weak and shaky, and his efforts to shrug Callum off were too feeble to be effective.

'You're not what I imagined,' Jasper said.

'Really? What were you imagining?'

'Someone arrogant and violent. Maybe even sadistic.'

'You ought to reserve judgement on that until I take what I came for.'

Jasper tried to wriggle free, but it was useless. 'And what is that exactly?'

Callum reached inside his coat and pulled out a glass vial stopped with a cork and sealed with red wax. Jasper stared at it while Callum fiddled with the cork. The impression on the wax was vaguely familiar, though he couldn't immediately remember when he'd seen it last. He tried to memorise it for later. He was in no condition to do any deduction right now—his head was swimming and he could barely focus on what Callum was saying.

'My trouble is, I don't know what I am. Once I dreamed of being a wizard like you. Now I'm willing to settle for just being a man rather than a feral beast. Even that meagre goal might prove to be beyond my reach.'

'Perhaps I can help?' Jasper said, the words sounding breathy and faint.

'You *are* going to help.' A knife appeared in Callum's hand.

'Wait—what are you doing?'

Jasper tried to pull away, but his legs felt like jelly and he slumped lower on the pew, almost falling onto the floor. Callum held him upright and steady. Jasper felt the knife flash across his skin, saw a blob of crimson blood on his arm, and passed out.

CHAPTER 27
TWENTY YEARS AGO.

CALLUM SPENT MOST OF the winter brooding on Murray's outburst while avoiding him as much as possible. Murray seemed content with this state of affairs and stopped nagging his adopted son to do more work around the farm. Whenever he could, Callum took the ferry to Campbeltown, spending hours in the library reading everything he could find about magic and witchcraft.

Murray had implied that Callum's mother had died in childbirth, but Callum tried not to think about that too much. When he did, the guilt became overwhelming. Instead, he focused on the fact that, despite his previous denials, Murray had clearly known his mother. What was the nature of their relationship? What were the real circumstances of her death? Was the story about finding Callum in a Moses basket true, or just something Murray had made up to avoid admitting the truth, whatever that might be?

Being abandoned as a baby had always felt like the defining moment of Callum's life, a shadow over everything that came after. How could he expect anyone in this world to love him if his own mother hadn't? But now he was starting to believe that she might have wanted him after all. Maybe she'd loved him with all her heart. Maybe she'd longed to survive and raise him.

Callum still felt angry at Murray for his deception, and for not loving him as a father should. But on those choppy ferry trips across the Irish Sea, he thought about the role the Cù-Sìth might have played in his mother's death. After all, it had admitted to devouring her soul. The more he thought about it, the more he came to believe that the Cù-Sìth had blighted all of their lives, even Murray's. It was a cruel monster that preyed on innocent people and took pleasure in their grief and distress.

In his research at the library, Callum gleaned a few more nuggets of information about the monster. It was an ancient fairy creature that lived in the Scottish Highlands and Hebrides. In some stories, it led wayward ghosts to their rest, much like Charon, the ferryman of Hades, who leads the dead across the river Styx in Greek mythology. That made it sound almost benign, but there were other tales in which the Cù-Sìth feasted greedily on the souls of the dead, growing fat on their anguish. Many accounts suggested it was invulnerable and couldn't be killed by mortal hands.

Callum found one account of a living person turning the tables on the beast, however. In the story, a young witch, consumed by grief after a Cù-Sìth slaughtered her younger brother, drank some of the beast's blood. Doing so gave her some of the monster's power, allowing her to kill it and avenge her brother.

Callum read the story many times, revelling in the witch's success. *What would it feel like to slaughter the beast and avenge his mother?* It might erase the years of hurt, or at least make them easier to bear. It would mean he was no longer a useless, bookish boy, but a fierce warrior who had confronted a monster from the darkest corners of the paranormal world and overcome it.

He began thinking about how he might do it. He could wear thick garden gloves to protect his hands from bites, and steel capped boots to kick the beast and protect his feet. He could take the large machete his dad used to hack away weeds. And he could enlist the help of his father's two fiercest dogs, a pair of mastiffs called Blaze and Shadow.

At first his plans were purely theoretical, more of a day-dream than an actual plan, but the more he ruminated on the Cù-Sìth and its evil intent, the more serious he became about taking action.

His relationship with Murray was as bad as it had ever been. On the rare occasions they found themselves in the same room, they ignored each other. Callum decided he needed to slay the beast for both their sakes. Murray would thank him when he found out, and then perhaps what was broken between them could be fixed.

One spring evening, filled with righteous anger and tooled up for the fight, Callum fetched the dogs and started out towards Kildalton church. Blaze and Shadow were not especially fond of him—none of Murray's dogs were—but they enjoyed a late night walk as much as any dog and followed him eagerly. It was a fresh, clear night and there was a crescent moon in the sky. Islay was dark, as always, but the sky was full of stars. Callum had brought a torch to light his way. His adopted father's machete was stuffed inside his coat. There was also a small gardening fork in his pocket that he'd spent days sharpening. He knew that what he was doing was reckless, maybe even mad. But he felt alive and purposeful in a way he hadn't in years, in control of his destiny at last.

As they neared the church, the dogs pinned their ears back against their heads and looked nervous, but they didn't turn back. They were big, powerful animals, and had yet to encounter anything stronger or fiercer than they were. Callum pushed open the rotten door of the church and shone his torch inside. The dogs nosed around the threshold curiously. The church was empty, although Callum thought he saw movement in a shadowy corner. His heart raced, but when he pointed the torch into the corner, he saw that there was nothing there—it was just his fear playing tricks on him.

They spent the next hour traipsing around the church graveyard and the surrounding area, but there didn't seem to be anything out of the ordinary. Rain fell in fat drops and the dogs stared at Callum with their big eyes and drooping faces, as if to ask how long he planned to stay out here. They looked like they wanted to return home and didn't understand why Callum was walking in circles.

Callum felt cold and foolish. Was the Cù-Sìth's appearance a once-in-a-lifetime event? Would he ever see it again?

He considered going home, but he wasn't quite ready to give up yet. He'd prepared so thoroughly for this moment, he wanted to wait a bit longer. He had hoped that, because of his personal connection with the Cù-Sìth through his mother, the beast would sense his presence and know he was searching for it. After a while standing outside in the cold, he led the dogs back into the church and settled on a pew. The dogs sniffed around the corners of the building with their noses to the ground.

Despite his frustration, hadn't he won a kind of victory just by coming here? Ever since the Cù-Sìth had cornered him, he'd been afraid of returning to this place, but now he'd over-come that fear. Kildalton church belonged to him again. No fairy creature was going to drive him out. With these thoughts in his mind he relaxed. He rested the machete against the pew, leaned back, and shut his eyes.

The first howl shocked him out of his shallow sleep.

The second and third howls filled him with terror.

As he'd predicted, the Cù-Sìth had sensed his arrival and was calling to him. Goading him. Challenging him. Callum was afraid, but mentally shook himself. This was why he'd come—to confront the beast and avenge his mother. He was ready.

He picked up the machete and whistled to the dogs. They were staring out of the church door, plainly wondering what kind of creature was howling. They seemed wary when Callum strode out of the church but they followed him. Despite his bravado, Callum was keen to encounter the Cù-Sìth in the open, not inside the church where it might trap him and cut off any escape, as it had before.

He saw the beast moments after leaving the church. Its enormous eyes were two bright green beacons shining at him from about five hundred yards away. It didn't approach, but simply waited and watched. Blaze and Shadow snarled and then started barking. Callum had half expected them to cower or run away, but instead they seemed aggressive and ready to fight.

We can do this.

Avenge my mother.

Prove to Murray that I'm stronger and braver than he thinks.

Before he could have any second thoughts, the dogs raced towards the Cù-Sìth. Callum chased after them, slowed down by the machete. The dogs stopped a few yards away from the beast and continued barking and growling. The Cù-Sìth was unmoved. It stared impassively at Callum and showed no interest whatsoever in the dogs.

'I spared you once, boy,' it said. 'But you seem eager to die by my paw. Very well, if that's what you wish. I will savour the taste of your soul.'

Anger flared hotly in Callum's chest. 'You won't. You're going to pay for hurting my mother.'

The Cù-Sìth shook its head in a disconcertingly human way. 'Her soul was full of regret and bitterness. I sense yours is too.'

The Cù-Sìth padded forwards a short distance. It was enough to make Blaze and Shadow pounce. They leapt forward, lunging for their enemy's throat, but the Cù-Sìth was so big that they had trouble reaching it. Blaze remained at the front, snapping and barking while dancing just out of range of its enemy's vicious teeth and claws. Shadow circled around the back and bit the beast's back leg. The Cù-Sìth whined in pain and twisted around, snapping at Shadow.

So it can feel pain, Callum thought. *It can bleed.*

With renewed confidence, he charged forward, swinging the machete and stabbing wildly with the sharpened gardening fork. He thought he landed a blow, but it was hard to be sure. The Cù-Sìth and the two mastiffs were a blur of black and brown fur, writhing and snapping, rolling on the ground.

Blaze sunk his teeth into the Cu-Sith's throat and clung on. The Cù-Sìth snarled and tried to shrug him off, but the dog clung on tenaciously. Callum saw an opportunity. With the Cù-Sìth's attention focused on the dogs, he plunged the sharpened gardening fork deep into the creature's flank.

It felt tough, like trying to punch a hole through thick leather. The Cù-Sìth howled in agony and roared up on its hind legs, lifting Blaze off the ground. Callum watched in awe. It clearly possessed enormous strength to be able to stand on its hind legs with a dog clinging to its throat while another snapped at its legs, all while a gardening tool was buried in its flank. It reminded Callum that this was no overgrown dog—it was a magical creature with immense strength.

With one of its huge paws, the Cù-Sìth took hold of Blaze and threw him off. Blaze flew through the air and landed several metres away. Blood sprayed from the wound on the Cù-Sìth's throat, but it did not appear to notice or care. Blaze whimpered and did not get up. With one opponent down, the Cu-Sith turned towards Shadow, who backed away, barking.

Sensing the fight was almost lost, Callum charged forward with the machete in his right hand. He didn't bother slashing at his enemy. He needed to end the fight quickly, so he thrust the machete sideways into the creature's abdomen, hoping to inflict a mortal wound. The Cù-Sìth turned and looked at him. Something like a smile curved its black lips.

'You cannot kill me, mortal,' it said. 'Death is my business.'

The machete quivered and dropped onto the ground as if the Cù-Sìth had ejected it. Callum noticed that the gash on the creature's neck was no longer spurting blood, and the wound he'd made with the machete seemed to be healing with unnatural speed. A cold, clammy feeling settled in his gut. The Cù-Sìth could heal itself at will. The stories that had said it was immune to any normal attack appeared to be correct.

Callum gathered what remained of his courage and picked up the machete. He saw that it was drenched in the monster's blood. Some of it was dripping onto the grass. Without giving much thought to what he was doing, he brought the blade to his lips and sucked in some of the blood. It tasted like oil mixed with ash.

He felt different immediately. The world looked different. Smaller. A place to dominate. A land that held no fear for the likes of him. He straightened up and smiled, knowing that he was a hunter now. An apex predator.

Shadow, undaunted, or perhaps enraged, by Blaze's injuries, appeared on the Cù-Sìth's other side, snapping and snarling. The Cù-Sìth turned towards the dog and Callum took his opportunity, hacking at the monster's legs while it was distracted. He struck blow after blow until the Cù-Sìth's legs buckled and it collapsed on the ground.

Summoning all his strength, Callum lifted the machete high above his head and brought it down on the beast's neck like an executioner. There was a wet, crunching sound. Callum looked down. The Cù-Sìth's head was barely connected to its body anymore, its neck reduced to a bloody pulp of sliced sinew and broken vertebrae. The eyes—which before had been blazing beacons alive with spectral energy—stared up at him, bulging and blank. Lifeless. Dull. Callum dropped the machete and fell into a seated position on the ground, his heart thumping against his ribs.

Against all the odds, he'd killed the Beast of Islay.

CHAPTER 28
PRESENT DAY.

CALLUM LEFT THE CHURCH triumphant. He had enough of Wychwood's blood to enable Valerie to brew her potion—the one that would end his suffering and merge the two warring sides of his personality. Hound and man, united at last.

A feeling of euphoria swept through him. To celebrate, he decided to transform. With none of his old potion left, the urge to become the hound again had grown into a painful ache that never went away. With Wychwood unconscious and defeated, it was an itch he felt safe enough to scratch. He took off his clothes and savoured the moment as his skin sprouted fur and he bulked out with muscle and claws.

It was the first time he'd transformed without reluctance or fear. On all fours, he scurried happily across the grass, his snout low to the ground, feasting on the scents he found there: the musty reek of humans, the earthy stink of farm animals, and the smell of ghosts, which reminded him of mist on a winter morning. How he longed to track down a ghost and devour it! The spirits would welcome his approach too. He could feel them calling out to him, longing to be released from this world.

But that was not his mission. It was hard, as the Cù-Sìth, to keep his mind centred on his real task. His human task.

Eventually, guided by his nose, he found the right spot. It had a certain smell that he'd never forget. He remembered as if it were yesterday, the spray of blood staining the grass, the Cù-Sìth whining in pain and expiring under the light of a crescent moon. The final chop of the machete that separated the beast's head from its body and Callum from his childhood.

Was there any need to rush? He'd found this place so easily and could return any time. *Why not hunt a few lost souls first?* There were so many of them on Islay that they'd chased him all over the island while he was in his human form. *They're an infestation that needs to be dealt with.* He could spend the rest of the night devouring them, then return here in the morning and complete his mission.

With the decision made, he used his front paws to dig a shallow hole in the ground into which he placed the vial of blood, which he'd been awkwardly carrying in his mouth since he ditched his clothes. When he raised his head from the hole, he realised he was being watched. There was a creature nearby. Not a ghost—a beast of flesh and blood. He saw its eyes flash silver in the dark, reflecting moonlight. The creature was a fellow canine. A pet. It stank of fear. It wanted to run away but was mesmerised by Callum's glowing eyes.

Callum smiled to himself. Dog flesh might be a nice appetiser before his main meal of ghosts.

The dog barked loudly and bared its teeth.

The sound jolted Callum out of his bloodlust. His human side reawakened.

What am I doing? Burying my precious vial of wizard blood in the dirt? Hunting ghosts and stray dogs?

He realised he'd allowed the Cù-Sìth to take over. If he spent the night hunting, he'd never turn back—he'd forget his humanity long before sunrise.

With a great effort, Callum transformed. It was painful, but it worked. He found himself naked and shivering, drenched in sweat, feeling sick... but human again.

That had been a close call. He couldn't let it happen again.

The dog had stopped barking and was watching him warily. Callum ignored it and dug up the vial of blood. Then he found the exact spot where his first transformation had happened, which he'd marked years ago with a small pile of stones—a monument to his own foolishness. He picked up one of the stones and went in search of his clothes.

It had been a difficult and dangerous night, but now he had everything he needed for his next, and hopefully final, transformation.

CHAPTER 29

JASPER DRIFTED IN AND out of consciousness. The pain in his abdomen was intense, but the feeling of dread was even worse. Would his magic abilities return after a while, or were they gone forever?

It wouldn't matter either way if he ended up bleeding to death in this derelict church.

Eventually, he dragged himself back to full consciousness. He still felt nauseous, but managed to open his eyes and sit upright on the pew. Daylight was streaking through the slit windows of the church. He'd spent the whole night passed out in this horrible place.

He took several deep, steadying breaths and stood up slowly. His arm was crusted with dried blood and he felt weak and wobbly on his feet. His memories of the night before were disjointed and disturbing. He closed his eyes and pushed the memories away. There would be time to make sense of what had happened—later. For now, he needed to focus on getting away from this church and back to civilization.

Getting to the church door—nevermind any further than that—was quite a challenge. He paused every few steps as his head swam and his stomach churned. It felt like the worst hangover of all time. And he should know.

Using the pews for support, he eventually made it to the door and staggered outside. He stood at the threshold for a while, enjoying the gentle warmth of the rising sun on his face. The island looked a lot friendlier than it had a few hours earlier.

'Jasper!'

A smile spread over his face as he recognised the young woman running towards him. He gave her a friendly wave as she approached.

'I'm so glad you're OK,' Alyssa said when she reached him. She was wearing a purple hoodie and trainers that were caked in mud. She went to hug him, then pulled back, her expression clouding over. 'Actually, I take it back: you look far from OK. What happened?'

Jasper smiled ruefully. 'A lot. Most of it bad. I'll tell you all the gory details after we find my car.'

'Sure. Where are you parked?'

Jasper opened his mouth, then remembered the Honda wasn't anywhere nearby. 'It's back at the ferry terminal.'

'OK. we can go there now, if you're ready. There's a ferry to the mainland due in a couple hours.'

'We'd better head to the Ardview Inn first, though. My suitcase is still there.'

A thumping headache started building behind Jasper's eyes as they walked back towards Port Ellen. He silently hoped they didn't run into Grace on the way. If they did, he'd be sorely tempted to put a nasty hex on her, and that wouldn't end well for either of them.

'How did you know where to find me?' Jasper asked.

'You said you were planning to come back to London last night. When you didn't show up, and stopped answering your phone, I got on a train to Scotland. I knew you were staying at the Ardview Inn, and the landlord told me you went to Kildalton church last night with an old lady and never came back. He didn't seem to like her much—implied she wasn't trustworthy.'

'Smart guy. I wish I'd asked for his advice before going.'

Jasper was touched by Alyssa's concern for him. She'd promised to come and get him if he stopped answering his phone, and she'd done exactly that. Alyssa could be stubborn and impulsive, but she was also incredibly loyal; if she promised to do something for you, you could bank on her doing it.

After about an hour picking their way through the countryside of Islay, with Jasper leaning on Alyssa for support, they reached the Ardview Inn. Jasper collected his suitcase while Alyssa ordered them a cab to the ferry terminal. The cab driver threw Jasper a wary look, but accepted the fare after being shown the plastic bag they'd brought with them in case Jasper was sick on the journey. Fortunately, the cab ride passed without incident. Alyssa sorted out the ferry tickets and soon they were heading back to the Scottish mainland. Jasper spent most of the trip staring at the iron grey sea while puking up over the side of the ferry.

He felt marginally better when they got back onto dry land, but his hands were shaking when he took out his keys and tried to unlock the Honda.

'I don't think I'm in a fit state to take the wheel,' he said with a sigh. 'Do you mind driving?'

'No worries,' Alyssa said, taking the keys.

'Thanks.'

Jasper did his best to relax in the passenger seat, but that became increasingly difficult as Alyssa struggled to master the

Honda's controls. She stalled twice on the way out of the car park.

'You *can* drive, can't you?' Jasper asked, checking his seat-belt was secure for the third time.

'I've been driving since I was fourteen,' Alyssa said testily. 'I'm just not used to this car.'

Things got worse from there. Alyssa handled the gear stick as if it was a chicken she was trying to strangle. She stalled three times in a row at a set of traffic lights, causing the cars behind them to blare their horns. Sweat beaded her brow; she looked stressed out.

'Just pull over for a minute, will you?'

Alyssa muttered something mutinous, but pulled over and turned off the engine.

'Would I be right in thinking you haven't driven a manual car before?'

'No, you wouldn't.'

'But you learned in an automatic?'

'Most people do in the US. I took lessons in a manual car when I first arrived in London.'

'How many lessons, exactly...?'

Alyssa crossed her arms over her chest, looking grumpy. 'Only three,' she admitted. 'I was going to do more, but it was too expensive to keep a car on the road in London. It was easier to just use public transport.'

Jasper blew out a long breath. 'OK. We'd better switch over.' But as he stepped out of the car he swayed on the spot, grabbed the car door for support, and threw up on the pavement. He got back in the passenger seat and looked at Alyssa. 'I'm not sure it's a good idea for me to try to drive.'

Alyssa chewed her lip. 'I think I can manage, as long as we stick to quieter roads. I just need a bit of time to get used to the clutch and the gearshift.'

'Why don't I deal with the gear stick, so you can focus on the pedals?'

Alyssa nodded in agreement, and they spent the next half hour driving slowly around quiet residential streets, with Jasper changing gear and coaching Alyssa through controlling a manual car.

'You don't want to rush off the clutch. Hold it on the biting point for a second before coming all the way off the pedal.'

Alyssa nodded tightly, concentrating with all her might. She wasn't actually a bad driver. She understood, in theory, how to work the gears and clutch, but lacked the confidence and finesse that comes with experience. After a bit of practice, they set off back to England, sticking to smaller roads and avoiding the motorways. The journey would take a lot longer, but they'd stand a better chance of arriving in one piece.

Alyssa's driving had improved significantly by the time they passed out of Scotland and into Cumbria, and Jasper handed over control of the gear stick. They rarely made it out of third gear, and several cars honked grumpily at them for going too slow, but the ride was much smoother than before.

As they entered Yorkshire, Alyssa said: 'So what happened on the island? I hope it wasn't a wasted trip?'

'Not entirely,' Jasper said, waking up from a snooze. 'It turns out we're not dealing with a werewolf after all, but a very different kind of shifter. Callum Kirk, otherwise known as Callum Murray, is a *Cù-Sith*.'

'What's that?'

'A type of fairy, native to Scotland. And not the Tinker Bell kind with pretty wings and a sassy attitude. A Cù-Sìth is an oversized dog that conveys people to the afterlife by devouring their souls. The whole island is teeming with ghosts, who are there presumably because they don't know how to enter the afterlife without the Cù-Sìth to take them there.'

'And this *Cù-Sìth*... Callum Kirk... is he the Whitehall spy you've been searching for? The one helping the werewolf packs?'

Jasper bit his lip. 'I'm not sure about that. I think there may be more going on there than I first realised.'

CHAPTER 30

As they drove south, Jasper tentatively tested out his magic. He tried conjuring a small ball of werelight—a basic, easy spell. The light was weak, barely visible in the afternoon sunshine, but it was there. The familiar tingle in his fingers told him that his magic was returning. He breathed a huge sigh of relief. It would probably be several hours before his abilities returned in full, but they weren't gone forever. The noxious poison Grace had slipped into his drink at the Ardview Inn hadn't destroyed his magic permanently.

Once he'd satisfied himself that he was still capable of casting spells, he relaxed and told Alyssa everything that had happened on Islay—from his encounter with Murray's ghost on the farm to Grace poisoning him and Callum Kirk stealing his blood.

'What does he want with your blood?' Alyssa asked, sounding unsettled. 'You said he was a supernatural hound, not a vampire.'

'I don't know exactly, but he must be planning to use blood magic, perhaps to help him control his transformations.'

'It's creepy. Drugging you, then taking your blood.'

'I agree. So what were you up to in London while I was busy being abducted in Scotland?'

'Things have gotten pretty wild over the last few days, actually. The werewolves are furious about what happened on Hampstead Heath and have been attacking seekers and other Paranormal Office employees. The *Uncanny Chronicle* ran an editorial condemning forced microchipping and calling for fairer treatment of werewolves.'

'Interesting. All grist to the mill for your podcast, I guess.'

Alyssa frowned. '"*Grist to the*"... er, what?'

'Grist to the mill. I just mean this is all useful material for your podcast.'

'Yeah, it is. I did an episode looking into the Paranormal Office leadership and their reasons for pushing forward the anti-werewolf laws. It turns out some of them have less-than-honourable reasons for wanting to strip werewolves of their rights.'

'Yes?'

'Well, take Patrick Grimshaw for example—the chief seeker, in charge of magical security. A werewolf killed his son a few years ago. Which is horrible, I know, but it means—'

'Grimshaw might be out for revenge.'

'Exactly. I found out he created a plan a few years ago to lock up all werewolves in kennels, even if they hadn't committed a crime.'

'I remember that. The plan was leaked to the *Chronicle* and eventually the government had to disavow it. I didn't know Grimshaw was behind it.'

'He was. And then there's Erin Mayhew, the Keeper of Coin. She's rumoured to have invested in a company bidding on a contract to privatise parts of Hampstead Heath. They want to convert part of the Heath into a "pleasure garden" and charge people for visiting.'

'That's interesting... but what does it have to do with were-wolves?'

'You remember telling me that the werewolves have tra-ditionally used parts of Hampstead Heath as a safe space where they can go to transform at night? The privatisation can only go ahead if the werewolves are forced off the land permanently—which is looking more likely than ever, since the crackdown. If that happens and the pleasure garden idea goes ahead, Mayhew stands to make a lot of money.'

Jasper smiled. Alyssa had the instincts and tenacity of an investigative journalist. Her podcast research had revealed that two out of the three members of the triumvirate—the powerful mages who had presided at Jasper's show trial—had unsavoury reasons to victimise the werewolves.

Alyssa seemed to read his mind, because she said, 'I don't know much about the last member of the triumvirate, Arthur Sallow, but I plan to keep digging.'

Jasper nodded. 'Sallow has always struck me as a straight shooter. But that doesn't mean he's not strongly motivated to crackdown on werewolves. Unlike the other two, he was elected to his position, and he stood on a platform of bringing werewolves under control. He's staked his political career on it.'

Although Jasper wasn't that interested in politics, he had once thought highly of Sallow, until the man wrote a nasty, werewolf-baiting article in the *Uncanny Chronicle* in the run up to the last election.

'So, all three have their own reasons for wanting to suppress werewolves,' Alyssa said.

Jasper stared out of the window at the passing countryside. Field after field of bright yellow rapeseed.

'What are you thinking?' Alyssa asked.

'Just about something Callum Kirk said. He implied he'd been taking orders from someone high up at the Paranormal Office. He assumed the same person had hired me to track him down.'

Alyssa took a moment to digest this. 'So... you think someone else is pulling the strings?'

'I didn't get the feeling Callum was lying or trying to trick me—he seemed to genuinely believe we were both working for the same person.'

'Any idea who they might be?'

'Not really. It makes sense that it would be someone powerful, with a strong motive to control or suppress werewolves. Callum said even he doesn't know their identity, despite working for them for years.'

'Maybe Rasmus can help? He knows the Paranormal Office and its people well, doesn't he?'

'He does, that's true,' Jasper said. 'He worked there for years. And I promised to keep him in the loop about my investigation.'

Jasper went to dial Rasmus's number on his Nokia, then remembered that Grace had stolen it.

'Here—use mine,' Alyssa said, handing over her iPhone.

After fiddling with the iPhone for a few minutes, with Alyssa barking instructions at him (Jasper hated smartphones and usually avoided them), he dialled Rasmus's number, activated the speakerphone, and placed the phone on the dashboard.

'Hello? Alyssa?' Rasmus said in a gruff voice.

'It's me, Jasper. I'm using Alyssa's phone.'

'I'm here too,' Alyssa called out. 'You're on speaker.'

'Um, OK,' Rasmus said. 'Hullo to both of you. Are you back from Scotland yet? How's it going?'

'I think it's fair to say my trip north has had mixed results. I tracked down the wolf of Whitehall—who isn't actually a werewolf at all. His name is Callum Kirk, and we think he has a handler at the Paranormal Office—someone much more powerful who is calling the shots.'

'We're wondering if you could help us figure out who that might be?' Alyssa chipped in. 'Someone with an axe to grind against werewolves?'

'Yes, yes,' Rasmus said distractedly. 'We should talk it through and discuss everything you've found out. But let's do it properly. In person.'

CHAPTER 31

Callum's euphoria had worn off by the time he reached London, replaced by a double dose of anxiety and dread. Was this really going to work? He was placing a lot of faith in a mad old witch who lived in a makeshift underground bunker. Maybe she was just trying to con him out of ten grand.

He found The Hide again without difficulty, but what remained of his optimism was crushed by what he found inside.

There were signs of a struggle: a stack of mouldy newspapers and several coffee cups had been knocked onto the floor. The bed, on the other hand, was made, and there was a person-shaped lump under the covers. Callum called out Valerie's name several times to rouse her, but she didn't answer, and the lump remained completely still. With a growing sense of dread, Callum approached the bed and pulled back the covers.

Valerie had obviously been dead for a while. Her eyes were blank and staring, her skin was cold and pale as tissue paper. There were black scorch marks around her neck. It looked like someone had choked the life out of her with magic.

Had she been attacked in her sleep? That seemed unlikely. Valerie wasn't an easy person to sneak up on. She had always seemed to know in advance when Callum was approaching her home, which suggested she'd rigged up some kind of alarm system to warn her of people approaching her home. Maybe she'd even raised magical wards around the bunker. She'd lived on Hampstead Heath in secret for years, after all, and had managed to remain undetected by the authorities. Callum always assumed she slept with a knife or a magic wand under her pillow.

No, she hadn't been killed in her bed. Someone had placed her there after death and tucked her up neatly under the bedclothes, as if arranging a body for a wake.

But why? Is this meant to be a warning?

Before he had time to think it through in any detail, Valerie started glowing.

Callum stepped back in shock. He realised it wasn't her whole body that was glowing, only a small section around her midriff. He pulled the blanket down and found a glowing glass sphere resting on her stomach, sandwiched between her rigid, veiny hands. The bunker had been so dark that he hadn't noticed the odd bulge under the blanket until it started glowing.

The sphere was pulsing with inner light. *It's a communication orb.* Although he'd never used one before, he knew what they did. This one seemed to be filled with glittering mist. Callum wasn't sure if touching it was safe. For all he knew The Boss might have placed a curse on it and left it here as a trap.

A strange voice emanated from the orb. 'Good evening, Callum. How are you? Did you enjoy your visit home to Islay? I hear the island is beautiful at this time of year.'

Callum had to resist the urge to run away. Could the orb be used to attack him? He didn't think so, but wasn't absolutely sure.

'Who are you?'

'A friend. The one who has been providing you with po-tions for the best part of twenty years. I was sorry to hear that they have been growing less effective recently.'

The voice was very odd. It kept changing: from low and gravelly to high-pitched and squeaky; from the voice of a young girl to an old man, and everything in between. Just when Callum thought he detected the hint of a regional ac-cent, the accent changed. If he hadn't suspected the speaker was a mage, and using magic to disguise their voice, he'd have guessed they were using an electronic voice changer.

Callum had been told that communication orbs usually showed the face of the person speaking, but there was no hint of a face in this one; it was full of swirling grey smoke that pulsed with light.

'Valerie's dead,' Callum blurted. 'Did you kill her?'

'Valerie's a loose cannon, as I'm sure you've noticed. She admitted she was planning to brew an alternative potion that would allow you to control your hound form permanently.'

'Is that why you killed her?'

There was a long pause. 'I regret Valerie's death,' the voice said at last, 'but she left me with little choice.'

That sounds like a yes, Callum thought grimly.

'Valerie no doubt encouraged you to break off your agree-ment with me. But you and I are kindred spirits, Callum. For years, the magical government has treated shifters as if they were normal citizens—the equal of wizards and upstanding mundane citizens. You know better than most how untrue that is. So do I. Werewolves brought death and misery to my family, and I've spent years trying to bring them to heel. I've long believed they belong in secure kennels where they won't pose a threat to the rest of us.'

'Thanks for the speech,' Callum said coolly, 'but I'm guessing you didn't contact me to wax lyrical about werewolves.'

'Quite so. The information and assistance you give me is invaluable, Callum. That's why I'm prepared to make you an offer better than Valerie's, if you're willing to continue working with me.'

'I'm listening.'

'I know you've obtained some of Jasper Wychwood's blood. It's of no use to you now that Valerie is dead, but it's useful to me. I want it. In exchange, I'll cure you of your affliction.'

Callum narrowed his eyes. 'You'll... cure me? What does that mean exactly?'

'It means you'll be free of the Cù-Sìth curse. You'll be fully human, with a human body and human instincts. And once you're cured, we can talk about your future. If you're still interested in becoming a wizard, I can ensure your next training application is looked on more favourably than the previous ones.'

Callum sat down on the bed. On the face of it, the deal The Boss was offering was everything he'd always wanted. He'd be rid of the infliction that had blighted his whole adult life. He could become a wizard, something he'd dreamed of since he was a child. All he had to do was give up a vial of blood he no longer had any use for.

But could he risk trusting someone he knew to be a killer—a traitor to their own government?

'I need to think it over,' he said.

'Please think quickly. Keep this orb with you and place both hands on it when you're ready to speak to me again. I'll be waiting.'

The disguised voice fell silent, and the orb went dark. Callum pulled the blanket back over the orb, to prevent The Boss from spying on him.

He needed time alone, in private, to consider his future.

He had a nasty feeling that if he refused his benefactor's offer, his career in the mundane government would mysteriously fall apart. The Boss had proven that he or she had powerful connections in both branches of government, and was able to pull strings to get people hired or fired. Furthermore, they'd now proven that they were prepared to kill to protect their interests. Did he dare refuse their offer? If they really could cure him of the Cù-Sìth curse, it might be worth swallowing his misgivings and continuing to work for them.

He considered leaving the bunker, but it was late and he was exhausted. He noticed that Valerie's Greek Fire device was still in the bunker. Could he afford to leave it where it was? He felt he should try to make it safe before leaving, if only to prevent it from blowing up and killing innocent visitors to Hampstead Heath. For now, he carefully detached the visible beaker of Greek Fire from the ignition. He still didn't know for sure if there was more Greek Fire buried in barrels underneath the bunker, as Valerie had claimed.

Once he'd satisfied himself that the Greek Fire device wasn't likely to explode, he lay down on a threadbare rug and tried to sleep. As he drifted off, he replayed every word The Boss had said in his mind.

Had they said anything that might provide a clue to their identity?

CHAPTER 32
ISLAY. TWENTY YEARS AGO.

AT FIRST CALLUM HAD no idea what was happening. He felt different, both physically and mentally. He found it was more comfortable to walk on all fours. His clothes were badly ripped from the fight with the Cù-Sìth, so he used his teeth to pull off the scraps that still clung to him. Clothes now felt more like an encumbrance than a necessity, anyway. He was larger and stronger than ever before, but also faster and more agile. He thrilled in sprinting across the island on all fours, stretching his legs and howling at the moon. Fields full of sheep took one look at him and scurried away as fast as their stubby legs would carry them.

A memory stirred at the back of his mind as he watched the sheep scattering. In a flash, panic quashed his exhilaration. *What's going on? What am I doing? Who am I?*

A part of Callum's mind—the boy that liked books, reading and schoolwork—knew what had happened, though not why. He tried to shake off the feeling and enjoy roaming the countryside, but the panicky feeling wouldn't go away. It gnawed at his insides.

What's happened to me?

He did the only thing that seemed to make sense. He went home.

Murray's dogs barked and bared their teeth, but also flattened their ears and backed away from him. Then Murray himself came outside to investigate the commotion. His eyes went wide with fear when he saw his son. Callum tried to speak, to explain what had happened, but the sound came out all wrong and Murray shouted threats before running back into the farmhouse and emerging moments later armed with a shotgun. Murray advanced with the dogs at his side and lifted the shotgun. Callum turned tail and ran away as shotgun pellets blasted the space he had occupied moments before.

Callum spent the next few days in abject horror, with no idea what to do. Kildalton church was the only place that felt safe, so he curled up there and tried to sleep. He was exhausted, terrified, and hungry. After about a week, driven wild by hunger and the instinct to hunt, he chased down a lamb and feasted on it. Its warm flesh tasted so good that for a while he forgot about wanting to be human again. His belly was full and his sharp teeth were smeared with blood. He slept contentedly beside the carcass.

When he awoke, he hated himself, hated what he had become. The truth was now undeniable: he'd turned into a wild animal. A dirty, vicious, monstrous thing.

He returned to his father's house, and Murray again chased him away. His father showed no sign of grasping the truth about this monster that was suddenly intent on invading his farm. Surely he knew his son was missing? Callum decided he must, at all costs, make his dad understand what had happened. So, every day, he sat on the grass outside the farmhouse, making no aggressive moves, and moving away when Murray threatened him with the shotgun or his dogs. But he kept coming back.

After a few weeks of this, Murray approached him empty-handed. The dogs barked from inside the farm-house—Murray must have locked them indoors. He stared at Callum from a few feet away.

'What do you want from me?'

Callum dipped his snout. He couldn't answer with words, he knew that by now, but he had to make his father understand. Somehow.

'Did you kill my son?'

Callum lay down, pressing his body against the cold earth. His eyes filled with tears as he looked up at his father.

Murray looked confused. He frowned and waited in silence.

Then Callum had an idea. He stood up slowly, all the while staring into his father's eyes, willing him to understand. Then he turned and walked a few paces away from the farmhouse before turning back to look at Murray. *Follow me.*

Murray seemed to catch his drift, and followed him all the way to Kildalton church, and then beyond it, to the place where the body of the Cù-Sìth—the *old* Cù-Sìth—lay, dead and decomposing. Blaze and Shadow were also lying nearby. Flies were buzzing around all three bodies. The smell was appalling.

Murray stood in the midst of this scene of death and decay, a look of shock on his craggy face. The old man had a strong constitution, but even so, he grimaced and covered his nose and mouth with his hand. After a few minutes, he dropped onto his haunches and examined the bodies more closely, lingering longest over the body of the Cù-Sìth.

'Did you do this?' he asked quietly, looking at Callum. 'Did you kill this monster?'

Callum could only bark in response, but Murray seemed to understand.

'And did you... drink its blood?'

Callum barked again. *Yes.*

There were no more questions. Murray had never been the talkative type, and he seemed to have deduced what had happened. He sat on the grass for what felt like a long time, thinking, before eventually standing up and saying, 'Follow me, boy.'

For the first time since his transformation, Callum felt a sliver of hope. Murray knew what had happened. He'd be able to help—he could put things right.

Callum expected to be led back to the farmhouse, but Murray instead returned to Kildalton church. 'In there,' he said. 'Go inside.' Callum was confused, but he obeyed. 'Good boy. Stay.'

And with that he strode off. Callum barked at his back, but Murray didn't turn around. He thought about running out of the church and after him, but felt compelled to follow his father's order. *Stay.*

Murray returned half an hour later with tools and planks of wood which he started hammering across the broken doorway of the church.

Callum barked in protest, but stopped when his father flashed him a fierce look.

'Don't fret,' Murray said. 'You'll no' starve. I'll bring you food and water. But you can't come back to the farm.'

Callum barked and barked but Murray ignored him and he didn't have the willpower to disobey. He lay on the ground between the rotten pews and watched as his father turned the church into a prison.

For the next few months, Callum was left alone with only his despair and regret for company.

He moped around the church, chewing on the wooden pews and staring at the tiny slices of blue sky he could see through the slit windows. There were times when the Cù-Sìth took over his mind completely and he clawed at the church door or fantasised about hunting animals and devouring human souls. When the human inside him re-emerged, he felt terrified at what he had become. His humanity was slipping away; he inched closer to the abyss every day. He cried and howled and fell into a deep depression. Murray brought him food and water regularly, but rarely spoke and refused to let him leave the church.

Would he ever be free of this curse?

CHAPTER 33
LONDON. PRESENT DAY.

RASMUS LIVED AT THE top of an enormous tower block in Stepney Green, East London. His flat was small, but it was packed full of clutter. The old wizard had a habit of collecting bizarre things—novelty ornaments, poisonous plants, sentient tea sets, paperback romance novels—which bordered on hoarding. Jasper and Alyssa squeezed into his sitting room and moved aside some dog eared books and a set of knitted cushions depicting the cycles of the moon so they could sit on the sofa. Rasmus made them all tea, which arrived on a silver tray that hovered in the air beside its owner.

Once they were settled, Jasper recounted everything that had happened on the Isle of Islay. Rasmus reacted with alarm when he heard that Callum had stolen some of Jasper's blood.

'There are many uses for a wizard's blood,' he said darkly, 'and none of them are good. This chap sounds like a nasty piece of work.'

Jasper blew on his steaming cup of tea. 'I'm not so sure about that. The funny thing is, even though he'd arranged for me to be poisoned, when we talked I actually felt sorry for him.'

'Really? Why?'

'Because he's an outsider. He's carrying this Cù-Sìth curse, but he isn't part of the supernatural community, so he's dealing with it alone. I don't think his motives are bad—he's just been driven to desperation by circumstances.'

'That reminds me,' Rasmus said. 'After we spoke on the phone, I searched for his name in the Paranormal Office records department. It seems he applied for wizard training five times and was rejected every time.'

'So he knows about the wizarding community but has been prevented from becoming part of it. Most likely his boss is his only connection to the magical world.'

Rasmus wrinkled his brow. 'His boss? Who might that be?'

'Your guess is as good as mine. Callum told me he was taking orders from a senior mage at the Paranormal Office. He thought I was working for them too—asked me to give them a message.'

'And that message was..?'

'To sod off, basically. I think he's fed up with being someone's lackey.'

'Damn,' Rasmus said, bringing his fist down hard on the cluttered coffee table. 'This means Callum Kirk almost certainly isn't the spy we're looking for—he's just a pawn. For a minute there I thought you'd solved the case, but this takes us back to square one.'

'Maybe not,' Jasper said. 'Callum collected my blood using a vial with a wax seal. The seal had a glowing symbol on it which I didn't recognise right away, but now I'm sure it was the symbol of the triumvirate.'

Jasper grabbed a biro off the coffee table and used it to sketch three interlaced arcs on a napkin.

Rasmus blew out a long breath. 'That's the triumvirate symbol all right. Sallow, Mayhew and Grimshaw use it to seal and sign official documents.'

'At least this narrows down our suspects,' Alyssa said.

Rasmus sucked his teeth thoughtfully. 'In theory, but the trouble is, all three are hostile to werewolves. It's hard to imagine any of them siding with the packs.'

'We think they've been stoking the werewolf rebellion just to provide an pretext for a crackdown,' Jasper explained. 'They probably don't sympathise with the wolves at all—quite the opposite in fact.'

'Ah.'

'We know that Mayhew and Grimshaw have personal reasons to want to suppress werewolves,' Alyssa said. 'Mayhew has a financial stake in a company that will profit if the wolves are cleared off Hampstead Heath, and Grimshaw's son was killed by a werewolf.'

Rasmus nodded. 'And Sallow's reason for cracking down on werewolves is well known. His political career has been built on the promise of bringing them under control.'

'So what's the next step?' Alyssa asked.

'I think our priority should be to find Callum Kirk and get Jasper's blood back, before he can put it to use. If we're lucky, he may lead us to his boss.'

'But how do we find him?' Alyssa asked.

'I've had an idea about that,' Jasper said. 'But we'll need to act fast.'

Alyssa left Rasmus's flat soon after finishing her tea. Jasper and Rasmus hung around for a while longer before making their way to *Wychwood Books*. When they arrived, Jasper made them both sandwiches, which they ate sitting on a plump sofa in a corner of the shop.

'This place looks better than the last time I saw it. So do you.'

Jasper smiled. 'That's what a month off the booze will do for you. Although I did have to break my sober streak in Scotland to ingratiate myself with the locals.'

Rasmus raised an eyebrow. 'It's not the right time of year for dry January, is it?'

'I'd been calling it dry July. I thought my liver deserved a summer holiday.'

'Good lad. After that nasty business last year with the liches I was seriously worried about you. Not because of the liches—I was worried you were wasting away in this bookshop, getting depressed and hitting the booze.'

'I was. Sitting around serving customers all day doesn't suit me. I need to be out there, doing some good, you know?'

Rasmus's eyes twinkled. 'I do. Why do you think I suggested you for this investigation?'

Around 9pm, Alyssa entered the bookshop with a middle-aged woman wearing ripped jeans and a checked shirt with a silver patch pinned to it. Alyssa introduced her as Milah Silverback, the new leader of Silverback pack.

'Thanks for coming,' Jasper said quickly. 'Can I get you something to drink?'

'No, thank you. I don't intend to be here for long.' Milah spoke with a French accent. 'I cannot accept your proposal. I came here out of respect for your friend Alyssa, who has done much to advocate for my people, but The Stray cannot join my pack. Not after he betrayed us.'

Straight to business then.

'I understand your concerns, but I believe Callum Kirk—whom you know as The Stray—has been acting under the influence of someone much more powerful at the Paranormal Office.'

Milah rolled her eyes. 'This does not surprise me. There is always the double-dealing when it comes to the Paranormal Office. But this does not mean The Stray is not responsible for his actions.'

'I agree, but if you were to accept Callum into your pack, we could use him to catch the person really responsible for the oppression of your people. If we can prove that someone at the heart of government has been playing both sides, we might be able to discredit the microchipping policy and get a fair deal for all werewolves.'

Milah still looked sceptical, but her expression softened. 'Alyssa said The Stray is not a true werewolf.'

'That's true.'

'Then he won't be able to learn our ways. Silverback pack has strict rules and severe consequences for those who disobey. Does he even want to join a werewolf pack?'

Jasper bit his lip. 'We haven't asked him yet, but I'm hoping to persuade him to join you and repay his debt to the werewolf community in the process.'

'What makes you think he wants to do that?'

'Because he's an outsider struggling with a debilitating curse who would benefit from guidance and support. He's isolated from other supernaturals at the moment. He needs a community.'

'It's a risk,' Alyssa said. 'But if we can get Callum Kirk on our side, we might be able to discredit the Paranormal Office's entire approach to werewolves. Otherwise, the crackdown will continue—and your rebellion will eventually be crushed.'

Milah looked like she wanted to argue, but then she sighed and seemed to deflate. 'This is true. My wolves want to fight, but we cannot win against the might of the Paranormal Office and its seekers. Very well. I will take a risk on this Callum Kirk—but only if he agrees to accept the discipline of the pack. It will not be easy for him. Many of my wolves will hate and distrust him.'

'I'll do everything I can to persuade him to accept your pack and its rules,' Jasper said, relieved to have gotten over the first hurdle in his plan.

'This discussion is all a bit academic if we can't find the bugger,' Rasmus pointed out.

Jasper looked at Milah. 'If you have a sample of someone's blood, can you track the scent?'

'Yes. You have some of The Stray's blood?'

'No, but he is carrying a vial of my blood, and I believe his clothes are stained with my blood too. Could you find him if I let you smell my blood?'

Milah looked sceptical. 'This is like finding a needle in the stack of hay.'

'I think we can assume Callum's come back to London,' Alyssa said. 'He knows he's being hunted by the Paranormal Office. What if you limited your search to places in London where a shifter might hide out when they're on the run?'

Milah still looked dubious, but after a slight hesitation she nodded. 'I suppose we can try that. There are places our kind go when we need to stay out of sight.'

CHAPTER 34
ISLAY. TWENTY YEARS AGO.

CALLUM LOST TRACK OF time and almost lost track of himself. There were moments when the beast took complete control of his mind and he thought of nothing but howling and hunting and savouring the sweet taste of lost souls. Other times he clung desperately to the tattered shreds of his humanity like a homeless man clinging to a soiled blanket. He had no reason to believe his body would ever return to its human state; it seemed inevitable that his mind would soon surrender to the Cù-Sìth as well. Eventually, after howling and barking until his throat burned, he curled up in a corner of the church, resigned to his fate.

Murray came regularly to bring him food and water and remove his waste. He did this without speaking to or even looking at his son, until one day, when he filled Callum's dog bowl with a gloopy, oil-like substance rather than water.

'Drink,' he said.

It was the first word he'd spoken in his son's presence for such a long time. Callum felt so relieved that his father was speaking to him again that he obeyed immediately, shuffling over to the bowl and lapping the strange liquid inside. It tasted foul, but he kept drinking until the bowl was almost dry. When he'd finished, he looked up at his father with sorrowful eyes.

Murray picked up the bowl and left the church, securing the door behind him.

Soon afterwards, Callum felt ill. He whined and groaned for hours as his body changed. If his mind hadn't been so foggy and confused, he might have realised what was happening and felt happy. As it was, he thought Murray had poisoned him.

Murray returned in the morning. He found his son naked, curled underneath a rotten pew, hugging himself, shivering. But the potion had done its job: Callum was human again.

'Come with me,' Murray said, tossing his son a dressing gown and a pair of trainers. Callum followed Murray in a daze, stumbling, a stranger in his own body. When they got to the farmhouse, he sat down unsteadily at the kitchen table and Murray put a strong cup of tea and a steaming bowl of porridge in front of him. Callum realised for the first time that he was ravenously hungry. Without a second thought he wolfed down the meal, eating and drinking so fast he burned his mouth with the tea and hot porridge. The pain hardly registered—it felt so good to be eating a hot meal again at home. He felt almost deliriously happy as the porridge settled in his stomach and warmed him from the inside. *Murray has forgiven me for my foolish mistake and is ready to have me home again!*

He was soon disabused of that idea.

When Callum finished his porridge, Murray pushed two vials of the black, gloopy potion across the table towards him. 'I found a witch in London who can get you more of this. She gets it from a supplier in the Westminster government.'

'Thank you,' Callum croaked.

Murray's expression was stony. 'I'm telling you this so you can deal with this problem yourself. These two doses will only last a few months, after that you'll need more. I expect you'll be happier in London, anyway.'

Callum blinked at his father. 'What do you mean?'

'I mean you won't be living here anymore. It's time you made your own way in the world. You're eighteen, after all.'

Callum dropped his spoon. There was a ringing in his ears, a numbness in his hands. Was he really eighteen? His birthday must have come and gone while he was imprisoned in the church. Murray hadn't marked the occasion and Callum had lost all sense of time while he was locked up.

'I'm your son, your only child. You rescued me from that horrible church as a baby. You can't kick me out now!'

Murray scowled and stood up. He retrieved a cigarette from a packet stashed in a kitchen drawer and lit it from the gas stove. He opened the kitchen window and blew smoke out of it.

'I didn't rescue you from that church,' he said quietly, staring out at his farm. 'That was just a story.'

Callum was simultaneously stunned and not surprised in the least. The Moses basket story had always seemed far-fetched, even when he was a kid. The admission that it was a lie still stung, though. *Why had Murray waited so long to admit the truth?*

'So you've been lying to me all my life?'

'Aye.'

'Why?'

Murray didn't answer immediately. He continued smoking and staring out the window.

When the cigarette had burned down to the filter, he said: 'I was in love with your mother, but she didn't feel the same way about me. I was young and stupid enough to think her feelings might change over time, but they didn't. She wanted things I couldn't offer—to travel the world and live in a big city.'

'She went to Edinburgh and shacked up with some journalist. I tried to forget about her, but one day she turned up at the farm, pregnant and distraught. The journalist had dumped her. Told her to get an abortion. Like a fool, I took her in, hoping she'd fall in love with me if I provided a home for her and her child.'

'The birth was difficult. She was airlifted to hospital. I soon realised from the look in the doctors' eyes that she wasn't going to survive. As she lay dying, she made me promise to take care of you until you were grown up.'

Callum had always suspected that Murray had known and loved his mother, despite his repeated denials, but the rest of Murray's story was unexpected and devastating. Callum, son of a feckless Edinburgh journalist, had killed his mother and forever poisoned Murray's heart. The truth squeezed his insides and made it hard to breathe.

'You can't send me away to London. You're my only family.'

'I'm not your family,' Murray said harshly. 'You've got too much of your father in you—your real father. I met him once. A smarmy, arrogant man. Very pleased with himself.'

'You're eighteen now and a man. I've fulfilled my promise to your mother. God knows I tried to do right by you. But now I want you to leave.'

Murray flicked the ash off his cigarette, tossed the butt out the window, then walked out of the kitchen. Callum found that his face was wet with tears. He wasn't sure when he'd started crying. He wiped his face with a tissue and tried to stop his hands shaking. There would be no point pleading with Murray. Once he'd made up his mind, there was no changing it.

Callum had always believed that learning the truth about his mother would set him free—that in some unforeseeable, magical way it would undo all the pain he'd felt growing up with a father who never understood him. Who barely even liked him.

He left the farm a few days later, bound for London.

CHAPTER 35
LONDON. PRESENT DAY.

JASPER SOON RECEIVED WORD that the wolves of Silverback pack had smelled his blood coming from a secluded area of Hampstead Heath. He and Alyssa jumped on the tube and arrived as quickly as they could. Rasmus met them there, after first collecting a seeker-quality topaz from one of his contacts at the Paranormal Office. Topazes were part of the secondary tier of magical jewels, useless for general magic but with the unique ability to force a shifter to transform from one form to another.

Milah, in human form, met them at Hampstead tube station. 'The scent is strongest near a suspicious-looking clearing surrounded by trees,' she explained, leading them down the bustling street, towards the nearest entrance to the Heath.

Alyssa frowned. 'Suspicious-looking in what way?'

'We think there's some kind of tunnel or bunker underneath it. The Stray may be hiding inside.'

They arrived at a large iron gate secured with a chain and padlocks. Jasper sent a spurt of magic into the chain, breaking several of its links. They passed through the gate, shutting it behind them. There were a few street lamps stationed along the main pathways through the park, but Milah soon led them into a wilder area of the Heath that was almost completely dark. Thanks to the pall of pollution that hung permanently over London, hardly any stars were visible overhead, only the blinking lights of a few aeroplanes. Milah moved quickly and confidently, no doubt guided by her sense of smell. Jasper moved more slowly, staying close to Rasmus in case he tripped over in the dark. The old man was tough, but even wizards were susceptible to broken bones and twisted ankles. Alyssa lit their way using her iPhone's torch.

For about twenty minutes, Jasper heard nothing but the sound of his own breathing and the occasional crackle of a branch breaking underfoot.

The first howl made his heart jump in his chest.

He stopped in his tracks, ice flowing through his veins. He felt a pressure on his skull, as if he'd plunged deep underwater. The first howl was followed by a second, then a third. The sound was unlike anything Jasper had heard before. It cut right through him and drove away all conscious thought. He forgot where he was and what he was doing.

In the silence that followed the howls, Jasper realised he'd grabbed Alyssa's hand. In most other circumstances he'd have dropped it in embarrassment, but now he clung on, calmed by her touch. She squeezed his hand as if to reassure him.

Rasmus conjured a ball of werelight and let it hover above them. It cast a more gentle, purplish light than the torch on Alyssa's iPhone, which, Jasper now saw, she had dropped on the grass.

Alyssa looked as scared as Jasper felt. Milah didn't look much better. Only Rasmus seemed to have kept his cool.

'Are we all OK?' he asked.

Jasper nodded, even though his hands were shaking with terror.

Milah said, 'I've never met a shifter who could make a sound like that. It was... disturbing.'

'I'm OK,' Alyssa said, her voice shaking, 'but I don't want to go any further. I think we should turn back. Hand over Callum's location to the Paranormal Office and let them deal with him.'

Jasper had never known Alyssa to avoid a confrontation, but he agreed with her on this occasion. His feet were rooted to the spot and his heart was still hammering. Moving nearer to the source of those howls felt impossible. Insane. Reckless.

'I agree—this is too much for us to handle. We should turn back.'

Milah looked from Jasper to Alyssa and frowned. 'The howls were unsettling, but surely that's no reason to abandon our plans?'

Rasmus pulled something out of his coat pocket—a red-and-white striped paper bag. 'Here—eat one of these, both of you.' Jasper dipped his hand inside and pulled out a black, spiral-shaped sweet.

'Ew—liquorice,' Alyssa said. 'No, thanks.'

'Eat it. Trust me.'

Something in Rasmus's tone made Jasper obey without questioning why his old mentor was suddenly offering them sweets. He wasn't the biggest fan of liquorice either, and this particular type of liquorice was unusually smelly and strong tasting. Alyssa huffed but took a piece of her own, making a face as she chewed it.

'I hope there's some point to this,' she said grumpily. 'Are you hoping to distract us from our fear by making us puke?'

Rasmus nodded. 'Precisely. Except for the puking part. Cù-Sìth howls are imbued with a rather nasty enchantment. They bypass the hearer's higher reasoning and force them to freeze in place, making it easy for the beast to hunt them down. I'm less vulnerable to the effect as I've heard the sound before and was expecting it. Werewolves like Milah here are also less susceptible.'

'But Alyssa and I are vulnerable to it?'

'I'd say so, yes. Fortunately, there's an easy antidote to the Cù-Sìth's howl.'

'Liquorice?'

'Indeed. Beef jerky or lemon juice would be equally effective. Anything with an overpoweringly strong taste and smell. It jolts your brain out of its fearful state.'

Jasper started laughing, then forced himself to stop when he realised he sounded hysterical.

'Great,' Alyssa grumbled. 'So now I have to confront a dangerous monster while having a disgusting taste in my mouth.'

'Better than being unable to move and getting eaten alive. Shall we continue?'

The howls continued as they moved deeper into the park. This time Jasper and Alyssa chewed on liquorice without complaint. It was weird but it worked. He still felt scared, but the smelly sweets prevented his mind from fixating on fear.

'Next time we face off against a Cù-Sìth, I'm bringing beef jerky,' Alyssa muttered mutinously.

Milah led them through some trees and into a clearing teeming with werewolves, some in human form, others transformed. There was a metal hatch propped open on the ground in the middle of the clearing. One of the wolves in human form came up to Milah and said, 'There's a bunker underneath the clearing. It looks like someone has been living there for some time. The Stray isn't here, but his scent is all over the place. We think he's still somewhere nearby.'

'We should have a look inside before continuing the search,' Rasmus said. 'If Callum's been living down there, he might have left clues about where he's gone or what he's up to.'

'Agreed,' Jasper said.

The hatch led to a narrow, vertical shaft with metal rungs driven into the sides. Jasper descended first, followed by Alyssa, Rasmus, Milah, and a couple of her wolves. The bunker below took Jasper's breath away. It wasn't just somewhere to hide—it was a fully kitted-out home. Not one he would care to inhabit, but still.

Was this Callum's home, or just a temporary refuge? Someone had clearly lived here for a long time. There was a camp bed covered with worn blankets, pots and pans hanging from hooks on the wall, and fragrant herbs dangling from the ceiling. Unfortunately, the pleasant smell of sage and rosemary was ruined by a rotting odour that pervaded the bunker.

'There's a dead lady in the bed,' one of the wolves said.

That explained the rotten smell. A body was decomposing in here. Jasper pinched his nose closed and approached the bed to look at the body. The woman might have been anywhere from fifty to eighty years old. She was wearing ragged shawls and there were black scorch marks around her neck.

'Do we think Callum killed her?' Alyssa asked. 'Maybe this bunker belonged to her, and he killed her so he could use it instead?'

Jasper shook his head. 'I doubt it. See those black marks? She was killed with magic, and Callum was rejected for wizard training. I don't think a Cù-Sìth could have caused those injuries. Rasmus, what do you think?'

Rasmus was standing on the other side of the bunker, examining what looked like a grey metal filing cabinet like you'd find in most offices. He said, 'I think we all need to get out of here. Immediately.'

'Why?'

Then Jasper saw why. There was a beaker of glowing purple liquid on top of the filing cabinet. Plastic tubes snaked out of the cabinet's drawers.

'Greek Fire,' Jasper said. 'Bloody hell. This place is booby trapped!'

'We need to leave—now!' Rasmus shouted.

'What's Greek Fire?' Alyssa shouted over her shoulder as they scrambled to escape the bunker.

'It's highly explosive,' Jasper said. 'Without a spell to counteract it, it can carry on burning almost indefinitely.'

They pulled themselves out of the hatch and into the clearing.

'We should keep going,' Jasper said. 'Get well clear of the bunker. Hopefully, we're only dealing with one flask of Greek Fire, but if there's more....'

They jogged to the edge of the clearing towards the dense trees surrounding it. Jasper was sweating and panting with the exertion. Alyssa—being fitter and younger—looked a little better off, but Rasmus had turned pale.

'You OK?' Jasper asked.

The old man was breathing hard, but he waved away Jasper's concern. 'I'm fine, just not as fit as I used to be. That device gave me a fright though. The flask of Greek Fire was wired up to a detonator, which seemed to be connected to—'

A deafening boom filled the air. The earth erupted around them.

CHAPTER 36

THE EXPLOSION SEEMED TO come from every direction at once. Jasper felt it in his bones, and in the core of his body. It lifted him off his feet and flung him into the air. He clamped his eyes shut and flailed his arms, trying, but failing, to get a grip on something that might break his fall. Something rough scraped against his legs, his back, his neck. His face felt hot. He opened his eyes. He was wedged into the branches of a tree, suspended a dozen feet or so off the ground.

The tree was on fire.

He craned his neck and peered between his legs, but it was hard to see clearly as the air was thick with smoke and dust. He sucked in a breath and coughed uncontrollably. His hands were shaking.

Keep calm, he told himself. *You're still alive, you just need to find a way down.*

Once he'd steadied himself, he got a firm grip of the tree trunk and tried to ease himself down, branch by creaking branch. It was nearly impossible to see—his eyes were streaming from the smoke, and he didn't dare wipe them for fear of losing his tenuous grip on the branches. Despite his best efforts, a branch snapped when he put too much weight on it and he dropped like a stone.

So much for a controlled landing.

He tucked his chin into his chest and protected his head with his arms. His hip hit the ground first. The wind was knocked out of him and pain lanced through his core. A moan tore out of his mouth, unbidden. It felt like he'd been beaten up. His hip ached, his neck felt twisted and strained. His ears were ringing. Everything hurt.

He scrambled to his feet unsteadily. As his hearing slowly returned, he heard wolves whining in pain. The clearing was now a churning mud pit, an open wound. Twisted rubble from the bunker lay scattered about, some of it alight with Greek Fire. Those fires would burn and burn. Men, women, and wolves lay clutching wounds, scrambling in the dirt, bleeding and whimpering. Jasper's hip ached where it had struck the ground, and he was covered in scratches and small cuts, but he hadn't broken any bones or suffered any serious injuries. *Looks like I'm the lucky one.*

He scanned the clearing and located his friends. Alyssa was covered in mud but otherwise seemed to have escaped the blast unscathed. She was tending to Rasmus, who had been closest to the explosion. He was lying on his back. His clothes were ripped and mud and bits of debris were clinging to his beard and hair. Jasper knelt beside him.

'Don't even think about kicking the bucket,' he said. 'That would not be your style.'

'Don't count on it,' Rasmus mumbled, but he winced in pain as he spoke and was having trouble keeping his eyes open.

'Callum laid a trap for us,' Jasper said, brushing dirt off Rasmus's face. 'The bunker must've been stuffed full of Greek Fire.' Purple pools of the dangerous substance were burning throughout the clearing.

'Should we do something?' Alyssa said. 'The whole Heath could go up in flames!'

She was right. Greek Fire was notoriously difficult to extinguish. A team of specialists would be needed to deal with this.

'We can't do much on our own. We need to contact the Paranormal Office.'

'How do we do that? Do they have a... phone number?'

Jasper shook his head. 'We need a communication orb.'

But they didn't have one, and fetching one would take too long. Already the flames were licking higher, creeping along branches, spreading rapidly.

'Or I could send up a werelight flare. They're only supposed to be used in emergencies, as they can attract attention from ordinary people—'

'Do it,' Alyssa said firmly. 'This is definitely an emergency.'

Jasper nodded, then stood up and drew power from his ruby brooch. A ball of werelight coalesced above his hand. He turned away from Rasmus and Alyssa so as not to blind them, closed his eyes, and increased the flow of power. He willed the blazing ball of light to float higher. After a couple of seconds, he opened his eyes. The flare hovered serenely above the clearing and remained there, pulsing rhythmically, bright against the dark, smoke-filled sky.

'How long until someone from the Paranormal Office sees it?'

Jasper shrugged. 'Damned if I know.'

Together, Jasper and Alyssa hauled Rasmus away from the nearest pool of Greek Fire, which was dangerously close and burning intensely. Jasper's bruised body screamed in protest but he gritted his teeth and ignored the pain. 'We need to get him out of here, before the fire cuts us off. Greek Fire won't stop burning until—'

Alyssa dug her nails into his shoulder and turned him around.

There was a dark, hulking shape on the other side of the clearing: a monster in the shape of a giant dog with velvety fur and intense, glowing eyes. A flaming branch fell just behind the dog, but it didn't react. Its gaze remained fixed on Jasper and Alyssa. On its prey.

Is there anything left of Callum, the civil servant? Or has he fully succumbed to the bloodlust of the Cù-Sith?

'The topaz,' Jasper hissed. 'We need to find Rasmus's topaz.'

Alyssa rifled through Rasmus's pockets while the old man moaned softly. 'I can't find it! The explosion must've thrown it out of his pocket.'

Great. Our trump card—gone. 'Get him away from here, if you can. I'll deal with Callum.'

Alyssa put her hands under Rasmus's armpits and pulled him towards the path that led back to the rest of the park. Jasper circled around the edge of the clearing, drawing Callum's attention away from his friends. 'I'm not here to hurt you, Callum. I came to offer you a deal. We have a common enemy—the mage who has been controlling you for years.'

Callum's tongue lolled out of his mouth. If there was any humanity left in him, it was hard to see. 'Run away little wizard.' His voice was a low growl, the words barely recognisable. 'Run away so I can enjoy the thrill of the chase before consuming your soul.'

'This isn't you, Callum! Remember who you really are: a civil servant with a high-flying career. A peaceful man burdened by a terrible curse. Let me help you break free of it.'

'Your words mean nothing, little wizard. I am what I am. A hunter. Bringer of death. Servant of the underworld.'

Callum padded forwards on all fours, weaving around the flaming wreckage of the bunker and the pools of Greek Fire.

Jasper blinked sweat out of his eyes. 'I'm not working for your boss, I swear. I'm on your side.'

But Callum wasn't listening. 'I wonder if your soul will taste of regret? Most souls do. Regret... and fear.'

There was no choice but to fight. If he could somehow incapacitate Callum, he might have a better chance of getting through to the man behind the monster.

Jasper bent his knees and turned to the side, presenting a smaller target. Duelling stance. Meant for fighting other magic users, but at least it got him into the right frame of mind. He sent a volley of concussions spells at Callum, one after the other, aiming for his snout, his chest, his paws. The spells fizzed through the air like firecrackers, shedding sparks. Callum made no effort to dodge. The spells struck him and bounced off. The attack had no effect; Callum's black fur looked as pristine and velvety as before.

'My power was created long before wizards walked the earth,' Callum growled. 'Your magic tricks are useless against me.'

The smoke was thicker now. It filled Jasper's nostrils, making him feel lightheaded. *What now?* Standard combat spells weren't cutting the mustard. He needed to channel a lot more power to have any chance of breaking through the natural protections of a Cù-Sìth.

'Maybe I can't hurt you, but your former boss can. They'll have far more power at their disposal. Isn't it better if we work together against them?'

Callum leapt forward, the powerful muscles under his black fur propelling him quickly across the clearing. Jasper crouched down and rolled to the left just as Callum reached him. He felt a searing pain across his back. There was a spray of blood, the sound of tearing fabric. Jasper's coat flapped around his shoulders, ripped in half. He shrugged it off and staggered away from Callum, trying to put some distance between them, but tripped and fell backwards. The cut on his back sang with pain.

'I can see this isn't going to be a memorable hunt. What are you without your magic tricks? Just a weak, frightened man. A bag of bones. A sack of soft flesh.'

Jasper was on his knees, breathing through the pain. *Stay calm. This isn't over yet.* He pulled the ruby brooch out of his pocket and held it between both hands. Normally, he'd only draw down a fraction of the jewel's total power at once, but now he tried to drain it in one go. It was risky, but it was worth it in dire circumstances. The pain in his hip and back vanished instantaneously, replaced by the hot rush of magic. He kept drawing power until he felt sick with it. The ruby sparkled and vibrated.

This has to work.

Callum bounded forward, teeth bared, claws already wet with Jasper's blood. Jasper pocketed the ruby, locked his hands together, and unleashed a surging cone of fire magic.

Callum dodged out of the way with more agility than should have been possible given his bulk, but Jasper moved his hands and kept him in the firing line. The magic swirled around Callum, enclosing him in a sphere of fire. Jasper willed the fireball to rise off the ground. Callum was lifted several feet into the air where his powerful legs couldn't reach the ground.

The giant fireball hovered in the air, casting an orangey glow over the clearing.

Pain flashed through Jasper, returning stronger than before. He fell to his knees. His head throbbed. He was drenched in sweat. His magic was used up. The ruby was a dead weight in his pocket, drained of all its power.

The fireball shrank in size, and Callum dropped to the ground. His velvety fur glistened as if covered in a thin film of dew. Jasper groaned.

'As you'll soon discover, there is a lot of fire in the underworld. I am built to withstand it.'

High above them, the werelight flare fizzled out.

CHAPTER 37

There was no hope of hiding in the clearing, so Jasper scrambled back towards the protection of the trees. But before he'd got more than a few feet away, his feet were torn out from under him and his head slammed into the ground. White spots burst across his vision. Soil filled his mouth. He spluttered and coughed, clawing at the ground with his hands to get away, but he found he was pinned down. Twisting round, he saw Callum was pressing down on his ankle with his massive paw, holding him in place. He shifted more of his considerable weight onto the ankle as Jasper tried to wriggle free. The pain was immense—the ankle felt near to breaking—and an agonised scream tore out of Jasper's throat.

He's toying with me.

'Are you done playing, little wizard?'

Jasper roared, half in anger, half in agony. He grabbed a handful of earth and threw it over his shoulder, into Callum's face. The Cù-Sìth recoiled enough for Jasper to squirm free and hobble towards the trees. He tried to ignore the shooting pain from his twisted ankle.

It was almost completely dark under the trees. Jasper stumbled around, bumping into several tree trunks. He thought about summoning werelight to help him see, but that would be like painting a fluorescent bullseye on his back. If he kept moving, he might get lucky and find his way back into the main part of the park.

What would he do then? Raise the alarm? Send up another werelight flare? Even if he escaped and alerted the magical authorities, he'd be leaving Rasmus and Alyssa to fend for themselves. How long before Callum found them and made a meal of their souls?

If only I had Rasmus's topaz, I could put an end to this.

Something glittered in the darkness between the trees: two large, glowing orbs. The eyes of a Cù-Sìth.

What are the chances Cù-Sìth can see in the dark?

The eyes disappeared, and Callum howled. The sound ricocheted off the trees. Jasper tried to steel himself, but he was tired, frightened, covered in mud, and had a twisted ankle. The terror felt like a drip of icy water trickling down his spine. Cù-Sìth howls were charged with an old magic that awakened fear in Jasper that he didn't know was there. The same fear his ancestors had probably felt before the dawn of civilization, when magical creatures like the Cù-Sìth were more common. When humans were little more than helpless prey.

Some of Rasmus's revolting liquorice would come in handy about now. Instead, Jasper dug his dirty fingernails into his palms. The sharp pain helped bring him back to his senses. He decided he couldn't risk leaving Rasmus and Alyssa where they were. They had to leave together, or not at all. He took a circuitous route back to the clearing, avoiding the place he'd seen Callum's glowing eyes, but there was no sign of his friends. Perhaps Alyssa had dragged Rasmus into the trees for safety?

'Will you die facing me, or cowering in fear? Either suits me.'

Callum was right behind him. Jasper hadn't heard him at all, but now he smelled the sulphurous reek of his breath.

Even if I could somehow force him back into human form, is there anything left of the man Callum used to be? Or has the monster taken over completely?

Shapes moved in the shadows at the far side of the clearing. The werewolves were gathering. Their eyes glinted in the light of the burning trees and their fur was wet with blood. Some were wounded, some were limping. But they were preparing to mount an attack anyway.

As the werewolves emerged from their hiding places, Jasper sprinted forward and dived behind a piece of burning wreckage. He watched as two wolves jumped on Callum's back while another sunk its teeth into his back leg. Callum growled and tried to shake them off, but the wolves held on, digging their teeth and claws into his flesh. The other wolves circled around him, nipping at his legs, splitting his attention, trying to overwhelm him with sudden, darting attacks. It was working: Callum twisted this way and that, but the werewolves were faster, and quickly danced out of range when he threatened them.

While the werewolves kept Callum occupied, Jasper searched for the topaz. He scoured the ground near where Rasmus had fallen, but there was no sign of the jewel. It seemed hopeless—the topaz could be anywhere. It might have flown away into the trees or been buried in the rubble and churned mud left by the explosion. Either way, it would be nearly impossible to find now.

He came across a rectangular metal frame half buried in mud—the remains of the camp bed he'd seen in the bunker. The metal was badly twisted and parts of it were burning with Greek Fire. It gave him an idea. A small metal rod, partially ablaze, was hanging off the frame. He yanked it completely off, protecting his hand with the cuff of his coat.

As Jasper looked up, he saw Callum catch a wolf in his jaws and bite down with a sickening crunch. Another wolf was squirming on the ground, bleeding out; a third was lying completely still some distance away. Probably dead. Three more circled Callum, trying to attack him from different sides, but they were getting slower and more cautious, protecting injuries. Meanwhile Callum seemed to relish the fight. One of the werewolves tried to sneak up on his flank, but he saw the attack coming and sent it sprawling with a swipe of his claws.

The tide had turned against the werewolves. They were losing.

Jasper got as close as he dared and waited for a break in the fighting. The three remaining werewolves were retreating, one of them limping on a broken leg. Callum stalked forward slowly, in no hurry. An easy target. Jasper took his chance and threw the burning metal rod.

It struck Callum on the shoulder. He barely noticed the impact, but some of his fur caught fire. Callum jabbed at it with his paw but the fire kept burning. Sensing an opportunity, the two werewolves still capable of fighting came forward again, looking for an opening to attack.

There was still a trickle of power left in Jasper's ruby ring. He drew on it, then raised both hands in the air and spread his fingers. Thin tendrils of magic emerged from his fingers, creating a swirling mass of what looked like glowing thread that hovered in the air. He hadn't used this spell for years, but it had come in handy apprehending suspects in his seeking days. When there were several dozen strands of the magic thread, Jasper urged it towards Callum. Each skein of thread latched onto a different part of his body—his legs and feet, his paws, his shoulders. Jasper pressed his hands flat on the ground and the ends of the thread fixed themselves to the ground in a circle around Callum, binding him to the ground. He looked like a circus animal lashed to the ground. He roared in anger and pulled against the threads; they grew taught but didn't break.

Jasper dropped to his knees, breathing hard, aching all over. The exhaustion from casting such a powerful spell threatened to overwhelm him. He reached for the ruby brooch in his pocket, but it felt like a chunk of ice. It was tapped out. So was he. *At least the spell worked.*

The two remaining Silverbacks darted forward, biting Callum's thrashing legs. Showing no mercy.

'Don't kill him,' Jasper shouted. 'Remember, we need his help to—'

Callum ripped one paw free of the magic thread, then dug his claws into his own shoulder and tore away a hunk of flesh. The flaming piece of meat flopped onto the ground and continued to burn. Callum was left with a nasty, glistening wound, but he was now free of the Greek Fire.

A werewolf appeared beside Jasper and transformed, becoming human before his eyes. It was Milah. She had a black eye and her body was smeared with blood and dirt. 'We should retreat,' she said. 'This monster is too much for us. There's no sense in sacrificing our lives when there is no hope of victory.'

'As long as Rasmus and Alyssa are nearby, I'm staying to protect them.' Jasper looked around, but he couldn't see his friends. Had they gotten away? Perhaps. Or perhaps they were hiding somewhere nearby.

The spell was losing power now, and Callum quickly tore free of the remaining threads.

'Jasper! I've found it!'

Alyssa emerged from the trees behind Callum, sprinting into the clearing from the other side. Callum heard her shouting and turned around.

She was too far away from Jasper—he wouldn't be able to reach her before Callum did.

But she had the topaz. He saw it glittering in her hand.

She threw it in a long, graceful arc over Callum's head.

Jasper reacted instantly, plucking it out of the air. He sent a surge of magical energy into it—every last ounce of power he possessed. The topaz exploded with light, illuminating the whole clearing.

Callum backed away from the source of the light, but, as he did so, his body transformed. His fur fell away in clumps, his claws receded. His wolfish features melted like hot wax, and in place of the mighty Cù-Sìth stood a thin, naked man shivering and hugging himself. Pale, frightened, and beaten. His mouth was dripping blood and his shoulder was an open wound where he'd gouged his own flesh. He tipped his head forward and spat on the ground. The spit was pink with blood. 'You win, Wychwood,' he said hoarsely. 'Go ahead—you might as well kill me.'

'As I tried to explain earlier, I want to help you.'

'Is that what you call it? Setting a werewolf pack on me? Hunting me across London?'

'You did steal my blood.'

Callum sat on the ground and brought his knees to his chin. 'You can have your blood back. I have no use for it, anyway.'

'Really? Then why go to all that trouble to get it?'

'Because my boss—the one you claim not to be working for—asked for it. And before you ask, no, I don't know what they want with it.'

'But you still have it?'

'Yes, yes. I haven't handed it over yet. I was having... second thoughts.'

Jasper sighed with relief. Not only because Callum hadn't used his blood for any nefarious purpose, but also because the civil servant sounded sane; and human. The man behind the monster still survived. There was hope for him.

'Perhaps we can work together. I want you to help me unmask the Whitehall spy—your boss. In exchange, I've persuaded the Silverbacks to take you into their ranks.'

Callum frowned. 'Why on earth would I want to join a werewolf pack?'

'Because, just like a werewolf, you have a human side and a canine side. Werewolf packs help their members to retain their human thoughts after they transform. They could do the same for you. You could be part of their community.'

Jasper was expecting a quick, sarcastic response, but Callum just stared at him for a long moment with narrowed eyes. He seemed to be genuinely considering the offer.

'What exactly are you asking me to do? Help you arrest the spy?'

'I'd settle for your help in uncovering their identity,' Jasper said. 'I can arrest them myself.'

Callum smiled faintly. 'That's easy enough. They've hidden their true identity from me for years, but a few days ago they slipped up. I now know exactly who they are.'

CHAPTER 38
ONE WEEK LATER.

THE FOREIGN AND COMMONWEALTH Office was housed in a beautiful building on Whitehall filled with marble floors, classical statues, and renaissance paintings. It was designed to impress visiting diplomats and showcase Britain's power and prestige. The secret government department buried underneath the Foreign Office was, in many ways, its opposite: hidden, secretive, designed to obfuscate power rather than advertise it.

Rasmus had arranged the meeting with the Triumvirate. He'd told them that he and Jasper were bringing a senior civil servant from the mundane government, without explicitly saying that this individual was the spy Jasper had been tasked with apprehending. But the implication was obvious.

Alyssa had decided to sit out this encounter. Although she was intensely interested in the outcome of Jasper's investigation, it would be difficult to justify including her—a mundane, and a stranger to the Triumvirate—in such a sensitive meeting. Paranormal Office officials were apparently growing more paranoid by the day, and bringing Alyssa here would have felt like dragging her into the middle of a nest of hungry vipers. Even powerful wizards were sometimes wary of visiting the inner sanctum of British magic.

There was a grand courtyard in the middle of the Foreign Office which contained dozens of free-standing, wrought iron candelabra, each holding about a dozen electric light bulbs. All the bulbs shed a soft, yellow light, except one, which glowed purple.

Rasmus surreptitiously unscrewed the purple bulb while Jasper screened him from view. Despite being at the front door of British magic, so to speak, they were surrounded by mundane Foreign Office workers. Callum looked on with a hungry expression as Rasmus fiddled with the bulb. Jasper remembered the many applications the civil servant had submitted for wizard training, all rejected.

'So this is where you wizards hide yourselves,' he said.

'Only the ones running the show,' Jasper said quietly, glancing around the courtyard to check there was no-one else within earshot. 'I haven't been here for years.'

In response to Rasmus touching a groove on the iron candelabrum, a circular disc of marble slid sideways, revealing a hole in the floor. A staircase spiralled down into the dark.

'After you,' Jasper said, twisting his wrist and putting up a distraction spell so that anyone looking at them would suddenly remember a pressing engagement elsewhere and forget anything odd they'd seen.

As they descended, Jasper's skin prickled. He'd come down this staircase hundreds of times in his early twenties, often to see Rasmus, who had been his mentor while he was a probationary seeker. He remembered the dark corridors with their bare stone walls lit by werelight sconces, the cold air with a mildewy tang to it. The Paranormal Office wasn't built to look glamorous, but to Jasper it had seemed so. Becoming an employee of this place had been a sign of his acceptance into a world that, as a child, he'd been excluded from. He came from a famous wizarding family, with magical ancestors stretching back to the Norman conquest, but for a long time he had shown no talent with magic. A mundane in a family of mages.

Arriving here for the first time, as a young wizard coming into his power, a seeker in training, had been one of the high points of his life. Leaving the Paranormal Office again a few years later—humiliated and stripped of his seeker's jewel—had been crushing. It was a wound that had never fully healed.

If all went to plan, he might return here permanently. Arthur Sallow might soon be pinning a brand new seeker's ruby to his chest. *Assuming Sallow isn't the spy, which is far from certain...*

Was that what he wanted? To become a seeker again? Jasper still hadn't decided, but even the possibility made him feel giddy with excitement.

'This isn't what I expected,' Callum breathed, sounding awestruck.

Jasper smiled. 'It wasn't what I expected either, the first time I came here.' Not for the first time, he felt a sense of kinship with Callum, despite disagreeing with some of his actions. They'd both longed for acceptance into the wizarding world and been denied it for a long time.

Rasmus led them through twisting, dark corridors, eventually taking them into a lift and down to the lower levels.

'I hope you two are going to get me out of here again, once this is over,' Callum said with a jump in his voice.

Rasmus grunted noncommittally and Jasper shrugged. He realised, as they stepped into the lift, that they hadn't seen a single soul since they entered the Paranormal Office. They'd passed dozens of offices, small and large, all empty. Normally these tunnels were bustling with activity. The Triumvirate must have used their authority to clear everyone else out. Which seemed ominous. The knot of anxiety in Jasper's stomach tightened a few notches.

Soon after they exited the lift, Rasmus led them into a large circular room. Jasper had expected the meeting to be held in a quiet office, but the room they entered was more like a courtroom crossed with a dungeon. The walls were bare stone and there was a smell of damp in the air. There were chains and metal cuffs fixed to the walls.

The Triumvirate were waiting for them in silence. Arthur Sallow, the Minister for Paranormal Affairs, sat in a throne-like chair at the far side of the room, his hands folded neatly in his lap, his goatee beard pointing at the floor. He wore a pinstripe blue suit and a mustard yellow tie with a matching pocket square. Erin Mayhew, Keeper of Coin, sat on his right on a slightly smaller wingback chair, dressed in a grey trouser suit, her hair pinned up at the back. Her hawkish eyes swept over the newcomers as they entered, her cool smile fixed in place.

Patrick Grimshaw had vacated his chair on Sallow's left and was pacing the room. As soon as he saw Jasper and the others he shouted at them in his thick Glaswegian accent. 'About bloody time! You think we've got nothing better to do than wait for you lot?' He was wearing black cargo trousers and a military-style khaki jacket.

Apart from the three chairs and a table for the Triumvirate, there was no other furniture in the room. That suited Jasper fine—he was buzzing with nervous energy and preferred to stand. He was relieved to note that, unlike his show trial a couple of weeks ago, there were no members of the public or the press here to witness this encounter.

However, now that he thought about it, it was a little strange that there were no observers whatsoever. No-one to witness proceedings or take notes. Even the seekers and wizarding officials who usually populated the offices and corridors of the Paranormal Office had been temporarily banished. Which all suggested the Triumvirate wanted to keep this discussion as secret as possible.

Any decisions they made—punishments meted out or rewards bestowed—would also be kept secret.

Jasper had to consciously stop his knee from jiggling. If the Triumvirate decided to interpret the law 'creatively', there was no-one else here to see it or stop them.

'Welcome Rasmus. Welcome Mr Wychwood,' Sallow said smoothly, his friendly tone in stark contrast with Grimshaw's. 'I see you've brought someone with you. Can we assume that this is the guilty party? The one who has been handing out government secrets like choice cuts of meat for the werewolf packs?'

Callum squared his shoulders and looked directly at the Paranormal Office minister. 'I'm Callum Kirk, principal private secretary to the prime minister.' He clearly meant to sound dignified and confident, but Jasper couldn't help thinking of a captured soldier giving his name and rank to an enemy commander.

'You *were* the principal private secretary to the prime minister,' Erin Mayhew said curtly. 'I think we can all agree you won't be returning to that position.'

Callum opened his mouth to reply but Sallow spoke first. 'I see that you've arrived unfettered by handcuffs or a binding spell. Can we infer, Mr Kirk, that you are willing to admit your crimes and accept the consequences?'

'It's not as simple as that I'm afraid,' Jasper interjected. 'Callum was involved in the leaking of secret information, but he says he was acting on the orders of another—a senior member of the magical government.'

'Oh aye,' Grimshaw said, raising a bushy eyebrow. 'In other words, he's trying to save his own skin by putting the blame on someone else?'

'I'm prepared to hear what you have to tell us, Mr Kirk,' Sallow said, as if he hadn't heard Grimshaw's comment. 'But I make no promises of clemency. You'll have to trust that we'll treat you fairly, according to the law.'

That's hardly reassuring, Jasper thought. Even if he was taking orders from someone else, Callum had likely committed treason by divulging government secrets. Under magical law, traitors could be executed.

'We can start with the identity of this supposed spy chief at the Paranormal Office,' Mayhew said tartly, adjusting her glasses and leaning forward in her chair. 'Who is it? A name, if you please?'

Callum glanced at Jasper, who encouraged him with a nod.

'The person didn't tell me their name, and went to great lengths to conceal their identity. We had a longstanding arrangement: I passed on information about the mundane government and, lately, the werewolf packs, in exchange for potions that suppressed my Cù-Sìth form. On their instructions, I also persuaded the prime minister to support anti-werewolf legislation.'

Mayhew's precisely manicured eyebrows knitted together. 'You claim to be a... a *Cù-Sìth*? A species of fairy?'

'A demonic hound that devours lost souls,' Grimshaw thundered, his arms crossed over his muscular chest. 'I've heard they savage the odd tourist as well.'

'I killed a Cù-Sìth as a teenager and drank its blood,' Callum said. 'I thought the blood would strengthen me. It did, but not in the way I expected.'

'So you're not a werewolf at all?' Mayhew asked.

'No.'

'Well, well. How interesting.'

'Can we get back to the main point?' Grimshaw huffed. 'This lad says he was doing someone else's bidding for an extended period, but claims to have no idea who they were. Are either of you buying this rubbish?'

'It *is* rather convenient that you don't know the name of the person who supposedly enticed you to commit treason,' Mayhew said.

'I don't know their name and I never met them in person, but I have been able to gain some idea of who they are. When their potions were delivered to me, through an intermediary, the vials were sealed with one of these.'

Callum approached the senior mages and held out a wax seal with the symbol of three interlocking arcs—the icon of the Triumvirate.

After a pause, Mayhew sniggered. 'So you're accusing one of us of being the Whitehall spy? I'll give you this Mr Kirk—you've got some nerve.'

'What nonsense,' Grimshaw huffed, apparently not seeing the funny side. 'He'll say anything to protect himself.'

'If this is a lie, it's a bold one,' Sallow said, glancing at his colleagues with narrowed eyes.

'A bold lie is still a lie,' Mayhew pointed out.

'True, but Mr Kirk has brought us this seal as evidence for his accusation.'

'Probably a fake,' said Grimshaw.

'I'm happy for you to examine it,' Callum said, handing the seal to Sallow. 'You'll find it's genuine.'

'Genuine or not, your theory doesn't hold water,' Grimshaw said. 'What possible reason could we have for helping werewolves? All three of us have tried to bring the beasts under control. We've passed legislation to that effect. Why would we undermine that by secretly helping them?'

'I think that's the point,' Rasmus said mildly. 'We think the spy—whoever they are—has been encouraging the werewolves to rebel in order to frighten the public and create a pretext for the recent crackdown.'

'And you all have good reasons for supporting the crackdown,' Jasper said. 'Ms Mayhew stands to profit from the privatisation of Hampstead Heath—but only if werewolves are evicted from the area. And Mr Grimshaw has personal reasons for resenting werewolves.'

'Yes, we're all well aware of the personal tragedy that befell Patrick's family.' Sallow shot Jasper a fierce glace, as if to rebuke him from bringing up the topic.

'I'm sorry to mention something so painful, but it is relevant.'

Grimshaw turned slowly towards Jasper like a tank pointing its gunbarrel at a new target. 'Werewolves killed my son and I detest them for it. Everyone who reads the *Uncanny Chronicle* knows that. That doesn't make me a traitor.'

'Are Patrick and I your only suspects?' Mayhew sneered. 'Or is Arthur also on your list of likely conspirators?'

Sallow shrugged. 'I should think it's quite obvious that I have a motive for suppressing werewolves—the simplest one of all. My political career only took off when I promised to deal with the werewolf problem. I wouldn't have won the last election otherwise.'

'This is nonsense, Arthur,' Grimshaw complained. 'That seal could easily be a fake.'

'As I say, I'm happy for you to test it,' Callum said. 'And I can bring you more like it. The spy has been using that seal on their potion vials for several years and I've kept all of them.'

Sallow tilted his head to one side. 'Indeed? I only joined the Triumvirate eighteen months ago, so I suppose that takes me out of the equation.'

'I know you're not the spy,' Callum said, sounding a touch impatient. 'I spoke to them a week ago using a communication orb, and they let slip something which made their identity clear. They said that werewolves had brought death and misery to their family, and that ever since that happened they have believed werewolves should be locked up in secure kennels. '

The room fell silent. All eyes turned to Patrick Grimshaw.

CHAPTER 39

GRIMSHAW WAS NEARLY SIXTY, but he was still a formidable physical presence. He was over six feet tall and heavily built, with muscles cording his arms and legs and bulking his neck and shoulders. He looked like a boxing coach—past his prime but still packing a punch—whereas Sallow and Mayhew had the physiques of lifelong bureaucrats.

Grimshaw planted his hands on his hips, his face turning red with rage. 'How many more lies are we going to listen to?' he demanded, spittle erupting from his lips. 'This self-confessed traitor thinks he can pull the wool over our eyes. Let me take him to the cells, then we can pass sentence and be done with this whole bloody business.'

He aimed the request at Sallow, who nodded thoughtfully and said: 'The wax seal is evidence that one of us was involved in Mr Kirk's treason, but I'm certainly not ready to believe that Patrick is a traitor. Even if I were entirely convinced of Mr Kirk's truthfulness—and I am *not*—the comments he quotes are rather vague and hardly conclusive.'

'Some common sense at last,' Grimshaw roared. 'Even if this traitor is telling the truth, the real spy could have mentioned my bereavement and the kennel proposal in order to cast suspicion on me.'

This is it, Jasper thought. Time to reveal all, and hope that their ruse had worked.

It would either succeed... or fail spectacularly. There was no in between.

'Mr Grimshaw is correct,' Jasper said, stepping forward. 'Although I believe Callum is telling the truth, the spy might have said those things in order to lay a false trail. That's why we came up with a back-up plan. In the same conversation, the spy asked Callum to hand over a vial of my blood that Callum had taken from me a few days earlier. We decided to give them what they were asking for.'

Sallow frowned. 'I hope you're not foolish enough to allow an adversary to possess your blood. You must understand what the consequences of that could be?'

Jasper nodded—he knew all too well. A dark wizard named Yarrow had once performed a ritual using Jasper's blood, turning him into an unwitting servant. Due to its use in facilitating blood magic, possessing the blood of a fellow mage was illegal.

'I understand the consequences very well. That's why we didn't give them my blood—we swapped it for Callum's. We left a vial of it in a safe box hidden in a phone box on Whitehall for the spy to collect.'

'Ha!,' Grimshaw said. 'So you tricked them?'

Sallow hadn't taken his eyes off Jasper. 'Explain.'

'Drinking the blood of the original Cù-Sìth is what first triggered Callum's transformation. When the spy asked for my blood, it was obvious they wanted to use it to cast blood magic or gain some sort of power over me. As you know, consuming the blood of another—especially as part of certain spells and rituals—often imbues the user with powers and traits from the one who gave the blood. The same thing happened to

Callum—he drank the blood of the original Cù-Sìth on the Isle of Islay and it triggered his transformation. .'

'Ah,' Sallow said, with the flicker of a smile. 'So you believe you've tricked our traitor into consuming Cù-Sìth blood—and suffering the same fate as Mr Kirk here?'

'That's the idea.'

It was a huge gamble, to say the least. They knew the spy had picked up the package from the phone box, but what if they hadn't gotten around to using it to cast blood magic yet? The original plan had been to wait another week or two to give the spy plenty of time to make use of the blood, but Sallow had been insistent that they come in now to update the triumvirate.

'It looks like your trick hasn't worked, Wychwood,' Grimshaw said. 'None of us have turned into a shaggy dog.'

'So your theory must be wrong,' Mayhew said tightly. 'The culprit isn't one of us. Frankly, I doubt anyone else was involved. This is all a transparent attempt to deflect attention from Mr Kirk.'

'That's what I keep saying!' Grimshaw said.

'Patience, my friends,' Sallow said. 'The transformation can be suppressed to some extent, I believe. Someone may be keeping up appearances...'

It was time to put the theory to the test.

Jasper caught Callum's eye. Callum nodded and quickly left the room.

Jasper thrust his hand into his coat pocket and pulled out the topaz that Rasmus had brought to Hampstead Heath. He focused his attention on it, drawing out its power. His hand grew warm and the electric tingle of magic danced up his arm. The topaz radiated waves of light and magic. The Triumvirate shouted in surprise and turned away from the dazzling light, shielding their eyes with their hands.

The topaz slowly dimmed as its power fizzled out.

Jasper looked around, his heart pounding.

Everyone still looked human. It hadn't worked.

Grimshaw, Sallow and Rasmus blinked and grumbled as they recovered from the explosion of light.

'Could have given us some bloody warning!' Grimshaw complained.

'Yes, I think we could have done without the theatrics, Mr Wychwood,' Sallow said dryly.

Erin Mayhew was the only one who didn't speak. She sat stiffly, gripping the arms of her chair, her eyes fixed in a thousand-yard stare. Her face had turned pale and there was sweat dripping down her chin.

Her shoulders shook, her fingernails scraped frantically against the arm of her chair.

Her face contorted with pain.

Hair sprouted from her skin. Her limbs grew longer, ripping through her trouser suit.

Muscles bulged. Claws extended.

Sallow and Grimshaw leapt out of their seats and adopted fighting stances, but Mayhew moved too quickly for them, ripping off her clothes and sprinting to the door on all fours. Grimshaw flung a stunning spell at her back, but it missed and thudded uselessly into the wall, sending out a puff of mortar. Before anyone else could ready a combat spell, Erin Mayhew was out of the room and tearing down the tunnel towards the Foreign Office.

CHAPTER 40

Jasper and Grimshaw sprinted after Mayhew, but she out-paced them easily and they soon lost sight of her.

'We need to cut her off,' Grimshaw said. 'There are only two ways out of these tunnels—the staff entrance, which leads to the Foreign Office courtyard, and the visitors' entrance. We should split up so we can cover both.'

'Agreed,' Sallow said, catching up to them. 'I suggest that myself, Rasmus and Mr Kirk go to the visitors' entrance, while you and Mr Wychwood exit via the staff entrance. You'll get there quicker than us, and the staff entrance must be the priority. If Mayhew goes that way she'll encounter mundane workers, who we must protect at all costs.'

'Fine,' Grimshaw said. 'Let's get moving.'

Grimshaw sprinted down the corridor and Jasper followed. He then turned into a vertical shaft with a ladder fixed to the wall.

'This is a shortcut,' Grimshaw shouted over his shoulder. 'It'll bring us out near the courtyard.'

'Does Mayhew know about this route?' Jasper shouted back.

'Yes, unfortunately,' Grimshaw said. 'But I'm guessing she's not thinking clearly right now. We have to hope she's gone the long way around.'

They raced up the ladder. Despite his age and bulky frame, Grimshaw moved with surprising speed and agility. Jasper breathed hard as he tried to keep up.

How would Mayhew react when she encountered defence-less mundanes? This situation had the potential to turn from a cock-up into a catastrophe. *This plan was too risky.* He'd assumed that between himself, Rasmus, and the two other members of the triumvirate, they'd easily be able to overpow-er the spy as soon as they transformed, but he hadn't reckoned with Mayhew's sheer speed.

The shaft emerged into a men's toilet cubicle. A civil ser-vant standing at a urinal gaped as Jasper and Grimshaw rushed out of the cubicle together. A minute later they arrived at the courtyard with the marble floor and iron candelabras. It was after normal working hours, so the place was mercifully quiet. There were only a handful of civil servants hanging around, carrying files or making phone calls. There was no sign of Mayhew, which meant either that she'd come through here already or...

Mayhew erupted from the secret hatch in the floor that Jasper had gone down earlier. She knocked over the cande-labra, smashing its bulbs and spraying the floor with glass.

One of the civil servants dropped her phone and screamed.

Mayhew's gaze fell on her, and something like a smile twisted her black, canine lips.

'I'll deal with her,' Grimshaw said. 'You evacuate the mun-dane workers and seal the exits. We can't let her escape this courtyard!'

Grimshaw sprinted towards Mayhew as she leered at the screaming civil servant.

A group of three other civil servants had formed a knot on the other side of the courtyard, frozen with terror.

'This way,' Jasper shouted, ushering them towards the nearest exit.

'W-what is that thing?' said the nearest civil servant, a woman with curly black hair.

'Has somebody called 999?' said the man next to her.

'Yes, it's all taken care of,' Jasper said. 'Please leave the courtyard and lock yourself in a meeting room. There's no need to call the emergency services—they're on their way already. Someone will be along to take statements from you soon.'

The false air of calm confidence in Jasper's voice was enough to persuade the civil servants to do as he asked. Jasper sealed the door they'd passed through with a spell. He worked his way around the courtyard sealing all the doors, occasionally distracted by the ferocious melee taking place between Mayhew and Grimshaw. He felt guilty for not helping Grimshaw to fight, but sealing Mayhew in was more important—if she escaped, people would probably die. As well as doors, there were a few open archways which meant Jasper had to erect magical barriers—which was trickier and more time consuming than simply locking a door. He watched out of the corner of his eye as Grimshaw flung spells at Mayhew. His efforts seemed to enrage her without doing any serious damage. Grimshaw was protecting his left arm, holding it close to his body. Blood dripped onto the floor from a nasty gash.

Let's hope she doesn't overpower us, Jasper thought, *or I might be sealing us both into our tomb.*

A couple of minutes later, Jasper sealed the last door. He turned his full attention to the fight. Mayhew was limping on her right leg, but Grimshaw was much worse off. His robes were shredded and he was leaking blood from several wounds. His left arm was either badly sprained or broken.

Jasper picked the topaz out of his pocket and aimed it at Mayhew. The jewel started glowing, but it was slow getting up to full strength. He'd drained most of its power using it downstairs. He could still use it if he pumped enough of his own magic into it, but that was a much slower process. He circled around so that Mayhew's back was towards him, hoping she wouldn't notice him until the topaz was fully powered up.

Unfortunately, Mayhew spotted the light from the topaz and spun around to face him. Grimshaw tried to distract her, but he was limping badly and his spells were growing less impactful.

Mayhew charged straight at Jasper, teeth bared, claws out.

Jasper dived to the side. Mayhew whooshed past him without connecting, but the topaz flew out of Jasper's hand.

Mayhew wheeled around, her eyes ablaze with purple light. She stared at Jasper, her eyes boring into him. He felt like he'd plunged into an ice bath. His legs felt like lead. Grimshaw advanced from Mayhew's other side, but she turned her glowing eyes on him and he collapsed on the floor, staring slack-jawed at the Cù-Sìth, mesmerised by her glowing eyes.

They were both defenceless.

Jasper tried to force his legs to move, but they refused to obey him. The topaz was out of reach, so instead he felt in his pocket for the seeker's ruby Rasmus had given him in the cells underneath the Royal Courts of Justice. In the week since they'd cornered Callum on Hampstead Heath, Jasper had recharged the ruby, in case he needed it again.

Mayhew stalked over to Grimshaw and placed a foot on his chest, pinning him to the floor. She crouched over him and bit into his leg, worrying the flesh with her sharp teeth. Grimshaw screamed.

Jasper was desperate to help, but he was still rooted to the spot by the mesmerising power of Mayhew's gaze.

If I can't move, I'll have to get your attention another way.

With the ruby in hand, Jaser sent a spur of magic into the nearest iron candelabra. It jerked off the ground and hovered beside him. He funnelled more magic into the candelabra and angled it so the light bulbs were pointing at Mayhew. The whole thing started vibrating until the bulbs exploded and magical fire erupted from each of the bulb holders.

Grimshaw screamed again. Mayhew lifted her bloody snout and prepared to savage Grimshaw's other leg.

Jasper gathered all his power and thrust the candelabra forward.

It flew through the air like a fiery missile.

Mayhew saw the candelabra just before it struck her. Before she had a chance to dodge, she was catapulted across the courtyard and pinned to the wall.

Jasper breathed hard, drenched in sweat.

The ruby brooch felt cool in his hand. He'd drawn most of its power out in one burst.

Mayhew threw the candelabra off herself and hobbled forward with surprising speed. She was badly injured—her fur burnt away in places and matted with blood—but was not beaten yet.

Jasper knew that there was no way to escape—he'd made sure of it. He'd sealed all the exits and it would take time to undo those spells.

Behind him, one of the locked doors flew off its hinges. Rasmus, Sallow and Callum sprinted into the courtyard. Sallow flung a volley of concussion spells at Mayhew, who wheeled around to face this new threat. Sallow continued his assault, the large sapphire around his neck glowing, his features fixed in an expression of intense concentration. The spells didn't seem to do much damage, but they at least slowed Mayhew down. Callum ran over to help Grimshaw, who was moaning and slumped in a pool of his own blood.

Jasper realised he'd collapsed in a heap without even noticing it. He tried to haul himself up to collect the topaz, but he could hardly move. His limbs were shaking. He was exhausted, unused to casting so much magic in one go.

'Rasmus!' he shouted. The old wizard—who was busy backing up Sallow's attacks—spun around to look at him.

'Are you hurt?'

'I'm fine,' Jasper said. 'Look over there.' He pointed to the topaz.

Rasmus collected the jewel and held it aloft. Yellow light filled the courtyard.

Mayhew's howls turned into anguished cries as she became human again. She backed into the wall, sinking to the floor and bringing her knees up to her chin, staring around wildly. Jasper offered her his coat to cover her nakedness. She shot him a poisonous look, but grabbed the coat and draped it over herself.

Grimshaw was still moaning in pain as Callum ripped up his own shirt to create a tourniquet.

'I knew you'd been involved in some shady business dealings,' Sallow said, his face pinched with fury. 'But I never imagined you to be a traitor.'

'I'm no traitor,' Mayhew croaked. 'I was trying to save us all. The werewolves are a menace to society—you know that, Arthur!'

'You encouraged them to rebel against us for your own selfish reasons. If they are a menace, it's because you made them so.'

'No—'

'The penalty for treason is death, Erin. You know that. I'm not about to mete out that punishment here, in the middle of the Foreign Office, but be under no illusions: the law will be followed to the letter.'

Sallow's words were formal, detached, but his face was bright with anger. He'd worked closely with Mayhew for many years, and was obviously taking her betrayal personally.

Mayhew's eyes were wide and bloodshot. 'Please—Arthur! It wasn't treason. You have to believe that. I did pass information to the werewolves, but only to make sure that decisive action would be taken against them. You both know that's true!'

'That is irrelevant. You've committed treason and will be punished to the full extent of the law.'

Jasper caught Sallow's eye. 'We can all agree that Mayhew has committed a serious crime, and deserves to be punished, but is more bloodshed really the best way to put things right? I have a suggestion—an alternative punishment that has a certain poetic justice to it.'

Sallow smiled bleakly. 'In my experience Mr Wychwood, justice is rarely poetic. However, I think you've earned the right to be heard. What is your suggestion?'

CHAPTER 41
THE ISLE OF ISLAY. A FEW WEEKS LATER.

JASPER MADE THE JOURNEY back to Islay alone. He met Callum in Port Ellen, and together they walked to Kildalton church.

It was a warm August day, but there was a fresh breeze blowing in from the sea that prevented it from getting too hot. It was obviously a popular time of year for tourists to enjoy the spectacular landscape, and they said hello to a few ramblers en route. Although Jasper hadn't enjoyed his last visit to Islay, he now understood why people flocked here on holiday and why many locals never dreamed of leaving.

As they climbed over a stile between two fields, Jasper said: 'Now that I'm not being hunted by a mythical beast or poisoned by a mad old lady, this place seems idyllic. Is any part of you tempted to return here permanently?'

Callum shook his head. 'No. Don't get me wrong: the island's beautiful, but I'm a city dweller at heart. I fell in love with London in my twenties—the architecture, the constant noise, the masses of people. The sense that something important is always happening. I hated growing up on an island. I always wanted to be around people. To be at the centre of everything.'

Jasper nodded. 'Being a farmer on a Scottish island isn't going to scratch that itch.'

'No. I knew that from quite a young age.'

'Does Grace still have possession of your father's farm?'

'Yes—and she's welcome to it. I heard she's already sold the land to a developer anyway. They're planning to knock the farmhouse down and build a hotel.'

Was there a trace of regret in Callum's voice? Surely, he was bound to feel some sadness that his childhood home—his late father's house—was being demolished? But then, his father had sent him away when the Cù-Sìth curse had taken hold, so perhaps Callum's feelings on the subject were rather complicated.

'No, I'll be returning to London as soon as possible,' Callum continued. 'I thought perhaps we could travel together, if you felt like it.'

'Absolutely. I'd appreciate the company.'

'Good. I wanted to thank you for persuading the Silverbacks to take me in. They've already started helping me to integrate the two sides of my personality. It's not been easy, but I am starting to feel different. Less... conflicted.'

'That's great. I'm glad it's working out.'

They passed through a kissing gate and passed over the crest of a hill. Kildalton church appeared in front of them. It looked less menacing in the sunshine, more of a quaint relic than a dark and menacing ruin.

'For a long time I wanted to rid myself of my monstrous side,' Callum said, 'but I think what I really needed was a community to help me figure things out. People who understood what I was going through.'

As they neared the church, they heard three booming howls, one after the other. They stopped walking and listened. Jasper tensed, but the howls no longer had the same power to incapacitate and terrorise that they once had. He felt nervous, but wasn't rooted to the spot or overwhelmed by fear.

'It sounds like she's fully embraced her predatory instincts. This is the third day in a row she's hunted ghosts on the island. A good job too—the spirit population was getting out of control. Once the number of ghosts goes down to a more normal level, she'll probably restrict herself to hunting at night, but for now she's got her work cut out for her.'

'Is there a risk she could return to her human form and leave the island?'

Callum shook his head. 'Unlikely. Even if Mayhew still remembers her human life—which I doubt—she doesn't have access to the potions she'd need to suppress the curse. Still, as a precaution, the Paranormal Office has arranged for a couple of local wizards to monitor her. Make sure she only preys on lost souls and not people.'

Jasper felt a twist of guilt in his gut. He'd persuaded Sallow to allow Mayhew to live out her life as a Cù-Sìth on Islay, rather than face execution. Had that been an act of mercy, or just plain cruel? Now that the punishment was being carried out, he wasn't so certain he'd done her a favour.

As if responding to his thoughts, Callum said, 'It could be a nice life, if she embraces it. Take it from me, being a lone predator on a Scottish island can feel thrilling. As long as she only hunts ghosts, she'll be doing good—ensuring lost souls find their way to the afterlife.'

Callum turned to face Jasper, his eyes glistening.

'I have a lot to thank you for, Jasper. Introducing me to Silverback pack, persuading the Paranormal Office not to throw me in jail... I owe you a debt I probably won't ever be able to pay. I feel truly free for the first time in decades.'

'You're welcome. And don't consider it a debt. Just a favour from someone who knows what it's like to feel trapped and hopeless.'

Callum smiled. 'Well, you've made a friend at the very least. If there's anything you need, you know where to find me.'

CHAPTER 42

BLOOMSBURY STREET, LONDON.

A SMALL, HEAVY PARCEL dropped through the letterbox at *Wychwood Books* a few days after Jasper arrived back in London. He peeked at its contents, then stuffed the parcel into a drawer of his desk. He felt strangely guilty about it, as if the parcel represented a betrayal. *Of who, though? Rasmus? The Paranormal Office? His family, who, if they'd taught him anything, had taught him to respect authority?*

Sallow and Grimshaw would be irritated, maybe even angry, with his decision, but he didn't care. He'd caught their spy, which meant *they* owed *him*, not the other way around. But he was dreading telling Rasmus about his change of heart. Would the old man feel betrayed? He'd always supported Jasper, even when virtually everyone else in the wizarding community had believed him to be a traitor. But it was more than that: Rasmus was like a favourite uncle, maybe even a surrogate father. It was more than a decade since he'd mentored Jasper through seeker training, but he still craved his approval.

Rasmus finally turned up on a rainy Friday evening, just as Jasper was shooing away his last customers. Jasper locked up the bookshop and poured them both a glass of red wine. Rasmus settled himself on the sofa while Jasper sat in his stained-but-comfy armchair behind the cash till.

'I hope I'm not messing up your routine,' Rasmus said, nodding at his glass of wine. 'Weren't you on some kind of detox..?'

'I'm done with that now. It was a bit too black-and-white for me—I felt like a failure anytime I had a sausage roll or a sip of beer. I'm taking a more moderate approach now, only boozing on weekends. It's strictly soft drinks during the week. This is my first taste of alcohol since last Saturday.'

'Bravo, I'll drink to that!'

They clinked glasses and sipped their wine.

Rasmus smacked his lips together with satisfaction. 'Not bad,' he said. 'Normally, when you offer me a glass of wine, the back of my throat stings for days afterwards. You must've broken the five pound barrier on this one.'

'I did—it cost six ninety-nine! I can't remember the last time I spent that much on a bottle of wine. But I thought this was a special occasion.'

'I'm honoured. And so to business. The Paranormal Office is extremely grateful for your help in dealing with Erin Mayhew. Thanks to your efforts, the werewolf situation has calmed down considerably.'

'The *Chronicle* has been reporting that Sallow is negotiating directly with the werewolf pack leaders.'

'Indeed. Compromise won't be easy, but at least they're talking. And the microchipping policy has been scrapped, which is a big step in the right direction. Microchips that were installed by force at Hampstead Heath are being removed by Paranormal Office officials as we speak.'

'Good.'

'As to your future, there's been disquiet in some quarters about the idea of bringing you back into the fold, given your less-than-spotless reputation. But Sallow says he'd prefer you—'

'—inside the tent pissing out, rather than the other way around?'

Rasmus grinned. 'Beautifully put. The long and the short of it is: they want you back. As a seeker. Investigating magical crimes, keeping London's supernatural community safe. Just like the old days. No-more selling secondhand books and drinking your life away. You'll be back out there, jewel-in-hand, doing what you do best.'

Jasper's mouth had gone dry. He wasn't sure how to phrase what he needed to say next. Rasmus had gone to such lengths to get him reinstated, but he had to be honest with him. He owed him that.

Rasmus cocked his head to one side. 'You're going to say no, aren't you?'

Jasper nodded slowly, rueing the disappointment in Rasmus's face.

'May I know why?'

'I don't mean to sound ungrateful. I know you've worked hard to get me back inside the tent.'

Rasmus waved the comment away. 'Never mind all that. I'm not angry, just surprised. I thought you wanted to become a seeker again?'

'I did, but this investigation—freelancing for the Paranormal Office, if that's the right word—has reminded me just how stubborn and stupid the bureaucracy is. It's all politics and personal agendas. Sallow will do anything to get elected; Grimshaw just wants to settle old scores. And that's just the tip of the iceberg.'

'Can't argue with that,' Rasmus mumbled, pulling on his beard.

'Ten years ago I put up with it. I was happy taking orders. I was more idealistic in those days... more naïve, as well. I just wanted to fit in. But now I've been outside the tent for so long, I'm not sure I want to come back in. I haven't always been happy, but at least I'm free to do my own thing. Be my own boss.'

Jasper reached inside his desk drawer and put the parcel on the desk in front of him. From inside, he drew out a business card. The address of the bookshop and a phone number were printed on it in small, black type, alongside the words: *Jasper Wychwood—Paranormal Investigator For Hire.* He handed it to Rasmus, whose bushy eyebrows shot up as he read the card.

'Arthur Sallow will burst a blood vessel when he sees this,' he said. But he was smiling.

'I know.'

'He'll try to shut you down. The authorities detest private investigators. Think they're all con artists.'

'I'm sure that's true.'

'Nonetheless, I think it's an excellent idea. Slightly mad, but excellent all the same.'

Jasper had been sitting forward in the armchair, coiled like a spring, but now he allowed himself to lean backwards and re-lax. Rasmus was the only person who could've talked him out of his plan. If he'd been dead against the idea, Jasper would've reconsidered his plans. Having his approval felt good.

'I'm not trying to ruffle any feathers, but I feel I need to strike out on my own. I've become used to being an outsider, I suppose.'

'Anything that pisses off the powers that be is worthwhile in my book. I think you'd have struggled with taking orders again as a seeker, anyway.'

'Do you think Sallow will lose his mind about this? Will he have me arrested?'

Rasmus stuck his tongue into the corner of his mouth, thinking. His lips had turned slightly purple from the wine. 'He'll tell you to stop. Might even put the word out that you can't be trusted—try to put off some of your potential customers. But your assistance in the Mayhew investigation should give you a bit of latitude. Most likely, he'll turn a blind eye.'

Jasper felt giddy, almost weightless. Now that Rasmus had given his blessing, he had no excuse not to proceed with his plan. Getting clients would be difficult. As far as he was aware, there were no other legitimate private detectives in London who specialised in the paranormal world, only charlatans eager to take advantage of vulnerable people. Despite the difficulties in setting up such a business, Jasper felt there was a gap in the market for an honest paranormal private eye. Someone who knew the wizarding world from the inside, but who was far enough removed to see its flaws and contradictions.

'Trying to think up a promotional slogan?' Rasmus asked, grinning. Jasper realised he'd been staring into space.

'Yeah. I was thinking: *Supernatural Sleuthing—No Job Is Too Weird.*'

'Dreadful.'

'How about: *Something Strange in Your Neighbourhood? Who You Gonna Call? Jasper Wychwood!*'

'Worse. And you might get sued by whoever owns the copyright to *Ghostbusters.*'

'True. Perhaps I need to give it some more thought. I'm sure Alyssa will have some better ideas.'

'Ah. Is she going to be your marketing guru?'

'Possibly. She's already promised to refer people who write in to her podcast. She talks about werewolves and vampires a lot, so people often ask for her help with supernatural issues. Some of her listeners are a bit unhinged, though...'

'One of the perils of podcasting, I imagine—dealing with oddballs. Then again, I've been accused of being odd myself, so I'm no judge.'

'I guess now I won't be working for the authorities, I'd better return the ruby you loaned me.' Jasper took the magical ruby brooch out of his pocket and threw it underarm to Rasmus on the sofa.

Rasmus caught it smoothly but then threw it straight back. 'I'd keep that if I were you. Might come in handy.'

'Won't the seeker's office miss it? It's a seekers' ruby, isn't it?'

Rasmus shrugged. 'They didn't miss it when I took it, so I don't see why they should miss it now.'

Jasper blinked. 'You mean you stole it?'

Rasmus spread his hands. 'You might say that. I thought you'd find it useful, so I *liberated* it without filling out the necessary paperwork. You didn't think you were the only one with a healthy disdain for authority, did you?'

JOIN THE READERS CLUB AND GET A FREE BOOK

Thank you so much for reading *The Wolf of Whitehall!* As an independent author, the support of readers like you means everything to me. If you'd like to sign up for my Readers Club, I'll send you a free copy of *A Night In Highgate*, which tells the story of Jasper's first night on patrol as a seeker. This story is exclusive to my Reader's Club—it's not available for sale on Amazon or anywhere else.

Visit **www.jackcuranwrites/free-book/** to claim your free ebook!

REVIEWS ARE REALLY HELPFUL...

If you enjoyed *The Wolf of Whitehall*, I'd be really grateful if you'd consider leaving a review on Amazon. Reviews from readers like you make a huge a difference to the success of authors like me. Even a short one-sentence review, or a star rating, is helpful.

Thank you!

Jack

THE SHADOW KEY
JASPER WYCHWOOD CHRONICLES, BOOK 3

A prison riot. A powerful artefact with mind-bending properties.

Jasper Wychwood must face his demons.

Jasper's brother Tristram is due for release from the *Wimbledon Centre for the Incurably Delusional*—a prison for wizards. But when the brothers meet, it is far from a happy family reunion. There is a dark conspiracy afoot in the prison, and Tristram is involved somehow. Jasper wants to help his brother, but what if doing so costs him his sanity?

Don't miss Jasper's next adventure!
Buy now on Amazon in paperback or ebook format.